The Woman Who Rode the Wind

To Angie & Joe —

Happy Flying —

Ed

The Woman Who Rode the Wind

a novel by

ED LEEFELDT

Lighter Than Air, L.P.

PRINCETON, NEW JERSEY

Lighter Than Air, L.P.
P.O. Box 2362
Princeton, NJ 08543-2362
www.lighterthanair.net
litenair@aol.com

Cover design by James R. Harris
Text design by Pauline Neuwirth, Neuwirth & Associates, Inc.

Library of Congress Card Number 2001117953

ISBN 0-9679535-1-0

10 9 8 7 6 5 4 3 2 1

"I am hostile to gravity . . . He who one day shall teach us to fly will remove all boundaries, all landmarks. He will christen the earth anew, and the earth itself shall be light."

FRIEDRICH NIETZSCHE, *Thus Spake Zarathustra*

Acknowledgments

TO LISA, WHO MEANS everything to me.

To Jodee Blanco, my unfailing publicist; Kent Carroll, my unerring editor; and James Harris, who did paint the wind.

To Jinny Baeckler and the Plainsboro Literary Group, who encouraged me to be true to myself. To the Princeton Toastmasters, who taught me to speak up for myself. To Nancy Nicholson, who helped me to believe in myself.

To balloonists John Burk, Brian Boland and Mark Schilling, who took me aloft and told me their stories. To the gang at Bloomberg for their good advice and help, especially those I've worked for and admire: Bill Inman and Ron Henkoff.

To Dave DuPell, Judi Brenner, Sandi Friberg, Steve and Joan Guggenheim, Jack Knarr, Mal Parker, Paula Plantier, Pat Twohy, Dave and Sandy Wilson, and especially Larry Tomar.

And last to my family: mom, Dorothy; daughters Maren Kravitz and Kristin Melendez and her husband, Anthony; sons Erik and Tim and his wife, Anja, and their daughter, Emma; Jen Hutchinson; Nancy Leefeldt; Ed and Marylan Marsh; John and Sue Scudder; and Jim and Ruth Chorlton.

prologue

*F*OR A CITY SO *proud of itself,* he thought, *Paris has more than its share of lousy weather. Searing heat in summer, rain all winter and now—on this of all mornings—fog.*

Harding looked up. The fog obscured the heights of the Tower over his head as he stood in the restless crowd waiting for the president of France to arrive. Waiting for an hour now. He glanced at the mob behind him. This was going to be a great show. Like inviting two thousand people to the theater—all waiting impatiently for the curtain to rise.

Bad enough for the audience, but what about the men on stage? Harding could see the mist drip off the girders above them and down their backs. It collected like a sheen on their black frock coats as they sat waiting. Twenty men too important to be kept waiting.

Harding knew some of them, like the Comte de Vaux. He'd fire his Bulldog revolver at beggars who didn't get out of the street when he thundered by in his new motorcar. And Fabian

Bouchard: short, fat and intense. He and Harding had shared a few women, a lot of wine, and one vital secret.

At the edge of the stage stood Henri Meurthe, the president of the Aéro Club. He looked most uncomfortable of all. The others were glaring at him, angry that he had dragged them out in this filthy weather—and then President Pouchet kept them waiting.

Perhaps Pouchet's waiting for the fog to lift, Harding thought. He's the kind who wants a backdrop when he makes his big announcement, and what better than a full view of the thousand-foot Tower, the world's tallest building and its greatest wonder?

But maybe not. There was a more grim possibility. Perhaps Pouchet was afraid of anarchists, like the one who had thrown the bomb into the Chamber of Deputies. From his position just below the stage Harding scanned the crowd.

Seeing no obvious bomb throwers, he began dividing the crowd by their hats. On the podium, of course, were the top hats, members of the exclusive Aéro Club and leaders of Paris society, sitting stiffly as if posing for a photograph. Around them, at the foot of the stage, clustered the journalists in round derbies clutching yellow notebooks. Beyond them stood the common folk and laborers in their peaked caps.

Outside the protection of the Tower, Harding saw a tall man pacing like a boxer ready for his match and paying no attention to the drizzle. The tall man wore no hat at all. His blond hair was plastered against his head, but he didn't look wet. Now he could be dangerous, Harding thought to himself.

"Henri!" called out one of the men on the podium. "Is your friend Pouchet ever going to show up? It's already 11:35."

Harding saw Meurthe yank the chain on his waistcoat and pull out his gold pocket watch, the kind that was so big they called it a "turnip." But Meurthe wasn't looking at the time. He was looking at the picture inside the top cover. Whose picture? Harding wondered. He had owned one like that too—with his wife's picture inside—until he had to pawn it.

Then he heard the clatter of carriage wheels and hooves on cobblestones. Pouchet had finally given up waiting for the weather to change. Three identical closed carriages arrived, attended by the horse guard. There was a brief flurry of speculation by the men on the podium and then the question was answered. The president jumped nimbly from the middle carriage, surrounded by soldiers.

Pouchet strode casually up to the podium as if it were his second home. He shook hands with several of the men in top hats, and glanced ruefully at the sky. He was a small, balding man, unimpressive in appearance, but a person who was going to make you take him seriously. He cleared his throat three times before the crowd quieted enough to hear him.

"It is with the greatest pleasure," his voice high-pitched in the damp air, "that I make an announcement of utmost importance to all Frenchmen.

"As a climax to our glorious Exposition of 1900, Monsieur Henri Meurthe and these other members of the Aéro Club, all leading citizens of France, have designated a substantial prize for a feat of aeronautical navigation never before accomplished in this or any other nation."

Pouchet paused. A murmur from the crowd subsided instantly as the president drew a long breath. Harding was impressed. *He knows he has their attention.*

"The contest," Pouchet said and raised his right arm over his head, "the contest is, quite simply, to fly around the Eiffel Tower."

A second murmur came from the crowd, a much louder one. All eyes followed the president's arm upward, except Harding's and the blond man at the edge of the crowd. The mist obscured the top of the Tower, making it seem even taller. All they could see were the long iron girders swooping in toward the sky. It looked like a voyage without end.

Pouchet had stunned the crowd into silence. Even the reporters fell silent. No one had ever flown, except in a balloon. And a balloon could not really fly. It was simply blown by the wind.

Then a reporter for *Le Temps* broke the silence: "The prize! What is the prize, assuming such a thing can be done?"

"Yes, the prize!" shouted another, and then another.

Harding watched as the president allowed the shouts to grow to a roar. Pouchet smiled smugly. He would not be rushed. He would wait for the crowd to coax him into doing exactly what he had already planned.

"The prize . . ." said the president, and there was instant silence, "is this solid gold medal," which he took off the lectern and dangled from its ribbon. The medal depicted a winged man in flight.

The audience moaned in disappointment: "Only a medal? Who will risk his life for a medal, even if it is gold?"

But Harding knew Pouchet was a better showman than that.

"This medal . . ." the president continued, "and one million francs!"

There was a gasp from the crowd. Some of the derby hats bolted for nearby buildings to find telephones. Those who remained pressed closer to the podium. They had shaken off the gloom of the day. Harding smiled to himself. The thought of so much money had warmed them in artificial sunshine. He looked up at Pouchet, who was beaming with pride.

"What are the conditions under which the flight must be made?" shouted the reporter for *Le Figaro*.

Pouchet turned to Meurthe. "For those questions I will ask Monsieur Henri Meurthe, president of the Aéro Club, to provide the answers."

Meurthe stepped forward. He was tall, in his late 50s and had drooping mustache, grizzled hair and a huge prow of a nose. It was a handsome, determined and intelligent face that reminded Harding of pictures he had seen of Lincoln. Meurthe deliberately avoided standing too close to Pouchet so that no comparison between the size of the two presidents could be made.

"The conditions are simple: one must circle the Tower in a flying machine of any kind, being above the ground at all times," he said.

Other reporters now jostled for a favored position in front of Meurthe, bumping Harding from his spot. There were hundreds of newspapers in Paris and, at this moment, all of them had questions.

"Why so much?" asked the correspondent for *Le Petit Parisien*, largest of the city's papers. "The Tour de Marseilles auto race offers a prize of 50,000 francs. The Tour de France bicycle contest awards only 20,000 francs."

"The size of the prize," answered Meurthe, "indicates the difficulty of the endeavor. In the Tour de France, we are guaranteed a winner, no matter how fast or slow the contestants. Here, nothing is assured and"—he glanced above him at the height of the Tower—"the risks are great."

A reporter for *L'Humanité*, a Socialist newspaper, had pushed his way to the foot of the podium. His clothes were rumpled, his striped tie askew, and his jaw jutted out.

"Are you saying, then, this task is impossible?" he sneered. "Is that why you and your rich friends have made the reward so handsome? So poor laborers and farmers will take their bedsheets and jump from the Tower?"

Harding saw Pouchet motion to the police at the edge of the crowd, but Meurthe caught the gesture and raised a hand to stop it. He looked down at the reporter and answered him:

"We do not expect anyone to jump from the Tower as a consequence of this offer and, indeed, it would not benefit him to do so, since he would die and collect no money. The sole purpose of the Aéro Club is to foster the fledgling science of aeronautics."

"But man cannot fly as you describe it—by making a circle in the air," another reporter yelled. "Isn't that correct?"

"No man has done so yet," Meurthe conceded. "But who would have thought a few years ago we would hear music from wax cylinders, or capture the image of life on a screen, or get light from the white magic of electricity? Every day, as the new century turns, we witness awakenings of the human mind. Why not encourage new discoveries?"

"Then you are saying someone will win the prize?" pressed the same reporter.

"Nothing is impossible," answered Meurthe, "and nothing is inevitable. Whatever we get we must strive for. Hence this prize."

"Is there any machine that could now make this flight?" shouted a reporter from the back.

"None to my knowledge," said Meurthe. "But there are balloons capable of raising themselves into the air and maneuvering by means of electric or steam engines. Now we have the light-weight gasoline engine that powers our automobiles. Why not use it to conquer the sky?"

"Of the million francs," asked the reporter for *Le Matin*, "how much is out of your personal fortune?"

Meurthe hesitated. "The greater part," he answered.

Tell the truth, said Harding to himself. It's all your money. None of the others put up a franc.

Pouchet stepped forward again. "We owe a great debt to Monsieur Meurthe and the Aéro Club," he said. "From its beginning with the earliest balloons, aviation has been a French science, and every advance has come from France. This reward will insure that we, and not our *friends* the Germans, will have the glory of the conquest of the air!"

As the crowd cheered, Harding saw the blond man make his way to the front. He did not push, but his size and self-assurance cleared a path for him. Now he raised his hand.

"Yes," said Pouchet.

"If you please, sir," said the blond man in clipped, precise French, "having heard what you said, I must ask: Is this contest open only to the French? Will you exclude the citizens of other nations to ensure a French victory?"

Careful, Pouchet, he's baiting you, Harding thought.

"We will not exclude anyone!" shouted Pouchet. "But the Eiffel Tower is sacred to France, and it would be a travesty if anyone else were to succeed before a Frenchman."

The blond man leaped to the podium, making Pouchet shrink back.

"I am Maximilian von Hohenstauffen, German military attaché, and I have a letter for you." He waved it aloft to the crowd. "It is from His Majesty the Kaiser's Imperial Government announcing that Germany will enter your contest to sail around the Eiffel Tower. And yes, gentlemen," he said, turning to the men on the podium, "there is a machine that can make this flight. And we Germans have it."

At that moment, as if by design, the sound of an explosion echoed down from above. The little cannon on the second level of the Tower, fired each day to signal the noon hour, had just sounded with a hollow boom.

The crowd reeled from the shadowy noise, and from the second stunning surprise of the morning. Germany, France's mortal enemy since their war in 1870, would soar around France's shrine and win the million francs from the fools of the Aéro Club!

Reporters spilled out onto the plaza, jostling one another, confused. Harding watched as Pouchet attempted to control his rage. His eyes widened, his mouth dropped, and his nostrils flared. His complexion turned dark.

Even the men on the podium were stunned—all but one. News of the contest was a well-kept secret. Yet at the exact moment it is announced, this German appears out of the mist like an evil magician. How did he know?

But Harding knew. He glanced at Fabian Bouchard. Fat sweating Judas, he thought. You didn't just tell me; you tipped off the Germans too, didn't you?

Bouchard was wiping the perspiration off his face even though the day was cool, and making swift, covert glances at the German on the podium.

Harding saw Meurthe staring down at Bouchard. Perhaps he suspects? God help Bouchard if he does. I wouldn't want Meurthe for an enemy.

Then he looked at von Hohenstauffen. The German stood poised, smiling ever so slightly. Only a long thin dueling scar down his left cheek marred his handsome face, with its high forehead and long aquiline nose. Harding watched as Maximilian contemptuously put a cigar in his mouth and flicked a match with his fingernail. The flame seemed to come out of his fist. He had no fear of the crowd . . . or anyone.

"You're enjoying yourself, aren't you, you arrogant son of a bitch?" Harding said under his breath.

And now, as the people dispersed, so did the fog. The sun shone down through the filigree of the Tower, bathing Meurthe in the mottled light, making him look like a saint.

For a moment Harding almost believed, wanted to believe anyway, that this thing could happen, that Man could fly. After all, Paris was a bottle that had freed many a genie, a place where vaulted ceilings, statues and steeples rose from the ground like a stone forest, a city that woke and groped for the sky each morning.

Harding caught himself daydreaming. Time to get going. First, a cable to Neville Bishop six hours away in New York. Was he in the office, or still asleep after a long night with his latest mistress? No matter. In a few days we'll all be drawn into this . . . and there'll be a price to pay. And then, a drink. It's past noon.

one

*F*ROM HER PERCH ON the dilapidated bell tower, Mary Ann could see the winds dance.

The winds were invisible to the others down below. But she could see them in everything that moved. Sometimes they sent the leaves funneling upward like cyclones, or touched the dirt road and set the dry soil to swirling like small, inoffensive ghosts. And occasionally she'd get a God's-eye view of the wind as rain clouds rolled up the valley beneath her.

From where she sat, she could see the entire valley: the western slope where the road came weaving out of the mountains, the small town of Jericho, Tennessee, below her, and then back up to the top of her hill. Down that road everything had to come. But nothing—not even the wind—ever seemed to leave.

Then her eye caught a cloud of dust at the other end of the valley. It was Hosea in the freight wagon, driving too fast as usual. And in that wagon—unknown to her—came salvation.

THE WAGON ROUNDED the crest of the hill overlooking Jericho and started down into the valley. Sides of bacon and sacks of seed slammed against its walls as it tilted sideways on the gravel road. Hosea, his face as red as his sweaty flannel shirt, cracked the reins and pushed the horses toward town. He was driving too fast and too close to the edge, and he was drunk.

Alongside him, Harding Cooper was taking advantage of a free ride into this hidden corner of the Great Smoky Mountains. Well, not quite free. Cooper and Hosea were finishing off Harding's whiskey.

Below them the town was spread out in ribbons of white like the sails of a fleet. It was the first Monday in May, and Monday was wash day. The housewives of Jericho had their boiled shirts and petticoats on the line.

The wagon skidded to a halt in front of the general store on the town's main street. People were already lined up on the plank sidewalk waiting for their dry goods. A big day in the small town, Harding thought as he grabbed his carpetbag and jumped down.

"Does anyone know where to find Doctor Samuel Pitman?" he asked.

No one answered. They crowded closer and stared at him.

Cooper turned back to Hosea. "Real friendly, aren't they?"

The driver shrugged. "They're friendly to me. But I don't ask 'em questions."

Harding walked on down the street and stopped in front of a woman washing her porch. He stood with one foot on the step. "I'm looking for Doctor Pitman," he repeated.

The woman took the bucket of soapy water and dumped it down the steps. Harding realized, too late, that he had a hole in the elastic of his congress boot and his foot was soaked.

"That's all the answer you'll get from me," she snapped.

MARY ANN WATCHED HIM through her father's old telescope. What's he doing here? she thought. Is he a drummer? A revenue agent? Another outcast? She felt a touch of sympathy for him, and then anger at herself for feeling it. It was none of her business.

Harding trudged on through town, his carpetbag banging against his knee. Then he spied hope.

On a long, ivy-covered porch at the end of the block, three elderly women sat in rocking chairs, looking like blackbirds on a telegraph wire, ready to swoop down and peck the eyes out of a dying animal. The old-biddy brigade. Better than the town newspaper. They'd know where to find Sam Pitman. Had he run off with the mayor's wife or advocated equality of the races? Harding wondered. And how would he get these old hags to tell him? It was time to be charming.

Harding took off his yellow straw boater. "Mornin', ladies. Hot day for May, isn't it?"

"Seen hotter," said the first. "Who might you be?"

"Just got off the wagon," he said, avoiding the question. "I'm looking for someone."

"Friend of yours?" asked the second, raising her jaw. He caught the glint of her spectacles.

"Doctor Samuel Pitman."

The first one laughed shrilly. "He's no doctor. Never cured anybody, not even himself!"

"You don't want him," said the second. "Not unless you're partial to strange noises, and huge bats and hellcats, not to mention the desecration of a House of God. Go away."

Harding had seen their kind before. No sense getting into an argument. He'd wait them out, shuffling his feet, looking like a poor relation on the doorstep. He knew that they would pay him with information to see him leave.

Minutes ticked by. The three of them fidgeted in their rocking chairs. Harding stood there in front of the porch, enjoying the silence. The whole town must be watching by now, he thought. He could suffer the humiliation longer than they could.

The third one, who had been mute, broke first. "Tell him, Eutheria," she ordered.

Eutheria pointed up the hill. "If you want Pitman, take the dirt road on your right just beyond the covered bridge. Follow it past the hayfield and straight up the hill to the church."

"Eutheria!"

"Well, it was a church," she snapped.

"How far is it?" asked Harding.

"Far enough so you'll wish you'd never made the trip," said the second, and all three cackled.

"Can anyone take me up?"

"Not in this town," said Eutheria.

He should have left then, but Harding had a nasty streak. He took the now-empty whiskey bottle out of his jacket and put it on the porch railing.

"Ladies," he said, "I seem to have gone dry. Could you tell me where a man can get a drink in this town?"

"That trough over there," said Eutheria, "the one the other pigs use."

"I thank you very much," said Harding. He bowed and walked away, leaving the whiskey bottle on the railing where it would be visible to the whole town. "Excuse me, I have a long walk ahead."

IN THE STEEPLE ON the hill above them, Mary Ann saw Eutheria point in her direction. Oh, God, she thought. Is he coming here? No one ever comes here. What do I tell him about Father? She hoped that he wouldn't and she hoped that he would.

IT WAS A LONG walk, so long that Harding thought seriously of abandoning his heavy bag. Three times buckboards went by, and later two carriages and a surrey. All of them turned around just above him and came back down. No one offered him a ride. In the distance two men on horseback watched him. One had a spyglass. Either someone must have put his picture on the post-office wall—or the front-porch telegraph had been busy.

He stopped at the top of the last and highest hill. Both he and the day were spent. The church had a lovely whitewashed look from a distance, a place where you would worship if you believed in brotherly love—as the dear people of Jericho obviously did.

But now that he was closer, he could see the damage. The cross in front of the church was dismasted and leaned on its side. A stained-glass window had been smashed and boarded up. Fifty feet in front of the church a rusty Civil War cannon had been dragged into someone's flowerbed and left there, its muzzle pointing at the double front doors. The carefully planted azaleas lay trampled.

The church that was not a church: bats and hellcats. Well, this was what Neville Bishop paid him for. Harding slung his coat over his shoulder and knocked on the double doors. No answer.

Then he banged until his fist hurt. He was about to give up when the right-hand door opened—slightly.

A pretty young woman stood in the shadows, staring at him with dark, intense eyes.

"What do you want?" she asked. She sounded surly . . . or maybe just lonely and afraid. Or maybe she'd caught the town disease, whatever that was.

Anyway, hell of a greeting, he thought. What he really wanted was a drink. But instead he said, "Sam Pitman."

"You mean Doctor Pitman," she corrected him. "And who are you?"

"I'm the man who wants to talk to Doctor Pitman," he snapped. "There, did I say it right?" His patience with these people was running out.

"Wait here," she ordered. She retreated, leaving the door ajar. Harding pushed his way inside.

For the first time he understood why the townspeople were afraid of the place. It didn't look like any church that he had ever been in, although—granted—his experience wasn't vast. Pews had been upended and turned into workbenches. A wood lathe competed for space with a sewing machine and a drill press. Designs were nailed on the walls: pictures of ancient flying machines, even an angel with angles and formulae drawn across its body and surprised-looking face.

A horseless carriage had been dismantled and pieces of those new internal combustion engines were scattered around the floor. That explained the noises. Rolls of white muslin hung down from the rafters like banners in a cathedral. A huge cloth mounted on one wall looked like the wings of a prehistoric bird, with curved, riblike fingers keeping the fabric stretched. So that was the bat. And the hellcat? Was he looking at her? And where was Doctor Pitman?

She was startled to see him inside the church. "He doesn't want to see you," she said.

"How do you know?" said Harding, looking around. "Have you asked him?"

They eyed each other across the tool-strewn floor, sizing each other up. She's too young to be his wife, Harding thought, and too innocent-looking to be a mistress. Probably his daughter. She was dressed in a collarless brown shift with denim pants peeking out from underneath, too baggy to show her figure. But her face was lovely. She had a small nose, freckles that accentu- ated her cheekbones, and sandy blond hair, almost strawberry blond. He judged her to be about 20.

Mary Ann felt Harding's eyes slide over her. She knew what he saw; a bunched-up dress, overalls, messy hair pulled back into a bun. Knowing this, she then sized him up.

She saw a man in his early 30s with a handsome but prema- turely aging face and washed-out, world-weary blue eyes that looked as though they had seen too much. He was wearing a white suit, now sweat-stained, and his wilted paper collar stood up like a bird about to take flight. He wasn't much to look at either, she decided, partly in self-defense. But in some strange way, his disheveled looks made her feel as if she could trust him. At least he's not one of them, she thought.

"Look," his voice broke the silent staring match. "We got started on the wrong foot. I had a rough time finding this place, and I'm sorry I walked in on you. But I'm here and you're here, so I might as well tell you what I want." He hesitated, and then launched into his speech.

"I represent the wealthy industrialist Neville Bishop of New York City, who sees the potential in flight. Your father . . ." and he paused, waiting for some recognition. She nodded, and he went on, "is famous in aeronautical circles. When I read his article in *Scientific American* last month saying that he'd built a heavier-than-air machine that could actually fly, Mr. Bishop told me to bring him to New York—all expenses paid . . ."

"That article was finally published?" she cut him off. "And he's finally getting the recognition he deserves? Now, when it's too late?" Then her voice choked and she stopped.

Too late? "Where is your father?" Harding asked again, but more softly now, almost afraid of the answer.

"Why should I trust you?"

Harding could see the late-day light fading through the windows and he lost patience. "I walked all the way up here to see your father," he snapped. "I don't know where I'll sleep tonight. I'll probably end up walking back to Knoxville. All right, don't trust me. Trust the yokels who dragged the cannon into your flowerbed and splashed paint on your walls."

She scrutinized him again with intense, brooding brown eyes, as piercing a look as Harding had ever endured. Then she turned.

"Come on," she said, and walked out the back door of the church. There in the small church cemetery was a freshly dug grave. "He died in February," she said simply.

Harding walked over and stared down at the unmarked grave. "You buried him by yourself? No help from down below?"

"They hate us. They hate everything about us. If they knew that he was dead, they'd come up here and burn us out."

Harding looked across the grave at her. She seemed small and vulnerable and very beautiful. There was a sheen of perspiration across her forehead and nose, and the scent of honeysuckle was almost overpowering. He thought for a moment of making love to her, right here on the ground by her father's grave. And why not? Who would stop him? If he didn't, sooner or later the bumpkins in town would find out, and one of them would have his way with her.

But most of his pity was saved for himself. He had spent all this time, come all this way, and ended up at the side of a grave with this lonely, frightened child-woman. How would Bishop react? Would he even have a job when he got back to New York?

When he looked up she was staring at him again. But in the few seconds that his mind had drifted, something about her had changed. She looked more confident, almost as if the worst had already happened and she could cope.

"You must be very disappointed," she said, and he could have sworn that there was a mischievous twinkle in her eyes. And then she said, very softly, "Do you want to see me fly?"

He turned, startled.

"You don't believe it, do you?" she said with just the hint of a smile. "You've come all this way to watch someone fly but you really don't expect it to happen. You're no different than the people down there. They see it and they hear it, but they don't believe it. Well, you're going to see it too."

She went back inside and came out holding those strange curved wings. They were three times the height of a man, but so light that she carried them with ease. There was a notch in the middle for her head, a padded yoke for her shoulders, and a place for her arms to come through from underneath and grip the willow crossbraces on either side. She looked at him, a little embarrassed. "Can you strap in my arms?"

To Harding, it felt strangely like helping a woman get dressed—or undressed—as she stretched out her arms and he tightened the straps that tied them into the frame. Once again he was uncomfortably aware of her. It was a warm spring evening, just before sunset.

As they walked to the edge of the hill overlooking the hay-field, he again tried to assess her. She was attractive, he decided, but more than that, there was an innocence mingled with ambition; she was just naive enough to believe that she really could go up in the air in this ludicrous swaying contraption. Was she going to kill herself while he watched?

The varnished cotton twill of the wings gleamed in the sunset light, and the first puff of an evening breeze snapped at them. It sang through the whipstrung cordage that ran to the wingtips, sounding like a wild Highland tune. Mary Ann glanced at the top of the bell tower where a rag floated from the weather vane.

"The wind is right," she said.

"It's coming right at you," said Harding, the doubt obvious in his voice.

"That's what makes it right."

"What can I do now?" he asked.

"Nothing. Just stand back."

He stepped back, reluctantly. She seemed to draw into herself for a moment, then took five running steps that carried her to the edge of the hill overlooking the valley below. She kicked once or twice and the whole contraption went over the side and out of sight. Harding ran to the side of the hill, stumbling on the flat white glacial rock.

And then suddenly he saw her rising, the wings catching the wind, in flight. It was as though she had been lifted by one of those new Otis elevators, but with nothing underneath holding her up. It had to be an illusion, or a miracle.

He reached the edge and teetered to a stop just before he went over. Ahead of him, Mary Ann was already 100 yards away, flying into the red-and-orange glow of the evening sun, those ungainly wings now translucent and elegant. Below her were haystacks, looking like friendly pillows.

As Harding watched, Mary Ann did an aerial dance, making lazy circles to the right or left by dipping or raising her wings. She was going down the hill that he had just labored up, seemingly without effort. It was the most graceful thing he had ever seen. Then she went skimming across the fields, kicking the tops off the haystacks for pure joy. Harding saw flight and fluff and a spring sunset, and he thought: Maybe I *can* pull this off.

two

*F*AR ACROSS THE 50-MILE-long lake, Maximilian von Hohenstauffen could see the Alps looming, their white heads—like grandfathers—still covered with snow.

Nearby was an equally majestic sight: a huge airship in flight. The late-day sun caught the massive shape and spread its shadow across a mile of water. The dirigible was approaching fast, but at a great distance; Maximilian could not yet hear the hum of its diesel motors. At this quiet time, the only sound was lapping water.

Behind him was the great hangar where the dirigible would sleep. Maximilian stood at the mouth of the opening—more than 100 feet high—looking like an actor at the front of the stage awaiting his applause. He felt the platform sway gently under his feet; the whole structure floated on the lake so that, whatever the direction of the wind, the dirigible could always enter.

Maximilian heard authoritative footsteps behind him and knew immediately who it was. He turned and saluted.

Kaiser Wilhelm strode up, his blue eyes dark and brooding, the small, pointed, upturned mustache on his broad face—as

Maximilian knew—waxed by a barber as it was every morning. He looked like every other member of every other royal family in Europe, thought Maximilian, except for that one imperfection.

Perhaps because he was on the Bodensee, the kaiser was wearing a British admiral's uniform today: white cap cocked over one eye, navy blue coat with gold braid falling from an epaulet on his right shoulder and, of course, a sword.

The kaiser does love his uniforms, Maximilian thought to himself. If the French ambassador arrived, Wilhelm would surprise him by wearing a French marshal's uniform, even though he had once called Paris "the greatest whore in the world." When the Moscow ballet came to Berlin, he attended in a Russian uniform, and after the Barnum & Bailey circus captivated the city, the kaiser had a ringmaster's uniform made for him. But all the uniforms were tailored to hide that deformity . . .

His arm, the withered left arm. Only a stump, really. The result of his breech birth. As a boy he'd been tortured by it. Doctors had put him in a machine that pinned his head while it stretched his arm. They'd given it electric shocks, even "animal baths," where they'd wrapped the carcass of a dead rabbit around it. Finally they gave up.

Wilhelm had mastered all the military arts in spite of it: riding, shooting, fencing. He had a grip like iron. Maximilian respected him for that. But there was still that imperfection in a world where imperfection wasn't tolerated. Perhaps that was why the kaiser kept it behind him in a sling. It made him look a little off-center. But, of course, no one was expected to notice it. Instead, Maximilian shifted his gaze to the distance, where the new electric lights glinted off the spike helmets and rifles of the stony-faced guards standing stiffly at attention.

For a moment they stood there, side by side, as if equals. Then Maximilian picked up his binoculars and scanned the shore. Two of his men had built a smoky fire so he could tell which way the wind was blowing. The smoke was drifting nearly straight up. Max nodded at the signalman at the side of the platform where the canvas curtains were pulled back, and he flashed out a message on the heliograph to the crew on board. All was going well, Maximilian thought, and—with the kaiser here—it had better.

"I was impressed by what you did in Paris," the kaiser broke the silence. "Your announcement could not have been more effective. You embarrassed the French president."

"Our intelligence was very good," replied Maximilian. "It came from Fabian Bouchard, a member of their own Aéro Club."

"Yes," said the kaiser, and now his voice was steely. "But you also committed Germany to this contest. You made a promise you must now fulfill."

Maximilian pointed to the dirigible. "You see what we can do." The airship was now turning her bullet head toward them for a final approach. She was enormous, with three tons of hydrogen inside, and, with no wind to obstruct her, she waltzed on the water like a dowager empress.

"I have seen many things in my life and heard many promises," said the kaiser. He sounded unconvinced. "I saw an airship explode over Berlin and the man inside drop three thousand feet. I heard him scream as he fell. And the problems you have had here . . ."

"We have solved them," Maximilian interrupted, and then added, "Your Majesty." The kaiser looked at him sharply. No one ever interrupted him. He was the master of the German Empire, the most powerful nation in Europe, and he considered only God to be his equal. But von Hohenstauffen's lineage was old too. It went back to the Holy Roman emperors. In a world where birth and breeding were everything, Maximilian did not have to humble himself.

"But your ship is 420 feet long and 38 feet high," challenged the kaiser. "How will you transport it? You can't fly it all the way to Paris."

"We won't. We will build another one. In Paris itself."

The kaiser gave a snort of surprise and then looked at Maximilian to see if he was serious.

"Arrangements have already been made through Monsieur Bouchard," Maximilian continued. "He's putting up a huge building in the city where a dirigible, similar to this, will be assembled."

"And the French?" asked Kaiser Wilhelm. "They may be degenerate, but they're not stupid. Will they be asleep while this happens?"

"Having opened the contest to other nations, the French now have no choice. Bouchard tells me that they will begin this contest on their Independence Day—July 14. That gives us enough time."

"And will there be other contestants?"

"An American named Neville Bishop claims to have a novel design for an aeroplane, a heavier-than-air machine that flies with wings," Maximilian scoffed. "Ridiculous."

"But what if the ridiculous happens, and the French or Americans fly first? They'll win, and we'll be humiliated."

"They won't," said Maximilian, watching the airship dip lower and lower as it approached. The crew had unfurled St. Andrew's Cross, red on a white banner, as a signal that they were ready to dock.

"You sound very sure of yourself, von Hohenstauffen," challenged the kaiser. "Are you prepared to do what is necessary to win?"

Maximilian laughed harshly. "I went to *kriegschule*. Do you remember what they made us do when we were 12?"

Kaiser Wilhelm nodded grimly. "My personal tutor made me do it too. You are thinking of the day when they take the boys to the stables where the yearling calves are to be slaughtered."

"Yes," said Maximilian. "They showed us how to pick up the sledgehammer, swing it over our heads, and strike the calf where the tip of the skull joins its neck. I was afraid the first time, so it took me several blows. I was so ashamed that I went back and asked to do it again. I have killed several times since then, and I have never hesitated."

The two men were silent for a moment, trapped in their own memories. Maximilian watched the crewmen at the front of the airship throw down the two 300-foot drag ropes that skimmed along the water. Thirty men lined up on either side of the hangar, waiting to pull them in. Now was the moment that could be most treacherous, when the dirigible lost momentum. At this moment it could dip or soar or catch a gust of wind. And it was at this moment the kaiser broke in with another question:

"What is the future for this flying machine, apart from annoying the French?"

Maximilian thought for a moment. "In 10 years, 20 at most, there will be only one great power in the world. And that great power will rule the sky. There will be fortified cloud cities, castles if you will, 100 times bigger than this airship. They'll be capable of raining bombs down on those below.

"Only the fiercest warriors and their women will live up

above the rest in these castles, men like myself . . . and you, of course. They will joust in sleek machines that streak through the sky, like the knights of old, except thousands of feet in the air. Because the gases we use to levitate will catch fire, these men will fight with the ancient and honorable weapons, swords and broadaxes, and save the gunpowder and poison gases to use on the inferior people beneath them."

The kaiser nodded. They shared a heritage with others of their class. They might insult each other, seduce each other's wives, cheat at cards and even kill each other in the occasional duel, but to the outside world they were united and, in their own minds, invincible. They were the sons of men who had taken their land at sword's point, and, if they could, they would do the same.

He liked the concept, but there was a small nagging doubt in the back of the kaiser's mind. He was the absolute ruler on the ground, with an army of soldiers who would shoot down their own families if he so ordered them. But who would rule in Maximilian's world? He thought about this as he watched the propellers at the back of the airship slow to a halt and then reverse direction. The dirigible began to fill up the opening, forcing both of them to move to the side.

"Excuse me," said Maximilian, "this is the most delicate moment." He turned his back on the kaiser and walked away.

This time, Wilhelm noticed, he didn't bother to salute. The kaiser walked in the other direction toward his yacht. He looked back just once to see Maximilian standing in the open door of the hangar with his back to him.

That bastard, thought the kaiser to himself. But I wonder . . . can he pull it off?

Maximilian was wondering the same thing. He remembered

the eyes of Henri Meurthe as he stood on the podium in Paris. Meurthe was not stupid or degenerate, and he would fight. It would not be as easy as killing a calf.

The turning of the water-borne hangar had placed Maximilian in a direct line with the Alps, and he remembered folk tales about the Bodensee. There was one that—as a child—had scared him. It was about the only time in the last century when it had frozen over. He could imagine that ocean of endless ice, stretching like a glacier all the way from those mountains. There was a man with a very fast horse and sleigh who foolishly boasted to his friends that he could ride all the way across the lake—even in the spring, when the ice was melting.

His sled had reached the middle when he heard the ice start to crack under his runners. Panicked by the thought of being sucked into the lake's dark center, he whipped his horse and flew faster and faster, all the while the cracking of the ice getting louder and louder behind him. Finally, just as the lathered horse was ready to drop from exhaustion, he reached the opposite shore. Then, when he looked back and saw the yawning chasm he had escaped, he died of fright.

But I am stronger than that, Maximilian reminded himself.

three

ONCE HARDING CONVINCED Mary Ann to come to New York with him, he moved fast. He helped her pack a few clothes and her father's log book of his experiments. They left that night, locked the double doors of the church behind them, and walked down into Jericho, where they rented a carriage. Mary Ann left Harding's address in New York with the local telegraph office—in the unlikely event that there were any messages.

Then they were off. Harding's stamina was amazing, thought Mary Ann. He drove the carriage all night, and reached Knoxville the next morning. There they caught an express train and arrived in New York City early the following day.

Both were exhausted, which was not the best way to face the city. First she saw the screaming headlines about men who used hypodermic needles to put young women to sleep and abduct them into white slavery. Then she tried to buy a bunch of violets from a young girl on the street and was told by Harding that the girl wasn't really selling flowers—but her body. She and Harding pushed their way onto a trolley car, only to have a man put his hand between her legs. Harding grabbed him and pitched him off the car headfirst.

"Maybe we should walk," she said.

She saw wonderful sights as they strode up the longhorn curve of Broadway: pink stone houses that looked like four-layer cakes, trains that ran on stilts over the streets, and the new Flatiron Building that seemed impossibly tall. But the traffic was horrible. Pedestrians pushed her off the sidewalk. Then a motorized runabout grazed her with one of its thin, spidery wheels, and the driver cursed at her as if it had been her fault.

When they arrived at Neville Bishop's office in the garment district at 10 A.M., Mary Ann was amazed. The whole building seemed to shake with the sound of machines. The racket made her put her hands over her ears.

"What is it?" she shouted to Harding.

"Shirtwaists!" he yelled back. "Bishop makes shirtwaists. Get used to it. It pays the bills for his little hobbies . . . like us."

Inside, jammed together in a long room with a low tin ceiling, she saw hundreds of women bent over their sewing machines, pedaling furiously. Supervisors in vests and ties walked the floor behind them. A fight broke out between two women who both grabbed the same piece of cloth. They started tugging and pulling, yelling at each other in a strange language. One of the supervisors backhanded one of the women, and pushed the other into her chair.

Harding took her up two flights of rickety wooden stairs to a small outer room. There a male secretary with rolled-up sleeves and bulging forearms motioned them to a hard wooden bench outside Bishop's office.

"He looks like a bodyguard," she whispered.

Harding nodded. "Bishop needs one."

The morning dragged into afternoon. Bishop kept them waiting, as a steady stream of worried-looking young men with green eyeshades and celluloid collars ran into the office. Then she'd hear shouting and they'd come scurrying out with their heads down. Mary Ann felt like she did the day that she had been called to the principal's office in grade school. For the first time in two days she had time to think. How had she let Harding talk her into this?

Part of it was his disarming manner. He looked as nervous as she felt. Harding reminded her of her father, she thought, flawed but basically decent and caring. At least, up until now. But what about Bishop? He sounded horrid. The vile smell of the secretary's cigarettes made her want to choke.

Harding could see she was upset. "The city hasn't lost any of its hustle since you've been here, has it?" he said, forcing a smile.

But Mary Ann noticed that his hand kept moving toward the hip pocket of his coat, and she knew what was there. "What's your boss like?" she said, trying to distract him.

Harding hesitated, sizing up what he could say without upsetting her. "Neville Bishop is a gentleman inventor," he said finally. "You've heard of gentlemen farmers, the kind who run sweat shops in the city, but love their horses and cows in the country. Well, Bishop makes his scratch in shirtwaists, but he wants to be remembered as a heroic inventor. He's sort of like Andrew Carnegie, the steelmaker. Carnegie used to shoot down his workers and then build libraries for their children."

Mary Ann nodded grimly. "You don't like him much, do you?"

"I don't have to like him. I just work for him."

The secretary rushed over to a door that opened to a small elevator. Now Mary Ann understood how Bishop avoided the noise and turmoil below. Two waiters came past, carrying covered serving dishes on silver trays. They smelled heavenly. She caught a whiff of roast chicken and her stomach growled.

"Lunch," said Harding. "But not for us."

The burly secretary ushered in the waiters. When they came out he glanced at Mary Ann and Harding. "Mr. Bishop will see you now."

Bishop's office was like stepping into another world. Heavy brocade drapes in the windows shut out the light and noise. There were three overstuffed leather chairs surrounding his desk. Paintings of hunting scenes covered the walls.

Neville Bishop was sitting at a mahogany desk with lion's claws for feet, eating oysters and roast capon and drinking chilled white wine from a silver ice bucket with a mermaid's figure as a handle.

"Where is Pitman?" he shouted. "I told you to bring him back here. Not some shop girl."

"This is his daughter, Mary Ann Pitman," said Harding.

Bishop didn't even glance at her. He turned the full force of his gaze on Harding. "I asked you to bring me Doctor Samuel Pitman, one of the leading aeronautical scholars, and you find this . . ."

"My father is dead," Mary Ann cut him short.

"Then you've wasted both my time and my money," said Bishop, still looking at Harding. God, thought Mary Ann, he doesn't even have the good grace to say he's sorry.

She started to get up to leave when she heard Harding say, "She knows how to fly."

"She knows what?" said Bishop. He was eating as he spoke.

"I saw her. She took a pair of wings and flew from a hill. She was 50 feet in the air."

"What does that prove," snorted Bishop. "I can take a paper airplane and do the same thing."

"Control, Mr. Bishop," said Mary Ann. "I've seen pictures of the heavier-than-air machines you've made. My father used to laugh at them. You think just because you've put a big engine on a pair of wings you can fight your way into the air as if you were driving a car. Well, you can't. Everything you've ever tried just hits the ground and crashes."

Harding looked at her, open-mouthed. No man had ever talked to Neville Bishop that way, and certainly no woman.

But Mary Ann was tired and sore and hot and mad and thirsty. The ice bucket with beads of moisture dripping off the mermaid didn't help either.

He resembled the vice president, Teddy Roosevelt, she decided, but a meaner version. He was a big man with a bulky figure, broad shoulders, full chest and a heavy paunch. Leonine was the way she would have described him . . . if she liked him. He was of an age where overeating was considered both a virtue and an art form. Much of his face was hidden behind pince-nez glasses and a big mustache that was beginning to streak with white, but his gray eyes were piercing.

And they were piercing her. For the first time, Neville Bishop really looked at her. It was like staring down the tunnel at the headlight of a train. He was trying to make her flinch.

Instead there was a straight-eyed look about her that he found unnerving. She wasn't the demure type he was used to when he had need of a woman. The thought occurred to him: What does she know that I don't? And how do I find it out?

"And you have solved the problem of aerial navigation that's baffled mankind for centuries?" said Bishop, not bothering to hide the contempt in his voice.

Mary Ann took a deep breath. She realized suddenly that she was out of her element. She knew what her father was trying to do his last few months in Jericho; she knew how he was doing it, but she didn't know why. The theory of flight had never been explained to her. Her anger with Bishop evaporated. Suddenly they were both looking at her, waiting.

She remembered an example her father had used. She grabbed the box of soda crackers from Bishop's tray.

"Did you ever watch a bird fly?" she asked.

Bishop looked blank; it had been a long time since he'd spent any time watching birds.

"When he wants to turn, he dips one wing and raises the other," she said. She took the box of crackers and twisted the center in two different directions. Crumbs exploded from both sides of the box but no one noticed. "It's called wing warping."

"It's that simple?" asked Bishop.

"Yes," she said, "but no one knows how to do it . . . except my father and me."

"Well," said Bishop. "I think you might be useful on our trip to Paris."

Paris? No one had said anything about Paris. Coming to New York was bad enough. She glanced at Harding, trying to keep the surprise out of her face. He was staring down at the pattern in the Persian rug.

Now Bishop was smiling, as if he were examining her teeth in a slave market. He had regained the upper hand.

"A few weeks ago in France, an extremely wealthy automobile-maker named Henri Meurthe offered a million francs to anyone who could fly around the Eiffel Tower. I am going to win that prize, and you are going to help me." The way he said it left no doubt.

Mary Ann shivered. "Harding," she said, "I don't want to go to Paris. I think I want to go back to Tennessee." Events had once again unexpectedly gotten away from her.

Bishop must have pushed a button under his desk because a moment later the secretary appeared. "Show Miss Pitman back to the waiting room," he said.

Harding rose, too. "No," said Bishop. "You stay."

"I think it could work," Bishop said when they were alone. "I could hire a private steam launch. We could be there in five days. The contest doesn't start until July 14, the French Independence Day.

"The Pitman girl, Marian or whatever her name is, will be critical. She's worked at her father's elbow. She knows something and we need to find it out. Until we do, you can't let her out of your sight.

"Do whatever you have to do to get her to go. Take her down to one of those fancy stores along Ladies Mile, you know, the ones with the cast-iron fronts, and buy her a new dress. You're single again, aren't you?" Bishop gestured with his paring knife. "Romance her. Take her to see *Floradora* or one of those Broadway musicals. Hell, make love to her if you have to. Where is she staying?"

"I don't know," said Harding.

"You've got an empty house. Keep her with you until she

agrees to go. Tell her about Paris. There's not a woman in New York who wouldn't trade her virtue for a trip to Paris. Believe me, I know." He chuckled, and for a moment Harding thought he was almost human.

"One more thing," said Bishop, and his voice turned steely again. "This is your last chance."

Harding flinched. "What do you mean?"

Bishop grabbed Harding's coat, yanked out the bottle and tossed it into the nearby spittoon. "That's what I mean," he said.

THE SQUARE-FACED GASLIGHTS were just being lit as they arrived at Harding Cooper's brownstone on 68th Street. Harding started to help Mary Ann down from the dogcart, but she pushed his hand away and jumped down herself. On the sidewalk an organ grinder played a song of young love:

> *I've a secret in my heart, Sweet Marie;*
> *A tale I'd impart, love for thee.*
> *Every daisy in the dell*
> *Knows my secret quite well,*
> *Yet I dare not tell*
> *Sweet Marie!*

Harding brushed past him, went up the steps and fumbled in his pockets for his key. He picked up a pile of mail in the foyer and opened the second door.

If Mary Ann was surprised by Bishop's factory, she was stunned by what she saw now. The walls were blank, except for dark squares on the wallpaper where pictures once hung. The oriental carpet had been rolled and jammed end-up in the corner. Sheets were draped over chairs and tables. They looked like ghosts waiting to receive them.

Harding stood near the doorway. "There's a bed upstairs for you," he said. "I'll sleep on the sofa."

He paused, as if wrestling with his conscience. "Listen, you can do whatever you want. Don't worry about Bishop. His only chance of dying an upright man is on the end of a rope. I'm sorry that I got you into this."

"There's a bar up the block . . . a blind pig," he went on. "I'm going to get a drink. My bottle was, shall we say, confiscated." The strains of "Sweet Marie" came through the still-open door. "Damn hurdy-gurdy," he said, "doesn't he know any other song?"

Harding started toward the door, the mail still in his hand. Then he stopped and turned around. "This one's for you," he said. "It's a telegram."

Telegrams had never been good news. She opened it reluctantly and read:

REGRET TO INFORM YOUR HOME IN JERICHO BURNED
TO GROUND. CAUSE SUSPICIOUS.
                            SHERIFF HEWITT.

She crumpled up the telegram, trying not to sob. "All my father's work," she whispered and ran up the stairs.

Harding picked up the telegram and read it. "They didn't waste any time, did they?"

She had almost reached the top step when she realized that she hadn't brought any light with her and was about to stumble into the darkness. She looked back at him. He seemed more dejected than she was, more in need of help. She didn't like

Bishop and couldn't trust Harding either, at least, not completely. But she didn't have many choices. She weighed each one of them as she walked back down the stairs.

"Maybe burning my home was a sign," she said. "Maybe we're supposed to go to Paris. Maybe we're even meant to win. All I know is, I've got no place to go back to."

She searched Harding's face for an answer. But he just flopped onto one of the overstuffed chairs. The sheet on top of the chair spread out around him as if to carry him off into the land of ghosts. He had apparently forgotten his need for a drink, and perhaps that was a good thing, she thought.

Mary Ann took an oil lamp and went upstairs, this time all the way. The double bed in the master bedroom had a sheet across it but was otherwise unmade. It looked as if it had been cold—and lonely—for a long time. On the dresser, lying facedown, was an ornate gold frame, the kind used for wedding pictures. She hesitated, and then picked it up. There was no photograph inside.

What should she do? She didn't know, and no one was going to tell her. She only knew that she couldn't sleep, not with all that was running through her head. She searched the night table for something to read. There were novels: *The Prisoner of Zenda*, *Choir Invisible*, *Tess of the D'Urbervilles*, and then she saw that Harding—or someone—had pressed flowers in between the pages. The last one was a thin volume covered in rich purple vellum. Almost against her will, she opened it.

It was *The Rubaiyat of Omar Khayyam*, a book of Persian poetry. Across from the title page was an inscription: "Paris, March 1899. To my beloved wife, Maria. Your devoted Harding."

She felt embarrassed, as though she had seen him naked. In a way, she had. And no well-brought-up girl ever looked at a book without her parents' permission, let alone one like this. But she read on. The lush Persian quatrains were illustrated with pictures in gold leaf of dark-bearded sensual men in turbans lying next to graceful women. The women seemed to be wearing only the sheerest of undergarments, and halters that barely covered their breasts.

Outside the organ grinder had started to play his song again, the lament about Marie. She heard a voice shout, "Shut the hell up!" and it took her a second to recognize the voice as Harding's. She had never heard him angry before.

She turned the pages until she fell asleep. And the last poem she read that night was the one that she remembered longest:

> *And that inverted bowl they call the Sky,*
> *Whereunder crawling, cooped, we live and die,*
> *Lift not your hands to it for help—for it*
> *As impotently moves as you or I.*

four

$\mathcal{T}$HE STORM CLOUDS WERE rolling in when Henri Meurthe arrived at the French military camp of Parc de Chalais in the hills south of Paris. The black thunderheads thickened on the ridge above him, jostling each other like cavalry preparing for a charge. The flashes of faraway lightning overwhelmed the sunset.

Meurthe saw the soldiers scurrying, battening down for the storm as if it were an artillery barrage. They deflated all the balloons, which dwindled into strange, humorous little shapes as the hydrogen hissed out of them. They dismantled a huge kite, threw it hurriedly into a wagon, and sent it clattering to shelter. They fastened windows and latches, for winds of up to 30 miles per hour had been predicted. Two sentries were even spreading canvas coverings over the twin hand-cranked machine guns that stood guard outside the main building as Meurthe came up the steps.

But some were oddly unaffected by the storm's warning signs. As Meurthe stood at the door, he saw a tall figure dressed in white shirt, blue military pants and boots stride across the parade ground toward the reviewing stand.

"What is that fool doing?" growled one of the guards at the door.

"That's the Wild Man," said the other. "It's Chevrier."

So much has happened in the last month since I announced the contest, Meurthe thought as he walked down the long, flag-draped hallway. And much of it has been good. But now comes the real test.

There is a saying that, for all their faults, God loves the French best. They are the leaders in conquering the air; ever since the Montgolfier brothers put fire under a paper balloon and sent a duck, a rooster and a surprised sheep into the sky. The French built the largest balloon. A Frenchman made the first parachute jump. A Frenchwoman was the first aeronaut.

But lately, Meurthe thought, God loves us less. A man-lifting kite is invented, but not in France. From across the ocean comes word: the Americans are flying gliders on the sand dunes of Lake Michigan. In the south of Germany there are stories of great warships gliding over the Bodensee, built by a kaiser who wants to rule the world.

And what of France, the birthplace of flight? Paris is a grand soirée. It is celebrating the Universal Exposition of 1900. Imitation Africans and pretend Turks mingle with belly dancers. The city is full of greasepaint and hustle. The big Ferris Wheel takes passengers 350 feet into the air, and who would want to go higher than that?

Yes, Meurthe thought, Paris is a great party. There are 10,000 balls every month. The best one, everyone agrees, was when Robert de Montesquiou had his pet monkey baptized. The balloons still fly, but now they are toy balloons fired by gunpowder from a little tin cup. Their luminous bubbles drift over the city at night, sputtering and crackling. How typical of the French to turn something so serious into a toy!

But Henri Meurthe has changed all that. He gathers the members of the Aéro Club and proposes a reward for a flight around the Eiffel Tower. One million francs. His colleagues are stunned.

"Why so much?" they ask.

"Because we have become satisfied with so little," Meurthe tells them.

Now the French have something to anticipate. The domino players, the drinkers at the petit zinc bars, the strollers at the kiosks, all argue about it: "Man can fly.—He can't.—The weight of the air will smother him to earth.—In 10 years we will dance on the moon.—A scientist in Serbia has invented electromagnetic waves that will neutralize gravity!"

Everywhere he goes now, Meurthe is recognized and applauded. An elephant at the Paris zoo is named for him. When he attends the theater to see a new play starring the actress Sarah Bernhardt, the house lights dim and a single spotlight shines on him and his beautiful daughter, Yvette. The great actress herself dedicates her opening night to him!

And when Meurthe walks the streets with his long limping gait, the result of a war wound, people clear a path for him as if he were the new Napoleon. At the Corn Exchange, where he owns a seat, the traders cheer him as he strides across the floor.

Even old Jules Verne, crippled and nearly unable to walk, comes to Paris. He hobbles across the floor of the Aéro Club and seizes Meurthe's hand. "I wanted to meet another man who sees the future," he says.

A whole new industry starts: balloon-shaped chairs too fragile to sit in, glass balloon chandeliers that fall and break, balloon-faced clocks that sometimes work! Lovers pose for photographers in a fake balloon basket, against a backdrop of clouds. The anarchists' bombs going off all over Europe are forgotten. Instead, drawings of strange ghostly galleons floating in the heavens appear in the newspapers; ships propelled by rotors instead of masts hover above the moon.

Cartoonists give up their favorite occupation of showing politicians rising from chamber pots like foul odors. Now they set their imaginations free and draw whole worlds of people in the air; a crowded sky over a city full of flying machines. Some of them look like bicycles, others like submarines, some even like broomsticks. Women in huge flowered hats go shopping in balloons, their baskets hanging below them. Men with propellers on their backs meet in the clouds to confer. Policemen chase robbers through the air.

Meurthe shakes his head in astonishment at all this, but he is not impressed. "If I fail," he thinks, "they will turn on me just as fast as I have become their hero. Men may ascend the sky like living angels, but their natures do not change."

He opened the door to the commandant's office. Major Vitary was waiting for him behind his desk.

Vitary was a shifty-eyed man with theatrical black mustache. The kind who hides his cowardice behind a uniform festooned with medals, Meurthe thought. I must get past him quickly.

"Well, Monsieur Meurthe," said Vitary smugly. "I see that you have finally come to seek my help."

"Alas, Major Vitary, I did not come here to see you, but one of your officers, a Captain Chevrier."

Vitary's expression changed. First to surprise, then to anger. "Well, Monsieur Meurthe, I am not sure we can accommodate you."

Meurthe wasted no time. "Of course you can. Here is a letter from President Pouchet telling you to do so."

Vitary scooped up the envelope, ripped it open, and searched the letter for any flaws. Then he looked up. "I will have him escorted from his barracks," he said.

"He is not in his barracks," said Meurthe, continuing to one-up the pompous major. "I saw him heading across the parade ground to the reviewing stand."

Vitary reached for the phone and rang the officers' quarters, wincing as the first crack of lightning hit nearby. Was it true that these wires carried electricity?

"Lieutenant LeRond here."

"This is Major Vitary. Come here immediately and take someone out to meet Captain Chevrier." He stared across the desk at Meurthe. Maybe he'd get lucky and Meurthe and Chevrier would both be struck by lightning.

At the officers' quarters, Lieutenant Guillaume LeRond put on his slicker and box cap and headed for the door.

Two young lieutenants playing cards looked up. "Did they tell you to find the Wild Man?" asked one.

"Yes," said LeRond.

"Why not just leave him out there?" said the other. "The sky is more his friend than we. If she kills him, he will only be getting his just reward."

"I have my orders," said LeRond.

They both laughed. "And you always follow your orders,

don't you, Guillaume?" said the first. "That's why you're still a lieutenant."

Guillaume mumbled an obscenity and walked out. Next time let one of them answer the telephone.

The wind whipped his slicker up around him. When the rain came, he would be drenched. He hugged the protection of the buildings as he made his way to headquarters.

Meurthe was waiting for him at the door. "Did he tell you why he was going to the reviewing stand in this weather?" Meurthe asked over the howl of the wind.

"He said that he was going out to review General Lightning and Marshall Thunder," LeRond shouted.

"Then let's join him," said Meurthe.

The two men fought their way across the field. LeRond looked typical of the French soldiers who worked here, Meurthe thought. He was disciplined, comfortable with authority, but afraid of new ideas.

By the flash of the lightning, Meurthe could see the four-story-high crane with two outstretched arms that was used to test one's flying ability. Meurthe knew the story. A primitive glider hung from the end of one arm, while the other held a weight. The glider went around in circles at seven times the force of gravity and made anyone who tested it sick to his stomach. Chevrier had gone around in it countless times.

Then he saw Chevrier. Alain was standing at the top of the reviewing stand, waiting for the storm. The wind had pulled his shirt back almost to the shoulders, the way a man to be guillotined had his shirt torn to expose his neck. It had blown his hair back from a high forehead, and forced his eyes to narrow slits. But it hadn't moved him. He stood with his heels just over the edge, a 25-foot drop behind him.

Guillaume stopped and took cover underneath the stand. He called up to Alain: "You must come down!"

"Why?" bellowed Alain above the noise of the storm.

"Major Vitary wants to see you."

"That old woman? If he wants me, tell him to come out here and get me himself."

Guillaume was under the reviewing stand now, which gave him some protection from the coming rain. "What are you doing up there, anyway?" he asked.

"The most important thing a soldier can do, conquering my fear," shouted Alain. A bolt of lightning seared the flagpole at the other end of the parade ground. Alain flinched, but only a little, and then caught himself. When he opened his eyes, he saw he was not alone. Meurthe had climbed the bleachers and now stood next to him, also facing the lightning.

"You must be Henri Meurthe, the richest man in France," said Chevrier with contempt in his voice. "I was told that you'd be coming. What do you want with me?"

"I think you know," said Meurthe in a voice that carried over the storm. "I want you to fly around the Eiffel Tower."

Chevrier laughed. "Why me? I break all the rules."

"Men who break rules also break records," retorted Meurthe. "I believe that you are the one man in France who can win this contest."

"Of course I can do it," said Chevrier. "I have two designs for man-carrying airships that would work right now."

"Then build them both," said Meurthe. "We have a huge

workshop in Saint-Cloud, just across the Seine from Paris, that will be ready for you."

Alain hadn't expected this. "And you expect Major Vitary to let me go?"

"Vitary has no choice," said Meurthe. "You will temporarily resign your commission here, but you can take whatever men you like to help you. My money, which you apparently despise, makes all this possible."

From his shelter below the stand, LeRond watched the two men talk. The wind whipped up and slashed at them, but for all the effect it had, they might have been in a restaurant. They stood straight, facing the coming storm. Meurthe was slightly taller, even though his top hat had blown off and tumbled across the parade ground.

"My mother told me about your family," Chevrier said.

"What did she tell you?" asked Meurthe.

"About you, nothing other than you're rich. But your father signed the death warrants for my family in 1871, when the Commune was destroyed. And now you want me to work for you?"

"Listen to me, Chevrier," said Meurthe. "We are very different men, you and I. But, I think, both honorable. Both sons of France. If we do not take action now, we will fail her. The contest starts on July 14."

Alain turned his back to Meurthe and watched for the oncoming rain. "I will be in the International Balloon Race later this month," he said. "After that, if I choose, I may enter your contest."

Meurthe started to speak and then held back. He would not beg. He turned and started down the steps just as the skies burst open. He looked back to see Alain, still standing at the top, rain washing over him, his shirt and hair plastered to his body, facing down the storm.

"By the way," Meurthe called up. "Tell your mother I said hello."

At the bottom, he saw LeRond looking up at Alain, dark envy in his face. And, in an office across the quadrangle, Meurthe saw a tiny square of light where Vitary paced the floor in anger at having been passed over.

Alain, Alain, he thought, you can face down the elements, but what can you do about their envy? Envy is more to be feared than lightning.

five

*D*OWN BELOW, A THOUSAND feet below, Mary Ann saw caterpillars turn into butterflies.

Brightly-colored skins on the grassy floor of the Champ-de-Mars suddenly took life, bobbed like corks on a wave, and then popped up as balloons. Sunlight reflected off their silver tops so brightly that it hurt her eyes. Colors of all descriptions blossomed below her; yellows, blue fleur-de-lis, indigos, scarlets.

"This is the greatest event in the history of aviation," said Henri Meurthe standing at the railing beside her. Then he paused and smiled. "Except, of course, for our own."

Our Own. So now she was part of it; in Paris, one of five privileged people standing at the top of the new Eiffel Tower and talking very calmly about flying around it.

Mary Ann looked closely at the tall, angular Meurthe, a man willing to give a million francs to anyone brave (or foolish) enough to do the impossible. People had told her that the president of the Aéro Club was distinguished, even fierce. But today, with the balloons about to go up, he looked as if he were a child holding them all in his hand, about to let go. He reminded Mary Ann of her own father, in the happy days before his self-imposed exile to Jericho.

"This is our annual International Balloon Race to see how far aerostats can travel," he told her. "I will start them as soon as atmospheric conditions allow. Watch now. They are sending up trial balloons to test the wind."

There was a sudden flurry below. It was as if seeds had been sprung from their pods. Mary Ann got the eerie feeling that she was on the ground and that they had dropped on her.

Then they rushed by, small colored figures of dwarfs, rabbits, misshapen faces, all stitched together from goldbeater's skin, the fourth stomach of an ox and the most airtight substance known to man. At the same time a flock of pigeons was freed just below them, their wings flapping the air like a drumbeat.

That's the way the world's been going by me, Mary Ann thought. For years I waited in that church for something to happen. Then it all happened so fast. A day ago she was on a transatlantic packet, an hour ago on a train arriving in Paris with Harding—a few hours ahead of the dour Neville Bishop, who was bringing along the dismantled aeroplane.

Meurthe had met them at the station and whisked them into his touring car. It roared through the crowded streets to the Eiffel Tower, where they rushed into the elevators, and out at the third level. Then a quick run up the circular steps to an even smaller platform. Inside a glass booth sat the weatherman who monitored the city's winds and temperatures. Outside, apart from themselves, there were only two other people on the platform, Maximilian von Hohenstauffen, the German military attaché, and Meurthe's daughter, Yvette.

Mary Ann thought that the German, who was there to watch his countrymen fly, was handsome in a self-centered way, except for a scar that ran down the left side of his face. But it was Yvette who caught everyone's eye, including Harding's, she noticed.

Yvette looked slender and elegant in a scalloped, rose-colored dress that brushed the floor. Her dark brown hair was pulled back and wrapped around her head. But, whether by accident or by design, a few strands had come loose and danced with the wind.

When the pigeons flew by, she turned and laid a hand on Harding's shoulder, seemingly for support, although it was obvious to Mary Ann that she didn't need any. Mary Ann could see Harding suck in his gut and throw out his chest. She felt a twinge of jealousy in spite of herself. He had never done that for her. She tried not to look, but Yvette's mannequin-perfect beauty was . . . well, intimidating. She focused instead on what was happening below.

"There are 21 balloons in the contest, 12 of them foreign," Meurthe said, stretching his arm across the field. "Some are named for their place of origin, such as *Pommern, St. Louis* and *Copenhagen,* while others have the names of their intended destinations, like *Cathay* and the *Far East.* Some are named for mythology: *Zeus, Minerva* and, of course, the giant *Centaur,* the one that looks like a four-poster bed with its huge balloon in the center and its four supporting ballonets, one at each corner."

"And the one over there at the far right of the field?" she asked, using the French that she had learned in school. "The one that's pure white?"

"Yes," said Meurthe, happy to speak his own language. "That's the *Conqueror.* Breathtaking in its simplicity, isn't it?"

She nodded, wondering who had made something that lovely.

Meurthe shaded his eyes from the sun and watched the clown-shaped trial balloons drift away. "The wind is from the west. That is good. No balloons out in the channel or bothering our friends the English. No one getting wet. If we start them soon, they may travel all the way to the Sahara, Bulgaria, or the Canary Islands. Last year's winner flew 1,200 miles and ended up near Kiev in the Ukraine. But the wind is still a little too strong to send them off."

"They must need a lot of supplies for that length of a trip," said Harding.

"Their baskets are stocked with clothing for every climate, thermos bottles, liquor, soup packed in lime so that it will heat when water is poured in, even Japanese travel guides with phrases like 'How much is that?' and 'Show me on your fingers.' You can find it all in your New York emporium Abercrombie & Fitch. It has a catalog just for balloonists. Ah, I see the warm weather has brought out our current crop of *flâneurs*."

Meurthe was pointing at a crowd standing at the edge of the field. Mary Ann saw a pool of dark clothes on the olive-green grass, dotted with the bright colors of ladies' summer dresses and punctuated with Panama hats and straw boaters.

"Do you see Alain Chevrier among them?" asked Yvette. She obviously has an interest in him, whoever he is, Mary Ann thought.

Meurthe scoffed. "One does not find a dolphin in a school of minnows. These people are idlers, loungers, out for a day from their clubs or salons. Chevrier is in the white balloon over there in the corner, the *Conqueror*."

All of the balloons had been inflated, their skins stretched tight, straining at their ropes, ready for the moment when Meurthe would fire his flare gun.

Mary Ann heard a tapping on the window inside the glass enclosure where the meteorologist sat. "Monsieur Meurthe," he called, his voice muffled by the glass. "The winds are now acceptable. Only six miles an hour."

"Down there," said Meurthe, pointing beyond the ponds at the base of the Tower, "we shall put up a landing field for airships. And around it a track for racing automobiles."

"Aren't you a little ahead of yourself?" asked Harding. "We haven't even seen a man fly yet, except in one of these gas bags that get bounced around by the wind."

Meurthe laughed. "Are you one of those people who believe that the earth's clock is running down and that there is no one left to rewind it? You remind me of children I saw playing on the street corner the other day. Each of them would pretend to be an animal. The largest boy would pick a word like 'Jump,' and they would go around the circle. The one whose turn it was would have to say 'Elephant doesn't jump,' or 'Monkey jumps.' All the other boys would hit anyone who made a mistake.

"When they got to 'Fly,' the smallest boy said 'Man flies,' and the other boys punched him. But wait," said Meurthe, "he'll get his chance to hit them back."

Mary Ann heard Maximilian snort. "The bigger ones will always hit the smaller ones," he said.

That seemed to upset Meurthe. "Are you suggesting brute force is the only answer?"

"There is something to be said for force," Maximilian retorted.

It was then that Mary Ann realized she didn't like him, and that Meurthe didn't, either.

"I agree," said Meurthe coldly. "Yvette, hand me my pistol."

Maximilian stepped back.

Yvette gave Meurthe an antique case that looked as if it held a dueling pistol. He snapped it open. Inside, burnished to a high gloss, was the brass flare gun used to start Aéro Club events.

Harding laughed. So did Meurthe. Maximilian didn't.

Meurthe leaned over the edge. Far below, faces turned up to him, the balloonists, their rope handlers, their wives and mistresses, the onlookers, the passersby.

The flare gun went off. Ropes shook loose and fell to the ground. The seven-story balloons rushed upward, revolving as they came. As the *Zeus* passed in front of them it turned, so the stormy face of the old god painted on its skin was toward them, his hair and beard disheveled, looking as though they had disturbed his sleep. Below the balloons were the long snouts that controlled the release of the hydrogen, the serious faces of the aeronauts, and then the willow and rattan baskets, so tightly woven that they could smash through a brick wall.

"Look, Papa, they're kissing!" cried Yvette.

Mary Ann noticed, however, it was Harding's arm she took—not her father's. By rising faster than the *Zeus*, the *Minerva* had bumped the top of its balloon against the side of the *Zeus*; a maneuver called "kissing." Again, Mary Ann felt a twinge of jealousy. She had been told that Yvette was "a Beauty," which, in Europe, had the status of a Countess or a Marquese. Now Mary Ann knew how Yvette had gained the title. It was her ability to manipulate men.

Below, the *Conqueror* was just taking off. As it did, a gust of wind surged across the Champ-de-Mars, blowing hats and dragging the *Conqueror* along with it. The crowd scattered. Men and women, forgetting their finery, dove for the ground. The *Conqueror*, the bottom of its basket only four feet high, fought for elevation as it neared the edge of the field. Looking down, Harding and Mary Ann saw it smash through a board fence.

"*Mon Dieu!*" said Meurthe almost involuntarily.

"You sound as if you had a personal interest in Chevrier," said Maximilian, who was looking over his shoulder.

Two bags of the sand ballast that hung outside the basket fell to the ground. Two others split open, dumping sand on the spectators. Freed of the weight, the *Conqueror* shot up past the three levels of the Tower. Mary Ann saw Chevrier only for a second. He was hanging onto the ropes leading up to the balloon as the basket swayed beneath him. But he didn't look scared. If anything, he looked . . . happy. And then, while she wondered what kind of man he might be, he soared beyond her and up into the sky.

"Did you ever fly in a balloon?" Harding asked Meurthe.

"Yes," he said, "but it was not for pleasure. Thirty years ago, back in 1870, we were at war and Paris was surrounded by the Germans." He glanced at von Hohenstauffen, who had moved to the other side of the balcony to talk to Yvette. "The only way we could get messages to our troops was to escape in balloons. I was on one of the last balloons to fly from the city.

"But then, as now, balloons went where the wind took them. Mine ended up on a hillside in Norway. My messages were never delivered, and the city surrendered. I failed, and the Germans won." Even now she could sense his frustration. Meurthe was a man who didn't like to lose, she decided. And for some reason, he didn't like this German in particular.

"Monsieur von Hohenstauffen," said Yvette, "or may I call you Maximilian? What brings you to our city?"

"You may call me your obedient servant," he said in perfect French. "I am the head of the German contingent that hopes to win your father's million-franc prize. I had hoped to introduce myself to him, but I see he is too busy. So it is my greater pleasure to talk to you."

"What are the women like in Berlin?" she asked him.

Maximilian paused to light a cigar. He flicked a match and the flame seemed to appear out of nowhere. "They are fat Lutheran cows," he said. "They wear muddy brown skirts, sack coats that look like traveling rugs, and square-toed boots."

Overhearing them, Mary Ann flushed with embarrassment. He might just as well be describing her clothes.

"Someday I will have to marry one of them," he went on. "But for intelligence and beauty, I prefer the women of Paris."

"Monsieur von Hohenstauffen, you flatter us," said Yvette.

"Flattery is the farthest thing from my mind. Seduction, perhaps, but not flattery."

Yvette smiled, but it was an amused smile. It was one of her talents, Mary Ann realized. She would flirt with anyone, but she belonged to no one. At least, not yet.

A sound like a thunderclap echoed in the cloudless sky. "Look!" cried Yvette. One of the balloons was falling.

Meurthe seized the telescope and tried to keep it focused. "It was one of the last to go up, and it is white. It must be the *Conqueror*, but there's a tear in its side. It . . . it looks as if it's exploded. It's shriveling up at the bottom like a dried apple!"

"It was going up too fast, wasn't it?" asked Mary Ann.

Meurthe nodded, trying to keep his line of sight on the plummeting basket.

"He's going to die, isn't he?" asked Harding.

Mary Ann started to shiver uncontrollably. So high up. She could imagine falling from that height. It would be a tumbling, turning world with no direction, like being at the top of a swing just before you start down again and knowing that you are absolutely at the mercy of gravity. Was it true what they said about your whole life passing before you in the last moments? She looked at Maximilian. His eyes were hooded, like those of a hawk watching a mouse in a sunny field just before . . .

"Look, Papa, look!" Yvette called.

Above her, Mary Ann saw what appeared to be a mushroom. Then she realized the cap of the mushroom was actually the white covering of the balloon, which was caught in the mesh netting that had surrounded it and tied it to the basket. The stem of the mushroom was the netting and the basket.

"Brilliant!" said Meurthe, sighing with relief. "He must have released the ropes that held the neck of the balloon inside the basket. Then air pressure forced the balloon up to the top of the netting, where it formed a parachute."

"It's the same as flying a kite, isn't it?" said Harding. "If you push hard enough against the air, it holds you up."

Meurthe nodded again.

"He's still coming in fast though," said Mary Ann.

She could see the shape of the wounded *Conqueror* grow larger, as could everyone in Paris. Inside the basket a tiny figure was throwing everything out: instruments, anchor, megaphone, even a portable toilet pitched over the side; anything to lighten the balloon and slow his descent. A set of long underwear billowed out and floated away.

And the wind was getting stronger again. Gusts battered the top of the Tower and turned the mushroom top of the balloon into a spinnaker, a concave sail like a crescent moon. Now it truly was like a kite. It leapfrogged over one line of buildings after another, traveling as fast as a car, but with no control, getting closer and closer to the inevitable moment when something would reach up from the city and snatch it back to earth.

"Does he have a chance?" she heard Harding call to Meurthe.

Meurthe shielded his eyes against the sun. "It depends on where he hits!" he shouted.

Mary Ann looked down. All around them were saw-toothed chimney tops, the sharp-sided red tile roofs, the bullet-headed towers and needle-nosed spires of steeples. There are no soft haystacks here, she thought. If you fall, you die.

The remains of Chevrier's balloon careened toward the tower of a big church less than a mile away. She held her breath and tried to shut her eyes, but couldn't. It hit with a pitched bang, an almost musical crash as the basket smashed a stained glass window. The balloon itself floated down toward the street. Suddenly there was a white flash and a noise like a cannon as a gaslight ignited the remaining hydrogen inside. It seemed to vaporize before her eyes.

"He's dead," said Maximilian.

"No, he's not!" said Meurthe. He pointed to the edge of the roof.

There, hanging from one of the gargoyles, was a tall, dark-haired man. He had jumped from the basket when it hit the window, skidded across the steep slate roof and caught himself just before he fell a hundred feet to the street below.

"*Quel homme!*" cried Yvette. "*Magnifique!*"

Mary Ann looked through the telescope. Chevrier's arms were clasped tightly around the ugly face of a gargoyle, one of the ancient stone carvings that hung over the edge of the roof of the church and were supposed to protect it from evil. Ugly or not, it saved him, she thought. But his legs were kicking the air, looking for a foothold and not finding any. How long could he hold on?

Then down below she saw a company of firemen, who appeared like medieval knights in their steel helmets. The bell on their engine was clanging as they fought their way through the crowd. They hoisted a ladder toward the roof. When it reached him she heard a shout from the mob in the street, and a sigh of relief from everyone on the Tower. Everyone, she noticed, but the German.

"Come, Papa!" cried Yvette. "I want to take a closer look at this marvelous man!"

She disappeared down the circular staircase with a rustle of petticoats and silk. Meurthe, despite his limp, followed her, taking two steps at a time. With both of them gone, the platform seemed almost empty.

But Mary Ann just stood there, watching. He is going to be all right, she thought. She felt as though she knew him, as if she had reached out into the sky and saved him. Don't be ridiculous, she told herself.

She looked across the balcony. The German, Maximilian, stood at the far corner, distant, aloof, and perhaps a little angry. He was wrapped in his gray army cloak as if he were hiding a secret.

She heard a step behind her and turned around.

It was Harding. "Pretty remarkable," he said. "Yvette hasn't even met him and it sounds like she's in love with him already."

"Along with every other woman in Paris," said Mary Ann, watching the crowd below her cheer Alain.

Harding looked at her. "Well, you'll get your chance to meet him tonight. Henri Meurthe invited us all to the Aéro Club."

six

MARY ANN STOOD ON the Place de la Concorde outside the Aéro Club listening to the distant splash of the fountains in the Tuileries. The square—lit by gaslights—was so bright that there was not even a shadow on the sidewalk. She felt out of place, as if she were an actress who had stumbled on stage during the wrong scene.

The members of the Aéro Club, men in silk top hats, had been arriving all evening, some with well-dressed ladies on their arms. Mary Ann was waiting for Harding because she didn't want to go in without him. Now she didn't want to go in at all. Where was Harding? Had he forgotten? Was he drunk?

She wore the same summer dress she had arrived in earlier that day, and the breeze off the Seine gave her goose bumps. For protection she pressed up against one of the statues that lined the square. She looked up at the stone figure of a seated woman with her feet resting on two cannons and her arm cocked defiantly on her hip. The figure was draped in a black robe.

A tall man came up to the double blue doors of the Aéro Club where two doormen waited. Then he changed direction and came toward her, walking with a forward-sloping gait. He circled the monument twice before he noticed her and stopped.

"Who are you?" he asked in French.

"No one," she replied, also in French.

"*No one* shouldn't be out at night unless she's with someone," he said authoritatively. "This is not a place where women should be alone unless they are horizontales."

"I'm waiting for someone," she said defensively.

"And you're waiting here, by Our Lost Sister?"

"What do you mean?" She thought he looked vaguely familiar, but she hardly knew anyone in Paris.

"This statue represents Strasbourg, one of the cities taken by the Germans after we lost the war in 1870. It will stay covered in black until we win it back."

"You French hate the Germans, don't you?"

The tall man smiled. "We French? Then you are not one of us. I thought not. Your accent is imperfect. To answer your question, not all of us hate the Germans, but it is our national pastime. Many mothers—grandmothers now—take their male children to the graves of those who died in that war—like my father. And there they make them swear that they will never rest until the day of revenge comes. A man who dies young for his country, they say, will know only life's roses and leave no orphans."

He stopped. In that instant, Mary Ann thought she had never seen such a handsome man. He had a tall and slender but muscular body, tanned by the sun and the wind, and the head of a war bird, with a long patrician nose. His blue-gray eyes seemed to look into the distance beyond what others saw. Now she remembered where she had seen him; from the Tower when his balloon shot by, just before it exploded.

"You're Alain Chevrier, aren't you?" she said, searching for something to say. "That means 'knight' in French."

"No," he laughed. "Your French is good but not that good. A 'chevalier' is a knight. A 'chevrier' is a goatherd. And you are obviously American. Are you Marianne Pitman? I was told that you'd be here. Marianne is a lovely name."

"It's Mary Ann," she took some pleasure in correcting him. "And where I come from it's pretty ordinary."

"Well," he said, "if I were your escort I would be here by now. Ready to go in?"

She stared at him. He had on a rough work shirt, blue serge pants and military boots, and would look as out of place among the stylish crowd at the Aéro Club as she would.

"Should we be dressed like this?" she asked.

He thought for a second. "Of course they'll let us in tonight," he said. "They have to. But generally the Aéro Club is the kind of place where they hire people like us to throw people like us out. So let's have a little fun with them."

He took her arm and led her across the square and down a side street. At the far end was a doorway. Alain leaned his back against the door and tried the knob.

"It's locked," Mary Ann said.

"No door is ever locked," said Alain. He looked up and down the alley, raised his leg and kicked backward. The door gave.

"But you have an invitation?" she protested. "Why do this?"

"For the same reason that I fly."

Inside it was eerily quiet. Above them, they heard the faint sounds of a banquet. "The pigs are at the trough," said Alain. "I'm not hungry, are you?"

Mary Ann was starving. She hadn't eaten all day, but she wasn't about to admit it now. She followed Alain down the darkened hallways like an acolyte. While the major rooms at the Club were huge and lavish, the back corridors used by the staff were narrow and winding. She felt as though she was in the fun house at an amusement park. She would see a figure coming toward her at the end of the hall and suddenly realize it was her own reflection in a full-length mirror. Doors were concealed behind elaborately painted panels. Gaslights shaped like two-poster candlesticks made Alain duck his head more than once.

They walked through the gymnasium. It reminded Mary Ann of a cave she had once visited in New Mexico where small corridors opened into huge caverns. They found the swimming pool, the steam room, the boxing ring, even a barber shop with four white porcelain chairs gleaming in the moonlight. Now she understood why Alain had broken in. She had begun to see things from the perspective of a burglar. Everything was more intense: the light, the shadows, the objects on the wall.

A circular staircase led up to the Aéro Club's library. Glass shelves filled with books lined two sides, and above the first floor there was a second floor of shelves, bounded by a walkway and a polished wooden railing. One side was filled with Gobelins tapestries, expensive bibelots, figurines by Watteau, Houdon and Fragonard, and Chinese porcelains. On the other were trophies of ballooning contests.

Above them was the world's largest chandelier, a huge mirror-covered balloon with gaslights underneath serving as the basket.

Leather couches and tables were scattered throughout the room, but it was now empty. Mary Ann was impressed in spite of herself. But then, what other club could hand out million-franc prizes?

"Come over here," whispered Alain as he pointed to the far wall. Mounted on it was the lid of the stone sarcophagus, the former resting-place of Ramses III of Egypt. Carved on the lid was a picture of the goddess Isis, crouching down with slender veined wings outstretched as if to protect the portraits of every aeronaut and aviator who died in an accident. The rows of illustrations ranging up and down the wall were long and gloomy.

They were both ancient and modern. A bas-relief showed Greek criminals, daubed with wings and feathers, being thrown from the cliffs off the island of Leucadia. Balloons aflame plunged toward the ground, the aeronauts inside them philosophical or frightened or whatever the artist had chosen to paint them. Beautiful women in bodices and tights twisted in midair, straining against gravity. At the end of the hall were pictures of bodies on the ground, as peaceful as if they were sleeping.

But more frightening were the faces of the dead aeronauts. They were daguerreotypes, highly polished, silver-coated plates with images of glowing delicacy and complex tones of light and shadow. They looked so real that they seemed to speak. They reminded her of spirit photography; pictures conjured out of darkness like phantoms.

Mary Ann stared at the melancholy portraits. "I almost feel as if I know them," she said.

"I do know them," said Alain. "I grew up knowing every one of them. They are my heroes." He pointed to a bearded man. "There is Otto Lilienthal, who flew gliders off his own man-made mountain. When he fell and broke his back, his last words were 'Sacrifices must be made.'

"And John Wise, with his big prophet's beard. He believed that there were tides in the sky that could fly you across the oceans. He was right, but he died proving it.

"Over here is a portrait of Madame Blanchard, the first woman to fly . . . and to die. She surrounded her balloon with a ring of fireworks called Bengal lights and set them off when she was in the sky over Paris. But the fire got too close to the balloon and it exploded. She made it safely to a roof and then slipped and fell to the street."

"And this one?" she asked.

It was a picture of a man jumping from the basket of a balloon while a woman inside watched, his tense face nerved for the certain death below.

"That is Thomas Harris," said Chevrier. "He took his fiancée aloft over England and was foolish enough to pull the wrong valve, releasing most of the gas. When they started to fall, he lightened the balloon and saved her the only way he could. He jumped out."

"He died for love?" she asked. They paused for a moment and looked at each other.

"Come on," said Alain. "I'm ready to eat."

They walked quietly into the banquet hall, their presence masked by a sudden burst of laughter from the other side of the room, and took seats at the back. The dining room ran almost the full length of the building, and its wide windows opened onto the Place de la Concorde. Mirrors on the opposite wall reflected the stars of the night sky and the slow-moving Seine.

After downing a dozen oysters each, the diners had finished

four of the five main courses and were now working on the breast of pigeon. The pigeons had been killed by some of these same men at the Tir aux Pigeons, a Paris shooting gallery where birds had their wings clipped to make them fly more erratically. Some of the shot remained in the birds, so the waiters brought small plates and the gentlemen and ladies delicately spat the bird shot out. They made a clinking sound, like the ball on a roulette table, when they hit the enameled china.

Then glasses were tapped for silence. Henri Meurthe rose from his seat at the front of the horseshoe-shaped dining room.

"My first happy function here tonight is to introduce the president of France, and, I might add, my good friend, Auguste Pouchet," said Meurthe. "We are honored to have him speak tonight."

Alain groaned from the back.

Heads turned. Pouchet heard the noise, although he couldn't identify the source.

"I will keep my presentation brief," the president said, glaring. "First, we owe Monsieur Meurthe a large debt for bringing about this contest. When he originally told me of the award, he wished to be anonymous. But I convinced him that the donor of such a munificent prize could not remain unknown for long. I am happy we can now call it the Meurthe Prize!" The diners clapped and cheered.

"When we announced the contest, we did not expect to have such international representation." Pouchet's eyes shifted around the room to see if any of the Germans were present, and then went on. "However, we are pleased this noble dream, coming as it does at a time when Paris is recognized as an international leader, will show the fecundity of our resources, the strength of our engineers, artists and workmen, and the genius of the individual Frenchman so brilliantly displayed . . ."

Alain began to clap as if the speech was over. The rest, taking his cue, joined in. Mary Ann giggled. As Pouchet attempted to start speaking again, Alain rose from his chair, still clapping. So did the rest of the club members.

"Bravo!" he shouted.

Pouchet clenched his fists so hard the tablecloth ripped—and then sat down.

Meurthe rose again. "Ah, I see we have our own French contestant for the prize, Alain Chevrier, with us tonight. Stand up, Monsieur Chevrier! Don't be modest. I'm sure that you have something you'd like to say."

Alain rose. He had not expected to give a speech. For the first time Mary Ann saw a look of doubt on his face.

"I suppose I should thank you," he started, "for allowing me to see these acres of gilt and velvet and tapestries . . . and for the thrill of going to dinner between two solid walls of flunkies in livery. As Proudhon said, 'All property is theft,' and you have shown me not only the thieves, but also their ill-gotten gains."

The well-fed and half-drunk audience grumbled, but no one rose to challenge Chevrier.

"I'm a soldier," he continued. "I have fought for France. And I will fly for France, but for the people of France, not those who exploit them. I . . ."

Meurthe stood and started to clap. So did the others at the head table, and then everyone.

Alain stared at Meurthe a moment, and then took his seat. The veins in his neck bulged as he tried to hide his anger.

"We thank Monsieur Chevrier for blessing us with his candid

point of view," said Meurthe with a wry smile. "And now I'm going to bring these speeches to a halt, before you start applauding for me, too."

The meal ended with the usual brandy, apricot tarts, petits fours and the traditional French ice cream served with a paper umbrella on top. Alain ignored the food and walked up to Meurthe, who still sat at the head of the horseshoe table. He leaned on the table, rattling the remaining dishes.

"I did not enjoy what you did to me," he said.

Meurthe leaned back in his chair. Alain looked as though he could easily hit Meurthe, but the Aéro Club president seemed relaxed. He stroked his mustache.

"Yes," said Meurthe. "All too often these after-dinner speeches get long-winded and interfere with the serving of the cigars. Would you like one of mine? As the philosopher says, 'A meal without a good cigar is a one-eyed beauty.'"

Alain knocked it out of his hand. Mary Ann gasped.

But Meurthe didn't react. "Please forgo the histrionics, Monsieur Chevrier," he said quietly. "You are a soldier. You know perfectly well that in a war, even a class war such as the one you are trying to fight, bullets are fired in both directions. Or, to put it biblically, those who live by applause . . ."

"We will see each other again," Alain broke in. He spun and walked toward the door.

"Undoubtedly we will," Meurthe called after him, "if you have the courage to stay in the contest!"

Mary Ann caught up to Alain when he reached the front doors. Just as they walked out, Harding walked in.

"You must be Chevrier!" he said. "I saw what you did today. It was brilliant."

"And you must be Harding Cooper, the famous writer," said Alain.

Mary Ann was taken aback. Harding a famous writer? "You're late," she told him.

"Bishop arrived and held me up," Harding apologized as they walked outside. "He was looking for a boat on the Seine. He doesn't want to waste any time."

Mary Ann saw a bottle in his pocket. "Have you been drinking?" she asked.

"Drinking, yes, but not drunk. Found a new beverage called 'eau-de-vie.'"

"The water of life," Alain translated. "Clear as water and tastes like ground glass."

"I'd liken it more to lye soap myself." Harding passed the bottle over to Alain. "It's 120-proof."

"Which car do you want to take?" said Alain. "There are three Renaults, two Pannards, a couple of Darraqs and one of those Teuf-Teuf motorcycles."

"Did someone say that you could use their car?" asked Mary Ann naively. "They're private property."

"All property is theft." Alain turned the crank on the Pannard. It roared to life. "We'll have them back before those fat bastards inside finish their *bombes glacés.*"

They were off before she could protest again. Harding in the open car, Chevrier weaving in and out on the motorcycle with Mary Ann in the sidecar. They bored through the streets of the city, their goose horns blaring.

In the Place Vendôme, courtesans and late-night partygoers called to them from the sidewalk. In residential areas, people, angry at their noise, threw bottles and curses from upper-story windows. Neither Harding nor Alain cared. They waved back happily at everyone.

Then came the attack on the omnibus on the Rue de Rivoli. They formed an impromptu skirmish line and made ready to charge the big, lumbering horse-drawn double-decker. When Mary Ann climbed in with Harding, Alain unhooked the sidecar.

Their car swerved around the bus. The passengers on *l'impériale,* the open upper deck, looked down and laughed. Then Alain rode his motorcycle up the back steps of the bus, lifted his front wheel and rolled onboard, screaming a strange curdling whoop. She could see him ride up the aisle, bounce down the front steps, and take off again, the conductor behind him shaking his fist.

They passed through Les Halles, where huge iron beams held up the glass ceilings that covered the city's market. The daytime crowds were gone, leaving only broken crates, yesterday's smells, and a few *bijoutiers* selling the refuse tossed out from fancy restaurants and banquets like the one they had just left.

Now they were in an area of winding streets that seemed to change names constantly. Occasionally they would pass through a lighted square, dodge a monument or statue at the center, and then swerve into another narrow alley.

"Where are you headed?" Harding called out.

"We'll see the sunrise from the hills of Montmartre," shouted Alain, still leading the way.

At each turn he swung either left or right, with Harding trying to follow. The motorcycle had no headlight and no one thought to ignite the acetylene torches mounted on the front of the car. They played a game of shadow tag.

Finally Alain made a wrong turn. He plowed over a picket fence, its splintering stakes running up and down the musical scale as he uprooted them. He clipped a chestnut tree and sent a shower of pink blossoms raining down on himself. The motorcycle, out of control, ran into the wooden front steps of a frame house.

Lights went on inside. A pretty woman in a nightgown and cloth cap rushed out on the porch carrying an oil lamp.

"What is it with you *automobilistes!*" she screamed. "I will call the gendarmes and have you arrested. Out all hours of the day and night, driving recklessly. I swear, you will kill my children!"

Alain picked himself up from beside the motorcycle, whipped off his cap, and bowed. "Madame," he said, "I will gladly give you more."

They abandoned the motorcycle where it lay, saluting the woman's porch and the wounded chestnut tree. Alain jumped onto the back of Harding's two-seater and they roared away before the woman could make good on her threat to call the police.

Soon they were lost in Montmartre. Harding flagged down the driver of a milk truck.

"Which way to the top?" he yelled.

"*Pardon, Monsieur?*"

"To the top, to the top," cried Harding, pointing up.

"Ah," said the milkman, showing a toothless grin. "*C'est à gauche, à gauche au moulin verte.*" He pointed to the left and made the sign of a windmill.

They took off in a cloud of fumes. Two turns later they were lost again.

"There's too many windmills up here," Harding complained.

"Yes," said Alain, "but it's not Montmartre's fault. It's so high above the city it's easy to catch the wind."

"Did he mean this windmill?" Harding asked as they flew by another. "This one's green."

"No, I think he meant the last one," said Alain. "They all look alike in the dark."

"Let's try the next one," shouted Harding over the roar of the engine. "Here it is . . ."

Suddenly they saw only space. Then they felt a bumping under their wheels. They had turned onto one of the streets in Montmartre, so steep that the residents had built wooden steps into the hill. They went straight down the board steps, bouncing all the way. Harding was suddenly very sober, trying to keep his foot from sliding off the brake, the wheel shaking in his hand. Mary Ann threw her arms around him, surprising them both.

It was well that he kept his foot on the brake. There was a drainage ditch at the bottom of the stairway. The car skidded to a stop with the front wheels just over the edge.

Then the car rolled in. Harding jumped from one side. Alain seized Mary Ann and leaped out the other. Both of them fell to the ground. The car rolled leisurely to the bottom as if it were taking itself for a Sunday drive, started up the other side, and then came back down, its shiny wheels settling into the mud.

Mary Ann lay still on the ground, Alain half on top of her. He was close enough to kiss her, and she hoped that he would. When he realized where he was, his eyes widened as if he was embarrassed by the unintended intimacy, and he pulled back.

From a few feet away came Harding's voice. "Look out there," he said, his voice strangely peaceful after their wild, terrifying ride.

In the distance, looking like an upright honeycomb glowing amber in the darkness, stood the Eiffel Tower. The Tower's 22,000 gaslights illuminated the slender spire all the way to its peak. They turned the ugly brown stewed-beef color of the Tower in daylight to the burnished gold of night.

But Harding wasn't pointing at the Tower. His face was turned upward to the night sky.

Mary Ann looked, too. She had not truly gazed at the sky since she was a child lying on her back in the summer fields. And now she realized why. It wasn't safe to look at. It was too open. It bent your neck back too far. And it scared her. It had infinite depths—or no depths at all. It was an open door to the universe, the whole ocean of air above them. The prow of the ditch where they lay was the last of Land's End, and all beyond was the Great Voyage. Out there, among bright stars, ancient nebulae fractured and new ones coalesced, smashed together by soundless explosions.

"It's a beautiful moment, isn't it, the sky just before dawning?" asked Alain, still lying beside her. "Once I had them lower me into the dry bottom of a 40-foot well in Algeria."

"What the hell for?" they heard Harding say.

"It was a trick that I learned from an old Arab," Alain replied. "I sat there for 12 hours looking up through that small hole, with darkness all around. But because of the darkness, I could see stars glowing in the daytime, when no one else could. And as day passed into night, I saw distant constellations that have yet to be named. That sky is like our lives. There are no limits except the ones we put there."

She heard Harding's voice again, skeptical this time. "You mean to tell me that big sky up there will allow Man to be its equal? And, if it does, do you really think it will be one of the three of us, sitting like fools on the side of this ditch?"

There was silence for a moment, and Mary Ann thought that this strange debate in the dark was over.

But then Alain rose. "Who knows?" he said. "No one ever knows anything for sure. But I believe that there's a star out there in the heavens for each of us, the born and the unborn. And I will find mine. Good night, Harding. And good night to you, Marianne."

"What about the car?" asked Harding.

"Leave it," said Alain. "The owner will find it . . . or buy a new one." He walked away into the night, whistling.

Mary Ann watched him go, watched him as long as she could see into the darkness. "Good night, Alain," she whispered.

"Look," said Harding. And, in that instant, a shooting star flashed across the sky and fell to earth, leaving a second's silvery glow behind it. "I wonder if someone has fallen from his place in Alain's heaven to some unknown hell below?" he said.

She shivered, perhaps because the night was chilly.

Harding wrapped his coat around her. "Come on, Mary Ann," he said, pointedly using her real name. "I'll take you back to your hotel."

seven

On Board the Bethanie—16 M<small>AY</small>

N<small>EVILLE</small> B<small>ISHOP LEANED BOTH</small> hands on his silver-headed cane, triangulating himself like a surveyor. He looked out over the boats beneath the shadow of the Pont Marie bridge. Mary Ann stood beside him, wondering what he saw. Was it the quaint, wooden-slatted washrooms built out over the river? Was it the scrawled graffiti under the bridge? "Gave herself to me—fully" boasted one inscription. Was it the ducks on the quays, standing on one leg preening themselves?

No, thought Mary Ann. What Neville Bishop sees are possibilities. He's the kind of man who looks at a forest and sees railroad ties. And what he's looking at now is that boat over there, the *Bethanie*.

"Are you sure it's the longest one on the river?" Bishop asked Harding.

"Longest and widest," said Harding.

"Then let's go get it," said Bishop.

He strode up the gangplank and onto the middle of the barge. There was a dog at the other end of the gangplank, yapping and trying to get loose from its chain. It wasn't a big dog, and it didn't look unfriendly, but Bishop pushed it out of the way with his cane. Behind him came his entourage: two big hired men, then Harding and Mary Ann.

Each boat on the Seine was home for a family that ferried cargoes up and down the river. They reminded Mary Ann of the little cottages and country gardens where she had spent her summers as a child. The rounded cargo bay, only slightly above deck level, went from the pointed prow to near the back, where a squared-off pilothouse spanned the width of the boat. Behind was a back deck that looked like a yard and extended all the way to the rudder.

The *Bethanie* was especially pretty. The boat had geraniums spaced all around the sides—obviously a woman's work. There was a little doghouse and a tree in a pot on the back deck. Even the anchor was well-placed. It didn't just lie on deck. It overhung the bow, mounted on a wrought-iron piece that looked like an inverted fishhook.

There were lace curtains in the window of the pilothouse. For a moment Mary Ann could see herself and Alain floating down a peaceful river in a boat like this . . . then she caught herself.

Bishop made the short step from the rounded cargo bay to the top of the pilothouse. The dog was still yapping. Bishop bent over at the waist and rapped on the window with his cane. Mary Ann saw his pants stretch as they rode up over his ample rump. His ankles were surprisingly skinny and white. She wondered what the person inside saw—an upside-down look at Bishop? Better than the view she was getting.

Someone opened the door to the pilothouse. Bishop and the rest, still playing follow-the-leader, came down the ladder and through the door.

They filled up the pilothouse, which already had a big wood and brass wheel higher than a man. Bishop took the only seat available, leaving the others to stand. The barge captain and his wife offered them wine.

Bishop refused.

"Don't mind if I do," said Harding, who got a dirty look from both Bishop and Mary Ann.

"Harding, tell this frog that I'm a very wealthy man who wishes to rent his boat for a month to travel up and down the Seine," Bishop said.

Harding translated, but left out the "frog," Mary Ann noticed.

The captain and his wife looked at each other and both shook their heads vigorously. Mary Ann was relieved.

Harding turned back to Bishop. "He says that he would never rent his boat to a Frenchman, let alone a foreigner."

"You've got to convince him. I *need* this boat." Mary Ann could see Bishop struggling not to raise his voice. "Offer him more money."

"That won't do it," warned Harding. He paused and thought for a second. "Put on your glasses, the pince-nez," he told Bishop.

"What!"

"Just put them on quick." Harding pulled a newspaper out of his pocket and showed it to the captain.

Mary Ann heard them talking and caught the words "San Juan Hill" and "vice president."

Then the captain smiled and grabbed Bishop and hugged him.

"I told him that you were Teddy Roosevelt," said Harding, showing the picture from the newspaper to Mary Ann. "Well, he does look a little like him."

Mary Ann turned away and faced the river, so as not to laugh.

"But Monsieur," said the captain in broken English, "the *Bethanie* is our home. Where would we live?"

"Tell him that in I addition to rent I will put them up in one of the best hotels on the Île Saint-Louis during the time that I use their boat," said Bishop. He took a gold money clip full of francs out of his pocket—with the hundreds on top—and started peeling off bills.

The captain and his wife eyed them hungrily.

"Monsieur is very generous," the captain's wife broke in. "But what about our dog?"

"We'll keep the dog," said Bishop. "Harding will take good care of it."

"What?" said Harding.

"All the details are in this lease agreement," said Bishop. "I had my French attorney draw it up for you. Please sign both copies."

The barge captain and Harding exploded into French, and Mary Ann—with only her classroom knowledge—couldn't keep up. She had a premonition, though. It reminded her of the time she had seen a weasel catch a chicken.

She looked the couple over. The captain was in his early 60s, a sturdy, bullet-headed man with a salt-and-pepper mustache. He looked like a lot of American farmers Mary Ann had seen: big and rough, but not nasty. When he signed the lease, he wrote his name in big block letters, like a schoolboy. He would be easy prey for Bishop.

The wife was short, round and had a full bosom. She was beaming at Mary Ann. She looked motherly, and Mary Ann wondered whether the couple had any children? Unexpectedly she got her answer. It was both yes . . . and no.

"You will take good care of our boat?" the captain's wife asked Bishop. "She was named after our only daughter, Bethanie Émelie. She died two years ago September."

She came over, pinched Mary Ann on the cheek and smiled at her. "She looked a lot like you."

Bishop had Harding reassure her. She bustled around polishing the crockery and Limoges collection on the wall before she left. An hour later the captain had their suitcases in hand and was walking down the gangplank, his wife waving goodbye to her dog, her boat and her flowers.

"*Au revoir, mes petits,*" Mary Ann heard her say. Harding went along to help them get settled.

When they were out of sight, Bishop said: "Go to work."

His two men started dismantling everything. They tore the pilothouse loose from the boat and pushed it into the river. The flowerpots went into the water. The dog was barking. It was kicked into silence. Bishop shouted orders. The mast came down. It too went into the water. The fishermen along the quay watched the destruction impassively, cigarettes dangling from their mouths.

Finally the *Bethanie* was leveled right down to the deck. Carpenters arrived with planking that was nailed crosswise the entire length of the boat. A huge catapult, looking like a siege engine, that had been resting on the quay was uncoverd and hoisted on board.

That evening, by the light of the moon, Bishop walked up and down the planking alone. He reached the prow of the boat and looked over the dark lapping waters of the Seine.

"I am the master of my fate, the captain of my soul," he said to the river.

Mary Ann drew a bucket of water out of the Seine and took it over to the dog, who was whimpering. "What soul?" she muttered to herself.

eight

*T*HAT NIGHT MARY ANN left her hotel and wandered around the city, trying to find sleep and—perhaps—forgiveness for her role in what had happened earlier in the day.

In the moonlight up toward Montmartre she could see what looked like glistening bones, the beams and rafters of the still-uncompleted Sacre-Coeur church. It was being built as an offering to God, France's self-imposed penalty for losing the war to the Germans in 1871.

She remembered Harding telling her about a play called *Mademoiselle Fifi*, in which a French prostitute plunges a knife into a German lieutenant after he pours wine on her head. She remembered too the way that Meurthe and Maximilian, the German, had glared at each other that day on the Eiffel Tower. Would either of them ever forget? she wondered.

She strolled past the bars and heard singing through the open doorways. The dance halls, some of them old windmills, were filled with sweaty men in straw hats and women kicking up their legs to show flesh-colored stockings. She did not go in.

She walked by restaurants and looked in open windows. Lovers sat, sharing food by a single candle, the light reflecting in their eyes. And then there were the prostitutes in bright dresses sitting on their front porches. The older ones knitted while the younger ones, some barely teenagers, played with dolls while they waited for their gentlemen clients to come and take them upstairs.

The French had a whole language of illicit sex, Mary Ann discovered. The women were called *les horizontales,* or "the unbuttoned," but like French society itself, they were divided into classes. At the top were the demimondaine, who were scarcely ladies of the night at all but very high-class kept women, the kind she had seen at the Aéro Club the previous night. Below them were the *maisons de tolérance* where ordinary prostitutes lived and worked. There were over 100 of them in Montmartre alone, with large illuminated street numbers to help clients identify them. The lowest class lived, worked and even coupled on the street, in alleyways or abandoned doorways.

There were many bums or *clochards.* Everyone tolerated them, if they were amiable. She saw them go to the bars late that night, when the owners were just putting the stools up, and stagger out with half-empty bottles that had been left on the tables. They would wave to their friends and walk down to the river where the midnight fires still burned.

Then she saw a familiar figure in a white suit come out of a bar—Harding. He seemed uncertain of his direction and then headed across the street, where he had seen a calico cat.

"Here, kitty," he said, holding out his hand a foot above the pavement.

The calico may have been an alley cat, but it had its dignity. It got to its feet, blinked twice, and sauntered away. Harding followed, and so did Mary Ann.

The cat jumped to a porch and then up to a board fence that marked the edge of a vacant lot. Harding did the same thing. If Mary Ann hadn't seen it, she wouldn't have believed it. His sense of balance, even when drunk, was perfect.

The cat was annoyed. Perhaps it felt it was being upstaged. Its tail twitched. It trotted nervously across the top edge of the fence. So did Harding, a trifle faster than he should have. The cat jumped for a wrought-iron second-story porch. Harding stepped on a first-floor windowsill and swung himself up.

Perhaps the cat saw Harding as a pursuer. Or maybe it just didn't want company. It leaped from window ledge to window ledge until it was on the roof of one of the low buildings. It turned again, its tail still twitching.

Harding was still behind it, mumbling "Good kitty." One of the tiles gave way as he scrambled up the roof. It exploded on the cobbled street next to Mary Ann.

There was a flash overhead. The calico cat had made a tremendous leap across the alleyway to the opposite roof. In a moment Mary Ann knew Harding would try the same leap. But he wouldn't make it.

"Harding!" she shouted.

Seconds later oil lamps flickered and brightened inside the houses on both sides of the alley. Voices yelled "*Chut!*" and "*Taisez-vous!*"

A face appeared over the edge of the roof. "Mary Ann, is that you?" Harding asked.

"Come down here," she whispered hoarsely.

THEY STARTED TO WALK, but all the starch had gone out of Harding. He leaned on her, his face scratchy against her cheek and smelling of bay rum. There had been times, many times before she met Alain, when she fantasized about what it would be like to have Harding touch her, but not like this. She almost had to carry him, and he was heavy.

She searched frantically up and down the boulevard. There were no cabs. There was nothing on the empty street. Even the *horizontales*, smelling no business, had gone in for the night. Then an empty glass-enclosed hearse came up the street, pulled by two big horses.

"Oh God," said Mary Ann. "What's he doing out tonight?"

"Coming for us, perhaps," said Harding. "He seems to be headed in our direction." Harding flagged down the hearse. "I'll pay you to take us home?" he asked.

"Why not?" shrugged the top-hatted driver. "But you'll have to ride in back."

Harding opened the two glass doors and lifted Mary Ann inside. Then he crawled in. They left the back doors open.

"This is actually comfortable," said Harding, leaning back. "You get a nice view, too. A shame the usual occupant never gets to enjoy it." He pulled out his bottle.

"You should put that away," said Mary Ann. "If you keep drinking like this, you're going to die."

"Yeah," said Harding. "I'll give a whole new meaning to Tennyson's 'Crossing the Bar.' You know, you remind me of a song I heard:

> *One evening in October,*
> *I was very far from sober,*
> *To toddle home to bed I vainly tried.*
> *When my feet began to stutter,*

I lay down in the gutter,
And a pig came up and lay down by my side.

Oh, we sang of stormy weather,
And the more we are together,
Till a lady passing by was heard to say:

"You can tell a man who boozes
By the company he chooses,"
And the pig got up and slowly walked away.
Yes the pig got up and hung his head in shame,
And slowly walked away.

Harding had a nice baritone, the kind that dominated a church choir. The driver turned around with a look of annoyance and gave the horses a snap of the whip.

Harding was silent for a moment, looking out. Then he turned to her.

"Sure, I'm a drunk," he said. "But I'm a pleasant drunk, a genial and well-meaning drunk. I'm never obnoxious and seldom piss my pants. Put me in a corner with a bottle and leave me; I'll be perfectly happy. So, as a drunk, I can highly recommend myself for your next party. Give your guests someone to point the finger at and say, 'At least I'm not as soused as that man over there!'"

"But you were a famous writer once, weren't you? I heard Alain say so."

"Don't believe everything Chevrier tells you," said Harding with a smile. "My father was a doctor, Ulysses Grant's personal physician. He wanted me to be a doctor, too. So he sent sonny boy off to the Sorbonne here in Paris for the best medical training.

"A lot of radical ideas were running around at the time and I got interested in Karl Marx. I was a little like Alain. Well, when I argued with my father about shooting workers just because they went on strike, he cut me off. Left me in Europe. Thought it would teach me a lesson. In a way it did.

"First I joined the 'wandering people.' No job. No home. Traveled across Europe with a guitar, singing for my supper. Then I settled in Paris and started painting. I'm not a great painter, but I know great painting when I see it. I started to write about the Impressionists just as people in America were starting to appreciate them. And that's how I became famous."

"And you ended up working for Bishop?" she asked.

"From writing about art, it's only a short step to buying art," said Harding. "I helped rich stupid Americans plunder the Old World's treasures. Manet, Monet, it was all Mon-ey to me. And that led me to Bishop, who fancies himself a Renaissance man, but couldn't tell a Courbet from a sorbet." He took a pull on his bottle.

"Why do you do it?"

"You mean, why do I drink? Or why do I work for Neville Bishop? I drink because I don't like what I do . . . you saw how he operates."

"So why do you work for him?"

"That's simple. A lush like me can't get an honest job."

"You're lying," she said. "Bishop needs you because you understand the French as if you were one of them. And they respect you."

"All the worse for them. Next thing you'll be asking me if I was married."

"You were. Her name was Maria. Why did it end?"

"Well, that gets back to my fatal flaw, doesn't it? It happened right here in the City of Love. She went to see an angelmaker . . ."

"A what?"

"An abortionist," said Harding. His voice was flat. "I told her that I wanted to paint. I wasn't ready to have children. The French call them angelmakers because they make little angels. Except this one botched the job, so I got two for the price of one."

"You mean . . ." She looked at him in horror, not wanting to hear him say it.

"Yeah. He killed her." He paused. "No, let me tell the truth. I killed her." His voice broke as he said it. "Do you hate me now? Probably not as much as I hate myself."

She didn't know what to say. She reached over to touch his cheek, and felt it was wet, but only for a second before he jerked his head away. The hearse rolled on. They were on a cobblestone street now.

"It's quiet, isn't it?" she said.

"Yup," said Harding, glad to change the subject, "this hearse has new rubber tires. I'm told these things are hitting lots of people because they're listening for the sound of the metal wheels. Creeps right up on you and next thing you know, you're lying right here in the back. More business for this man.

"So what's your story? An only child?"

"I am now. I had a brother. His name was Samuel, just like my father. People used to call them 'First and Second Samuel.' Second Samuel and my mother both died of typhoid when I was 15. That was just before my father left Harvard."

"I seem to remember something about them running him out."

"They said he was doing 'unauthorized experiments.' He was trying to learn how to fly. They told him to stop."

"And instead he took you to that godforsaken church down there in Tennessee," said Harding, stretching out on the floor of the hearse.

"Yes. He'd wander in the hills, day after day, climbing the rocks and watching the eagles and the hawks. He could tell every bird just by the way it flew. Watching them fly, he thought about his dreams when he was a child. He made flying machines, first gliders and then wings with engines. And then one day he didn't come back. I found him out there in the hills among the rocks. He was frozen. His eyes were open. He was still watching the birds."

"Monsieur and Mademoiselle, we have arrived," said the hearse driver with mock courtesy.

They went inside Harding's apartment house.

When she asked the sleepy concierge where to take him, he said, "Third floor . . . and a half."

As they trudged up the narrow steps, Mary Ann understood what he had meant. She hadn't expected much, based on the way that he lived in New York, but this amazed her. "The owner cut every floor in half, didn't he?" she asked. "He turned six stories into 12."

"Yeah," said Harding, puffing up the stairway ahead of her. "I used to ask him how the other half lived, but he never got it." He opened the door. The famous high French ceilings were so low now that even Mary Ann almost had to stoop under the beams. The bed was only a pallet on a box, a foot above the floor. Papers were scattered everywhere.

"Why do you live here?" she asked.

"That's a simple question and deserves a simple answer. I own this place. I owned it back when . . . when Maria and I were living here, young and poor and in love."

"And you kept it even . . . even after."

"Yeah. I used to lie on this bed thinking she'd come walking through that door. And after I left Paris, I kept thinking if she ever came back I wanted her to have a place to stay."

She laid him gently on the bed and took off his coat. He was wearing crossbraced suspenders, a surprising luxury for a man who couldn't remember to keep his suit cleaned. One of them had snapped and he had knotted it. A garter strap that held up his sock had also snapped and the sock was flapping around his ankle. He used his necktie as a handkerchief when he sneezed. His shoelaces were gnarled, and it was obvious from the broken-down heels that he seldom tied them. If he changed his celluloid collar once a week she would be surprised. He was falling apart. She started to pull off his shoes . . . and found that he was up on his elbows, looking at her.

She looked back. The shoes dropped to the floor. Slowly, and with surprising tenderness, he brought his face up to hers and kissed her.

For a second she let him. Then she heard him say "Maria." Not Mary Ann. Maria.

She pushed him back down on the bed and stood up—as best she could.

"I'm that good?" Harding said.

"You called me Maria," she retorted. "You're still living on guilt, aren't you? Guilt and rotgut."

Harding rolled his eyes back toward the low ceiling. "It's been years and years and nobody's ever taken out the sutures. But you, Mary Ann, should definitely be kissed."

Mary Ann's eyes caught fire by the light of the single oil lamp. "I've been kissed . . ." she said defensively.

"And will be again," he broke in. "But not by me."

His eyes were suddenly clear and perceptive. "You love him, don't you?" he said.

"Who?" said Mary Ann, knowing whom he meant.

"Alain," he said. "You love him, don't you?"

"What difference does it make?"

"The truth?"

"No."

"Come on," said Harding. "Whatever else we've done, we haven't lied to each other tonight. The truth."

"Maybe. Maybe a little." She was sitting on the edge of the narrow bed now. Harding reached out and stroked her hair. She hated Harding. He was a big drunken oaf who had just chased a cat off a roof—and still he could read her thoughts.

"How did you know?" she asked.

"It shows," he said. "For one thing, you get this stupid expression on your face every time you hear his name."

She picked up one of his shoes and tried to whack him with it. He fended off the blow with his shoulder, still surprisingly agile.

Then he grinned. "He invited us to visit his workshop in Saint-Cloud tomorrow . . . I mean this morning. Want to go?"

"Isn't he afraid that we'll see his flying machines?" she asked. "After all, we're rivals."

Harding laughed. "I don't think either Bishop or that German worry him at all. Are you coming?"

"No," she said, walking quickly toward the door. Perhaps he would stop if she left. But his voice followed her.

"I'll stop by your hotel at seven to pick you up. And Mary Ann! . . . wear a dress. Not that brown one with the bleach stain. The one that looks like it came from a nunnery."

She picked up the other shoe to hit him, and saw that he was already asleep, his mouth open, snoring gently, unaware of the turmoil that he had awakened in her.

"Bastard!" she said to herself. She went out and shut the door softly.

nine

*A*N HOUR AFTER THEY started out the next morning, they were lost in Saint-Cloud.

Mary Ann and Harding had gone in search of the Parc de Aerostation, that fabled place above Paris where Alain Chevrier was building his magnificent aircraft. The entire city seemed to know where it was, and every newspaper had published pictures of the big churchlike structure with its high gambrel roof. As they crossed the Seine at the Aqueduct Bridge and followed the rushing water toward the heights overlooking Paris, she assumed it would be easy to find.

But the fog descended on them like a net as they got higher. "Now you know why they call it Saint-Cloud," said Harding.

"Did you bring a map?"

"I lost it," said Harding, rubbing his forehead. She could see he was nursing a hangover.

"How did you ever find your way when you were wandering across Europe?" she asked bitingly.

"I didn't have you along," he retorted.

Saint-Cloud was a series of narrow, twisting roads running progressively upward. Streets kept changing names. The old joke about Paris was that every street has at least one alias. Harding and Mary Ann turned up and down side streets, hoping to cut across and find the Park. But the slopes were so steep that Alain's building could have been nestled anywhere without showing a turret or a peak.

Then Harding began to sniff the air.

Mary Ann thought he had gone crazy.

"Sulfuric acid," he said. "Someone's making hydrogen." He ran to the edge of the hill and looked straight back toward Paris. "There!" he shouted.

She looked. The figure of a man appeared through the fog where no man had a right to be, rising out of the mist in thin air, defying gravity.

The figure was almost level with them, 100 feet away from the steep side of the hill, and Mary Ann could see it was Alain. He was standing, holding ropes like reins, guiding what appeared to be an enormous prehistoric creature beneath him as it reared its way up through the fog.

As Alain rose, she could see he was standing on the front of a blue dirigible, steering it with guide ropes connected to a rudder far in the back. The rising sun refracted on the mist, breaking it into rainbow colors that arched over the top of the flying machine. Then the dirigible rose higher, and cast its shadow across them and the mountain.

"The workshop's down below," Harding pointed. "Ready to go?"

Mary Ann stood there, unmoving.

"Let's go!" he repeated, loud enough to break through her reverie. Then he took her hand and walked her slowly down the grassy slope toward the big open door. As they did, they watched Alain lower the big dirigible gently into its berth inside.

"What's Alain really like?" she asked Harding.

"People have called him a Marxist, an anarchist, or a Communard, but I don't think that any label really fits."

"Well, what is he?"

Harding stopped for a moment, mulling what he should say. "An individualist," he said finally, "who happens to be lucky enough to do exactly what he wants."

"Why?"

"Because France needs him. He's the only hope this country has of winning the Meurthe Prize and, even more important, keeping it away from the Germans."

"The common people love him," said Mary Ann. "The newspapers call him the Magellan of the Air. He gets cheered wherever he goes. Maybe that's because he has the courage to thumb his nose at the rich and powerful. Or maybe it's just because he looks like a hero. He's young, handsome . . . and intelligent."

Harding looked closely at her. She started to blush. "A lot of women want him, don't they?" she asked.

"And a lot of men are sharpening their knives for him," Harding shot back. "What interests me is the way Chevrier keeps crossing swords with Meurthe. He hates him. But it's Meurthe who has put Alain in the spotlight. Before the Meurthe Prize, Alain was just an obscure officer doing experiments at an army base, a man who never would have risen past captain. Now he has Paris at his feet. Yet he despises the man who put him there."

"What about women?" she asked. "Do you think he has a special one?"

"I think he has a million opportunities. But Alain is like a steam kettle. All his energy comes out through his work. He's a genius, so he sees things that are far away, like stars, but misses what's up close . . . like you."

He waited for a reaction from her, but she deliberately walked on ahead. He wasn't going to read her thoughts this time.

The fog had burned off. Looking westward they could see first the blue ribbon of the Seine, then the green of the Bois de Boulogne, the city itself and finally, the distant Tower, its base lost in the haze.

By the time they had reached the huge doors to the workshop, Alain was waiting for them. "Harding! Marianne!" he shouted. (This time she didn't bother to correct him.) "Come in. Meet my ladies."

Mary Ann felt a flash of jealousy. Then she realized who his "ladies" were. They were made of gossamer, bamboo, linen and aluminum.

They passed the big blue airship, the one they had just seen outside. "This one is *La Grande Dame*. It is similar to what the Germans are building," said Alain with a smile. "It is a rigid framework of aluminum girders with 12 gas cells inside, instead of just one big one. For today's experiment, we even built a platform to see if it could be steered from the front. We are still trying to find the proper engine for it."

"How do you know what the Germans are doing?" asked Harding. "They've been very secretive."

Chevrier smiled again. "In Paris there are no secrets."

"Have you considered one of the new rotary engines?" asked Mary Ann.

Alain seemed surprised by the information, as well as where it came from. "But don't they get too hot?"

"They're air-cooled," said Mary Ann. "If you are traveling at 15 miles an hour or more, they won't overheat."

Alain was impressed. "How do you know so much about them?"

"My father and I investigated different types of engines when we were planning to build an aeroplane," she said.

"I envy you. A balloon is just a cloud in a bag. Propelling a dirigible through the air is like pushing a sausage through a brick wall. And trying to control it is like waltzing with a jellyfish. All you see here . . ." and he swept his arm around the huge barn, "is just trying to improve the existing technology. You and your father discovered new ways to fly. When this foolishness is over, I would enjoy working with you."

Mary Ann shot a triumphant look at Harding. At that moment a bulky man with big hussar's mustache, which rolled back into the folds of his neck, came up behind them. He was holding a heavy ring with crossed swords and a ruby inset.

"Here comes my assistant, Guillaume LeRond," said Chevrier.

LeRond held out the ring. "I found this next to the gas tank . . . again." He was glaring at Alain, who didn't seem to notice.

Alain took the ring from his hand. "This is my St. Cyr ring from my days at the military academy," he said. "I don't know why I haven't lost it." He looked at Mary Ann. "You like it?" He tossed it to her. "Keep it for me. Now let's take a look at the *Bitch* . . ." He saw the look of shock on her face and added, "No, it's not what you think . . ."

At the back of the workshop, looking almost like an orphan stepchild, was Alain's other airship, the *Bitch*. Mary Ann could see it was his favorite by the way he patted its torpedo-shaped balloon as he went by. Both ends were pointed. It looked like one of those aerodynamic racing cars except that instead of wheels it had a triangular rudder at the back for steering.

Below the balloon was a two-seater bike frame. There was an engine up front, then the handlebar to steer the rudder, pedals to start the engine, and a seat for the driver. Behind that was another set of handlebars riveted to the frame, a passenger seat, and then a propeller. And that was all.

"It's like that song, 'A Bicycle Built for Two,'" she called out.

"Except this bicycle will take you up in the sky," he answered.

"How does it work?"

He took her hand. "I'll show you."

Mary Ann hesitated. The only thing holding the bicycle frame to the balloon was piano wire. She looked at Harding.

He shrugged as if to say "Why not?"

"Come on," said Alain. "Have a little courage."

He didn't wait for an answer. He put both hands around her waist and lifted her slowly, effortlessly into the rear seat. It felt so sensual that she didn't object, even though she was frightened. But if Alain was in the air, she decided that she didn't want to be on the ground. He slid into the front seat and pedaled to start the motor. The windmill-shaped propeller started to churn behind her as they passed through the open door of the barn. Then they were up in the sky.

Alain reached over his head to where a huge coil of rope hung from a slender pole under the balloon and moved it backward.

"What's that for?" she asked.

"Elevation!" he answered over the roar of the motor and propeller. "When I slide it back, the front of the balloon goes up; forward and it goes down.

"It's called a drag rope," he went on. "When I let it fall, it keeps the balloon at a certain altitude. The more rope that drags on the ground, the less weight in the balloon."

"How long is it?"

"Three hundred feet. The drag rope can also tell you where you are at night—if you listen to it. When it's over trees, the leaves rustle. Through cornfields it has the sound of rushing waters; in an orchard there is a little jerk as it leaps from tree to tree. Over a rail fence it imitates a buzz saw. On a housetop it's a cello, when it hits a barn it's a double bass, and in the water it splashes and then is smooth."

"Does it ever catch anything?" she asked.

"There's a legend about the balloon people," said Alain. "One time, long ago, at a certain church, the people were coming out of mass when they saw a rope caught around one of the tombstones, stretched tight. That rope went up in the sky beyond the clouds.

"They waited, and soon a strange man, looking like no one they'd ever seen, came down hand over hand to free it. The people seized him and he died. You see, he couldn't live in our air any more than we could live under water."

Below her the earth was a concave saucer, the horizon lifting up to a rim that melted into a hazy sky. Nearby three clouds, looking as if they had business to the north, scudded silently by. Above them the artificial sky of white balloon captured the glow of the sun.

"How can anything be this beautiful?" she said, forgetting her earlier fright.

Alain looked back at her over his shoulder as if to say he understood. She had been initiated into a society where beauty was won only at the price of letting go of your fear.

"There are those who say a balloon is just an overstuffed condom," he shrugged, making light of the moment. "Did you know they're made of the same material? But others say a balloon is magic."

It was magic: distant villages and woods, meadows and castles. Dots of white imbedded in green foliage became a cemetery. A train was a snail on a silver thread, shooting off little cannonballs that exploded long before they reached their height. The wail of the locomotive was very faint, and then it was gone. They had moved above the range of earthly sounds.

"Most people don't appreciate this," Alain called back. "They're like those people who held the airborne mariner on the earth until he died. One time, I was testing a gyrocopter . . ."

"A what?" Mary Ann shouted over the noise.

"I put a small gasoline motor with a propeller on it on my back and started it. It went up fast and came down even faster. I broke three ribs. While I was lying there, my superior, Major Vitary, came over and laughed at me. Told me I would never fly again. Today, when he visits President Pouchet, it will be my turn to laugh at him."

Alain pointed ahead. Mary Ann saw the dense fog of a cloud coming at them. The air was suddenly cool, damp and milky white. They had lost sight of the earth. They had lost sight of the balloon over their heads. Even their faces were indistinct.

Then they were out again. Mary Ann squinted as she saw the sun. It was a brighter, purer light than she had ever seen from the ground. The trip through the cloud had caused the gas in the balloon above them to cool, and they had dropped a thousand feet. They heard dogs howl.

"We are coming over the city," said Alain. "The dogs can sense us."

Looking down, she could see the Eiffel Tower, closer now, the broad flat field of the Champ-de-Mars behind, framing it. The whole city was spread out under them in boxes and carrefours. "Take a look down there," said Alain. "Houses piled on houses, a huge prison for a million people who've been told all their lives that they can't do what they want—that they can't fly. The only difference between them and us is, we don't believe it."

He pressed the throttle and the *Bitch* did an aerial dance. Mary Ann was amazed. This was no sausage or jellyfish. Alain's ship twisted and turned with utter grace.

Then the motor cut out. Alain looked back, twisting in his seat as though he was sitting at a table. "Are you scared?" he asked.

Mary Ann looked straight down. Nothing but an iron bar was beneath her feet. Nothing but Alain's skill kept her aloft. And Alain, she reminded herself, was l'Homme Sauvage, "the Wild Man." So why did she trust him?

"A little," she confessed.

"One time when I was a boy in New Caledonia, I started to climb a cliff. When I got up 30 feet, I suddenly realized I was bending outward; the cliff was going straight up. I froze with my fingers in the rock, the crashing surf below me. I thought I was about to die.

"I didn't die, of course, but I've never forgotten that feeling. It was the most alive I've ever been. To me, fear is the most exquisite thing in the world."

He threw the rope all the way forward and the ship started to dive. Mary Ann caught her breath, wondering if it were her last one.

Below, covering a whole city block, was an enclosure surrounded by a wrought-iron blue fence with golden spikes. It was the Palais de l'Elysée, the presidential palace.

Pouchet was taking no chances. There were guard posts at the 20-foot-high gates. Inside under the trees, soldiers camped out in tents. Machine guns and a cannon with rotating barrels were mounted on the roof. Other machine guns covered the walls. The windows were barred against bomb throwers—should one get past the spiked fence.

But guards, gates and fences meant nothing to Alain. He came in silently from the clouds and swooped down on the president's palace like an owl about to pinion an unsuspecting bird, not even disturbing the soldiers who were brewing their morning coffee on the lawn. Mary Ann was amazed at his piloting. And she was scared. What was Alain going to do?

They were 50 feet above the ground; only 10 feet above the top of the Palais de l'Elysée. They were moving toward their own shadow. She saw a small man emerge from the front door, followed by a crowd of others, all in dark coats. A soldier in a blue coat and red trousers was coming up the driveway to meet him.

"Shall we give the president a salute?" asked Alain.

He didn't wait for an answer. He pulled out a flare gun and fired it. It went off with a bang. The sputtering flare rose in the air and popped.

It was as though someone had dropped a firecracker in a squirrel cage.

Shouts of "Who goes there?" came from all four sentry posts. Soldiers scurried about, bumping into each other, searching for the intruder, looking everywhere but up. The officer in the red pants had run behind a tree.

"That's Major Vitary," said Alain with a chortle.

Pouchet's aide had pulled the president to the ground when

he heard the gun go off. So, Pouchet himself, lying on his back, saw Alain first. He pointed up. Alain waved at him.

Blue coats swarmed out on the roof and cranked the cannon upward to aim at them. Machine guns swung around. Rifle bolts clicked. An officer seized a gun from one of the soldiers and aimed it at Chevrier.

Mary Ann screamed.

Alain simply sat there, hanging in midair. He looked back at Mary Ann, as poised and cool as if he were lecturing to a class.

"You see, even though you are part of a system, it is necessary to challenge and even defy its authority. It is what makes us free."

She could barely hear the words over the din at the time, but she would remember them later. She could see that he wasn't terrified the way she was. He was laughing. He's absolutely crazy, she thought. And she knew in that moment that she loved him.

Alain was facing down the officer who stood on the parapet of the palace, aiming his rifle across the narrow void at him. The officer would have to either shoot or lower the gun. If he shot, as he wanted to, he would be shooting down France's hope of winning the Meurthe Prize. Finally he lowered the gun.

"This is restricted ground," he bellowed, red-faced. "You have no right to be here."

Alain was not intimidated. "The ground may be restricted," he shouted back, "but the air is free."

ten

*E*ACH DAY AT DAWN a new package would arrive. On the first day a basket of orchids, on the second, a box of Swiss chocolates. On the third, nothing, and she was annoyed. But on the fourth, a small but exquisite piece of Limoges china. Each of the packages was marked: "For Yvette."

Yvette Meurthe was accustomed to receiving gifts from admirers. But they always announced themselves, and expected something in return, even something so small as a smile. The mystery man who leaped the iron-spiked fence surrounding the Meurthe estate and then climbed to the second-floor porch to leave his treasures outside her bedroom door was, to say the least, romantic. It reminded Yvette of that new play taking Paris by storm, the one in which the long-nosed man, pretending to be someone else, woos his lady from a darkened courtyard.

Yvette set her maid to find out who the man was. It turned out not to be a man at all, but a scrawny 12-year-old boy. And because of his size, he looked even younger.

The maid caught him the next morning delivering a package.

He wouldn't talk. She fed him two croissants, a brioche and a petit beurre. All of them went down fast. Then he talked.

The boy had been sent by one of the *hommes oiseaux*, the birdmen who were flying to the Eiffel Tower. This man had seen Yvette and fallen in love with her. Which one? The boy said he didn't know, but he turned his eyes to the floor when he said it. The maid didn't believe him.

Then Yvette came in. Her eyes sparkled and her dark hair shone from brushing. She asked him if he would like to have some milk.

"Coffee," said the boy. "I am a man now."

In the kitchen, while the cook ground the beans, heated the water, and then put the combination through a plunger, Yvette opened the latest package. It was a beautiful silver brooch with a note that said, "From A. Wear it if you care for me."

"Give me a hint," she pleaded with the boy. Where was this strange man who had sent these presents?

The boy pointed eastward, in the direction of the park that bordered the Meurthe's home. Across the park, on the hills rising above the city, was Saint-Cloud, where Alain Chevrier was based. Alain! The man every woman in Paris wanted. Alain! Who despised society, wealth and privilege. Secretly sending an urchin to woo the most glittering woman in Paris. The maid giggled. What a story for her friends in the market!

The boy hopped on his bicycle outside the gate and rode back toward Saint-Cloud. Yvette and the maid watched from her second-story balcony until he disappeared.

What would Yvette do about her new love? the maid asked.

Nothing—for the moment. "Let him come to me," Yvette said, looking across the park at the distant hills. "And he will."

The boy didn't ride all the way to Saint-Cloud, though. He stopped much closer, in the Bois de Boulogne, near the twin man-made lakes, where a man standing under the willows was watching Yvette through binoculars.

It was Maximilian von Hohenstauffen.

"Did you let them catch you?" he asked.

"Yes, the maid did."

"Did you tell them what I told you to say?"

"Yes."

"Good," said Maximilian. "She will be curious. And we will feed her curiosity with baubles. Let us see if she is wearing the brooch."

PARIS WAS A SMALL town cloaked in the finery of a big city, like a little girl wearing her mother's dress and wobbly high heels, Maximilian thought. Everyone knew everyone worth knowing, so it was simple to find out things, particularly about someone like Henri Meurthe.

Maximilian already knew the details: Meurthe came from a distinguished family, leaders in France for generations. But Meurthe didn't live off his inheritance, he was also a successful man on his own; he had invented a gasoline engine and made millions speculating in the new oil market.

But not just a rich man, Maximilian thought, also a dangerous one. He had won medals for bravery, including his desperate balloon flight out of Paris in the winter of 1870, and he had killed a famous duelist in a sword fight one cold morning after the man had insulted his future wife's honor.

But everyone has cracks in their armor. Maximilian was a soldier, and a soldier attacks the enemy's weakest point. Meurthe's weakness was Yvette. She was his only child, and since his wife was dead, there would be no more. What would Meurthe sacrifice for his daughter? Probably everything.

And no wonder. Yvette was one of the great beauties in a city that produced many beautiful women. When she entered a room children stood on the tops of chairs just to get a look at her. She was applauded at the theater as if she were one of the actresses.

Yvette was stubborn, too, and willing to flout convention. She had once made an off-handed remark that she would like to masquerade for one night as a *horizontale*. She never did, but the comment sent many men to the nether reaches of Paris in search of a woman who looked like her.

But legends can also be true. One time she and her friends had gone into Maxim's, wrapped up the restaurant's most expensive champagne in burlap sacks—the same way the workers drank their cheap wine—and drank it out of the bottle.

Another time Yvette was at an outdoor cafe when it started to rain, and refused to move. Neither would her admirers. They sat through the downpour, continuing their party. Gradually the other patrons who had run inside for shelter came out and gathered around her. And then the sun reappeared, vindicating her.

But there was also a darker side to her personality. Fabian Bouchard had told Maximilian that when Yvette was 15 and still at boarding school, she and another girl had fallen in love with one of the professors, who had encouraged both of them. The three-way tryst ended when the girls found out about each other, and Yvette threw the other girl down a flight of stairs. She would want what she couldn't have, Max thought, and be determined to get it.

And what did she want now? She had been fascinated with Chevrier the moment she saw him from the Eiffel Tower. Meurthe wanted Chevrier too, but not as his daughter's lover. Chevrier meant "goatherd," didn't it? The conjunction of events, like the stars in their courses, always had its purpose, and could be put to good use.

Maximilian watched through his binoculars as Yvette looked up, beyond him, at the heights of Saint-Cloud. She was beautiful, standing there with breasts embonpoint against the shimmering eau de-Nil-satin of her gown, her hair cascading across her delicate shoulders, the sun glinting off her new silver brooch, the one Maximilian had just sent her. The kind of woman he wanted, and would someday have. Her good bloodlines were obvious.

But not now. Now he had a different use for her.

eleven

MARY ANN WAS ALSO watching the hills above Saint-Cloud and thinking about Alain Chevrier. But there was no time for further visits, even if Neville Bishop would have let her go. They were assembling the aeroplane on the boat, working hard by day and even harder by night, tightening bolts and rigging guy wires by feeble lamplight.

Then, late in May, a note came from Alain inviting Mary Ann—and Harding—to hear him speak at the Place de Grève.

Alain received many invitations. He had been asked to speak in France's House of Deputies, where he was being called "the keeper of the Oriflamme, France's sacred banner, which he will carry for us into the skies."

Women—many women—sent him their gilt-embossed calling cards. Among them was a can-can dancer known as La Goulue, the Greedy Gal. Kings had drunk champagne from her shoe. Another was a famous demimondaine who, it was rumored, had sequins woven into her pubic hair. A third was Meg Steinheil, a notorious woman whose talents with lips and tongue caused a former president of France to have a heart attack and expire right in his office, his pants undone and his fingers frozen in her curly hair. Or so gossip had it.

Chevrier had turned them all down, saying he was too busy. But he couldn't refuse his mother Louise, who had asked him to speak before the veterans of the War of 1870.

Alain's speech was at a workers' hall. The Place de Grève— Place of Grievances—was where workers had come in earlier times to demonstrate against their employers. It was hot and swarming with people when Mary Ann and Harding arrived. Some of them were *mutilés*, ex-soldiers who had lost arms and legs 30 years ago in that war against the Germans.

"Don't step on that foot," Mary Ann heard one of them say, "it's the only one I've got." Harding called them "The Legion of the One-Legged."

Louise met them at the door and kissed Mary Ann on both cheeks, which surprised her because it was the first time they had met. Louise was tall, ramrod-straight and, even at 50, still a beautiful woman. She took them to the front row and motioned Mary Ann to sit next to her.

She saw Alain come in, surrounded by workers in cloth caps, calling many by their first names. He was friendly and modest, with nothing to prove. He nodded to Mary Ann as if to say that he would see her later.

The meeting opened with the singing of "The Internationale," the workers' anthem. Surviving members of the Paris Commune, who had revolted against the government in 1871, were introduced. Then Alain got up to speak.

"Many of us already know each other," he started. "And I hope by the end of the evening you will all know me better, and

I will know many more of you. I am Alain Chevrier, a contestant for the Meurthe Prize. One million francs. I will win the prize. But I won't take the money. I renounce the money, which was stolen from people like you.

"When I win the prize, I will give it back to the people to whom it belongs. I will reclaim the workers' tools from the pawnshops. I will free the musicians' instruments. Then I will take what is left and go up over the Zone, that region of poverty outside our city walls, and let it fly in handfuls. And that is my answer to Meurthe and all the others who think they can buy men with money!"

There were shouts and the stamping of feet as reporters headed for the door. They could see the headlines now: "Chevrier Renounces Prize."

"Please light the magic lantern," said Alain. He was standing with his back to a whitewashed wall.

"Tonight I want to talk of a great philosopher named Aristotle. Aristotle never took flight, as I have, and as your children will, but he had some remarkable theories.

"Aristotle believed that there were levels of lightness in the sky. The layer closest to earth was comfortable and heavy, like a good blanket. The second layer, the layer of water, was cold and wet and turbulent. It was this layer that one reached on the highest mountain peaks, or among the clouds.

"Then, above this, was the Region of Fire. It was hot and dry and peaceful, a region where all troubles vanished. Here flames could not burn, only warm. In this high place were birds with no feet or claws, because they slept, ate and mated in the air. It was a region of perfect tranquility . . . perhaps heaven itself. I don't know.

"But I know of the other two regions (and Mary Ann saw the magic lantern show a picture of a snowcapped mountain with the shadow of a balloon on it). This is the top of Mont Blanc. How many have died climbing it? Yet I surmounted it with ease. I stepped out on its peak.

"And this is your region of water (and the magic lantern showed a picture of what looked like icebergs floating in a foaming sea). It looks as if you could step on them, too. But they are clouds, the way they look when you are on top of them.

"And here," he said, "I show you the region of earth as it looks from above: fields and cities like a patchwork, rivers and distant seas. And from this height, I see with a new perspective. What is a fence, a wall, or a barred gate? What is a border? It means nothing. My fellow Frenchmen, I have German friends, and I tell you, the German people are exactly like we are."

The crowd rumbled. Hating the Germans was a religion here. But Alain went on.

"Most of them—like us—are forced to live in hovels like the Zone where families are jammed into one room. When there is no running water, they call us dirty, French and German alike. When we are too ill-fed to work, they call us lazy. When our daughters sell themselves to feed our families, they call them whores. When we seek refuge from this unhappy life in a bar, they call us drunks.

"We all know who they are. They are the few who own all the wealth, who enjoy what we work 14 hours a day to produce. They are the ones who talk to us in a loud voice because they assume we are too stupid to understand. And for them I have a few simple questions:

"There is food enough in the world for all. So why do children go hungry?

"There is land enough in the world for everyone. So why are so many without a home?

"Man is born free but is everywhere in chains. Why?

"We have more wealth than the Conquistadors brought back from America or the British from the Indies. We have the automobile with the power of 60 horses; we have the white magic of electricity with the power to light cities and run factories; we have refrigeration, the telephone, even a machine to type the words I say.

"But none of these inventions help us. They are more chains around our neck. In America, they use electricity to shock people to death."

Harding laughed, and Mary Ann skewered him with an elbow to the ribs.

"It is not enough to find a way up into the sky. That is the easy part. What we must do is make sure that this invention, unlike all the others, is not corrupted and made to serve the rich and the warlike.

"And this is where I need your help. Throw off the chains that bind us. Where the law discriminates against the poor, or the sick, or those who believe differently than we do, make new laws.

"And as you do your part to break these chains—chains that we have been forced to forge ourselves—I will find a pathway to the sky. In our lifetime we will see flying machines for everyone, as common as bicycles are now. And this is what it will do for us:

"Each person will be free to go wherever he wishes—with his own flying machine, who can stop him? You ask, 'How can man be free?' And I say, 'How can he not be free, with the whole earth and sky below him?'

"War will end. The men who provoke wars will no longer lie safe behind their armies, while others do their fighting for them. Now that anyone can rain bombs down on them, they'll seek to save their own skins.

"It will end class distinctions. How can you look down on someone when he is in the sky?

"It will change all concepts of distance. The infinite highway of the sky will come to every man's door, bringing fruits from South America, spices from the Far East, and news from everywhere in the world—uncensored and untaxed by any government.

"People will rise above the smoke of our soiled cities and there will be enough land for everyone. Trackless jungles will become habitable and perhaps even vast stretches on other planets that we now see on clear nights. Property will become of so little value that men will sneeze at it.

"Even time may change if we invent ships that fly fast enough around the Earth and Sun. We could become immortal, build city-stars of materials yet unknown to us, and fly them to distant constellations. And even the poorest man here on Earth will be wanted. 'Join our star,' we will say."

The picture behind Alain had shifted to the night sky.

"And so I leave you," he said, "not with an ending, but with a beginning. We now live in the Region of Earth. And we are beginning to explore the Region of Air.

"But I believe—and you should believe too—that somehow, some way, we will find this place where there are no more sufferers, no more oppressors, where love will reign among people. This place Aristotle dreamed of—the Region of Fire."

THE APPLAUSE WAS DEAFENING. Looking around, Mary Ann saw one man who did not applaud. It was Maximilian, standing by the door. What is he thinking? she wondered. It was better that she didn't know.

I will have to kill him, Maximilian said to himself. The others, like Bishop and that girl, I can dispose of in various ways. But this Chevrier, I must kill. And it will not be easy. If I try and fail, nothing will stop Chevrier from killing me. Nothing. Not society's feeble version of justice, not all the armies, or all the rules, or all the morals of men. Nothing. If he is close enough, not even a bullet in the brain will stop Chevrier.

And why must I kill him? Maximilian thought. The reason (why hide it from yourself) is that there is not room enough in this world for the two of us.

twelve

*A*FTER THE SPEECH, Mary Ann found herself walking the streets with Alain, Louise and Harding, too excited to sleep. She had a thousand questions she wanted to ask Louise. Where was Alain's father? Had he died during the war?

But Louise, with her simple black dress and her hair pulled back in a bun, had a dignity and a distance about her that made it impossible to pester her with questions.

"Let's find a cafe," suggested Harding. "All that speechmaking has made me thirsty."

"Too much and too long," said Louise, teasing her son. "Why not go to the Café de la Paix? We can watch the crowd come out of the Opéra. That's always good entertainment."

Alain chuckled. "You see them strutting across that lopsided plaza like giant blackbirds after you throw the crumbs out in the yard. Pretending they're not interested, but all the time eyeing each other to see who has the fancier clothes and carriages."

They sat at a table on the open terrace of the cafe, catty-corner to the opera house, and ordered pastis. The sweet anise-tasting liqueur seemed to make all of them more talkative.

"You know the opera house and I were born in the same year," said Alain. "Unfortunately, I didn't get to see it. I was in prison camp." He stopped for a moment to get their reactions. Mary Ann's mouth opened in surprise, but Louise laughed.

"Yes," he went on, "even at that age I had criminal tendencies. Tell them the story, Mother."

Louise scoffed. "He makes me tell that story to everyone he meets. Alain, I'm sure your friends aren't interested in things that happened so long ago."

"I'd like to hear it," said Mary Ann.

Louise looked at her, and all pretense of being casual suddenly stopped. Mary Ann felt she was being judged to see if she was worthy of this honor.

"All right," Louise said. "You have heard how we blundered into war with the Germans in 1870 and lost our army. Here in the city we waited for a new army that we heard was coming. But the Germans came first. They surrounded the city and tried to starve us out. They were too cowardly to come in and attack Paris, and we were too few and weak to go out and attack them.

"So we endured the coldest winter in years. We cut down the trees for fuel; we killed the rats and hung them up in the butcheries. Surrounded by soldiers with bayonets, women would line up early in the morning to buy one. My father set sparrow traps on the roof. Even the zoo animals were killed for their meat. I cried when the beloved elephant was shot so that wealthy Parisians could eat steak that night. We would all have starved, even ones like myself who were pregnant, before giving in to the Germans.

"The only thing we would not eat were the homing pigeons, because they brought news from the outside on the little microdots on their feet."

"Microdots?" asked Mary Ann.

"Yes, miniature pictures of military documents from our forces outside the city to let us know how close the Germans were and when they would attack," said Alain.

"Whoever thought Parisians would be grateful to see a pigeon?" Louise smiled. "But we were. People would hang out their windows in the evening, searching the setting sun for a pair of wings.

"For me it was a happy time. I met Alain's father, who had been wounded in the cavalry charge at Sedan. As I nursed him back to health, we fell in love and leaped over the fire."

"That means they got married without the benefit of clergy, because their families wouldn't approve," Alain explained. "In villages, when a man and woman hold hands and leap over a bonfire, it means that they are committed to each other."

"My husband tried to fly a balloon out of the city to take messages to the army," Louise continued, "but it was lost over the North Sea. And the army that was supposed to rescue us never came.

"Still we would not surrender, but our government did. And then, to escape the anger of the people, it moved to Versailles, where it was out of touch with the people and could do the Germans' dirty work." She almost spat out the words.

"The Germans ordered the Versailles government to disarm the people of Paris. And that was when war started again. This time the people were against both the puppet government and the Germans, who were still camped outside the city.

"Inside the city we set up a Commune that would make all men equal. Even women would have equal rights. Our principles were good. But we were too democratic. Our assembly spent days and days debating while the Versailles government marched against us.

"At the end though—the time we call Bloody Week—we were very brave. When the troops came, we gathered up stones from the streets, and built barricades. Frenchman killed Frenchman more mercilessly than he had ever fought the Germans. The air was thick with the smell and smoke of burning buildings. The Hôtel-de-Ville and the Palais-Royal, even the Tuileries, were in flames. We burned down the hated guillotine.

"Men and women mounted the barricades together and loaded and fired their scarce rifles. Every house was a fortress. Every window and roof blazed defiance. The troops of the puppet government paid dearly for every yard of the city they took. But most of them were Catholics from Brittany, ignorant country boys but deeply religious. They were told we were the Antichrist, and it was their duty to destroy us. So they pushed blindly onward."

"Tell Harding and Mary Ann what you did," said Alain proudly.

Louise shrugged. "I was unimportant. My family was important, though. My father was a colonel in the National Guard that fought the Versailles troops; my brother Theo was an assemblyman in the Commune. I was only a nurse. I did not want to fight, particularly when I learned that I was pregnant.

"But I could not let the men of my family go to battle without helping them. I turned the two-wheeled buggy we owned into an ambulance. Every day I drove out to the barricades to collect the wounded. We had converted the first floor of our home into a hospital and, at one time, nearly 40 men lay on that floor, wounded or dying."

"And you were six months pregnant then," Alain added.

Louise shook her head. "Yes, but it made no difference what I did, or anyone else, either. There were too many of them, and we had too few guns. All we had were the stones of our houses and a will to fight. In the end, the barricades crumbled. The crows came down and pecked the eyes of the dead, and we didn't even have the ammunition to shoot them.

"At the end of May, when all was lost, I went out with our soldiers to their last stand in the Cemetery of Montmartre. How clear it was that night! The shells fired by their cannon lit up the marble statues in the burial ground, making them seem as if they were moving. Our side had no cannon left, but we answered theirs in our own way.

"Someone began to play the organ in a nearby church, and it made a louder noise than the dance of their bombs across the cemetery. The enemy fired and fired at the church, but they weren't able to stop the sound of the organ. It gave us hope.

"Then they attacked, wave after wave, coming across the graveyard in the moonlight. Our men fired until their ammunition ran out; then they fought with rifle butts and bayonets. I took one man who had been shot in the chest and carried him, his arm over my shoulder, toward the gate. We must have lost our way, because the last thing I remember is tripping over something and hitting my head.

"When I awoke, it was dark all around me, but light above, so I knew it was morning. I was lying inside an open tomb. The man I had tried to help lay on top of me. I knew that he was dead. Underneath me, in a coffin splintered by shellfire, lay another man who had been dead much longer. Yet between these two I had lain safe that night, when all the others had died.

"When I climbed from the grave, the battle was over, and there was no sound. The ground was covered with white as if it had snowed. But I knew it was May. The white powder was quicklime, which had been used to cover the dead; the new dead of last night and the old dead who had been tossed out of their tombs by the shells. Now they lay together, so thick that I could barely step over them.

"I must have looked like a ghost in my white dress covered with blood, because no one challenged me. As I walked through the streets, I could see our men being marched away, their hands over their heads, guarded by the soldiers of Versailles. I reached our house to find my mother inside, sick with fever. She had just been told that my father was killed on the last barricade, and that my brother had gone into hiding."

Louise's voice choked and she stopped, unable to go on. Alain started to order another bottle of pastis, but Louise raised her hand. "No . . . water," she said. They waited while she caught her breath.

"The rest of the story is even harder to tell. I spent the rest of the day trying to nurse my mother. She was delirious. I don't think she wanted to live.

"The next day the soldiers smashed their way through the door and came upstairs. The officer wanted to know where my brother was. I told him that I didn't know. Then he said that if my mother didn't tell him, they would take me away. They seized me by both arms and dragged me to the door. My mother, still delirious, tried to rise. She mumbled something about Rue

Saint-Sauveur two blocks away. Then she stumbled and fell to the floor.

"But the soldiers took me anyway, leaving my mother lying on the floor, where she died that night. And, within a few hours, they had my brother, too.

"They kept us overnight in a stockyard, and the next day we marched to Père-Lachaise, the great cemetery of Paris. There was a long column of us. I found my brother Theo, and we linked hands as we walked.

"When I saw the pockmarked wall and the bloodstains on the ground, I knew what was about to happen. My brother gave my hand a last squeeze and went up first. I searched for something to say, and finally I shouted 'Good luck!' It was stupid, I know, but he smiled at me as they took him to the wall.

"Theo threw his hat down in front of him. They offered him a blindfold. He took it and threw it into his hat. They tied his hands behind him and stood him against the wall. Then the soldiers fired. But most of them missed. Only one or two struck him, but they did not kill him. He fell, and then struggled to his knees. He could not get to his feet because his hands were tied behind his back. 'Shoot me, you pig!' he shouted at the captain in charge of the firing squad. 'Put an end to it!'

"I can still see that officer. He wore big cavalry boots, the kind that came up over his knees, and he carried one of those big nine-shot revolvers. He walked up to Theo casually, as if he wanted to talk to him, and placed the muzzle alongside Theo's head. He fired twice. After my brother lay in the dust, he kicked his body. Then he looked at me and said, 'Take the sister next.'

"I was marched up to the wall and turned to face the firing squad. I too refused a blindfold, but I shut my eyes tightly because I didn't want to die with them open. I heard the same officer give the order to aim, and then a strange thing happened. The sergeant told the captain that his men would not shoot a pregnant woman. They were good Catholics from Brittany, so they believed the unborn child was innocent of sin, and had a right to life.

"Instead they took me into the crematorium at the top of the hill. I looked up at the domed roof and its high black smudged smokestacks, and wondered if they were going to burn me alive. They forced me inside, where three men in civilian clothes sat, looking bored amid the bones and ashes in the ovens. They heard what the officer said and then ordered me to the French convict labor camp at New Caledonia in the South Pacific. 'All memory of you will be erased from the records,' said one of them. 'It will be as if you died at that wall.'"

"HOW MANY PEOPLE did die?" asked Harding.

"More than 25,000- that we know of," said Alain. "But so many others were never found."

"And never will be, until the earth gives up her dead," said Louise. "Down in the catacombs under Paris, where the government chased the Communards with torches and dogs, are many new skeletons among the ancient bones. Brother turned against brother, and children were promised bread if they gave up their fathers. It was a time of betrayal. Even today in the corners of abandoned cellars or in newly dug ditches, a broken skull will be found and people will say, 'That must have been a Communard.'"

"But you lived," said Alain.

"Yes," said Louise, looking at him. "We lived."

"This opera is a long one," said Harding.

"But my opera is even longer," said Louise with a small smile. "Are you sure you want to hear the rest of it?"

"Yes," said Mary Ann. "I do."

"I GAVE BIRTH TO Alain on an old rotting prison ship as it sailed to New Caledonia. When it arrived, we were given a cottage on the shore of Nouméa in the midst of the penal colony. All around us were volcanoes. Gray clouds of locusts would descend on the island once a year and eat everything but the gum trees. Cyclones would whirl in from the ocean, destroy our grass huts and send the tin roofs flapping off like butterflies.

"But life could also be good. Crops grew easily, and there was plenty to eat, even when the bread ration was cut. Everyone kept a garden and a hen house. The fruits of the forest, the tomatoes and figs, mulberries and yellow plums, were smaller than the European kind, but sweeter.

"When Alain grew old enough to walk, he and I would climb the western slope of the forest overlooking the colony. We would play hide-and-seek on the enormous rocks that had collapsed like ruined fortresses, and watch the gypsy cormorants swoop and soar over the island. 'Look out there,' I would tell him. 'The whole world is yours. Reach out and take it.'

"When Alain's time came for school, I knew that I would have to teach him myself. So I started a school, and taught the black Kanaka children of the neighboring village too. Every morning the children and I would go to the beach and find a place where the tide had washed the sand smooth so we could practice our sums and letters. I found a broken piano with hammers missing, and taught them to play by humming the note when they struck a dead key.

"Finally, 10 years later, the French government declared an amnesty for all the remaining Communards and we were sent home."

"What about your school?" asked Mary Ann.

Louise laughed bitterly. "What is a school without children? The French brought their cattle to New Caledonia, the cattle brought ticks, and each year the tick fever killed more of the Kanaka children. Finally there were none left."

She stopped. "And that is the end of my story."

Harding winced. "Couldn't you give it a happy ending?"

"But I did." She smiled and touched Alain on the shoulder. "This is my happy ending."

"You must hate the Germans," said Harding.

"I do not love the Germans. But I reserve my hatred for the betrayers of my country, the rich men like Thiers and Meurthe who sat on the tribunal that terrible day at the crematorium and signed the death warrants . . . or sent us off to prison."

"Meurthe?" Mary Ann blurted out. She couldn't believe that the man she had met at the Eiffel Tower was capable of that.

"Yes, Paul Meurthe. He was the father of the one who is offering the prize."

"They're coming out now," said Alain, his eyes on the marble stairs of the opera house.

A forest of top hats appeared at the door as men in evening dress trooped down the steps, sweating heavily, a few even removing their coats. Barkers, who had waited all night for this moment, hailed cabs for the very rich, then waited with their hand out for a tip. Drivers of the rakish black landaus for the wealthiest families butted into the crowd, calling out, "You're blocking my way, Rothschild!" or "Move the hell over, Wagram!" Women, who had mercifully loosened the stays of their corsets during the performance, now adjusted themselves, hoping everything was in its proper place.

Mary Ann watched the tired faces and the weary bodies stuffed into their expensive clothes as they made their way across the square.

Harding nudged her. "Louise is right," he whispered. "This is quite a show. The rich inconveniencing themselves to be seen by the other rich."

And, at the far end of the crowd, came Henri Meurthe and his daughter Yvette. She looked cool and unruffled. Even at this hour she still turned heads, as she stood there, poised in the gaslight underneath the stone wings of an angel's statue. But Yvette was not looking at the men in their starched shirts with diamond stud pins winking from their cravats. She was looking across the square—where Alain sat.

"Father," she said, "some friends of mine are meeting at Maxim's shortly. You take the carriage and I'll go down the block and meet them."

"But the hour is late," Meurthe protested, "and Maxim's is a mile away. I will give you the carriage."

Yvette kissed him on the cheek. It was a kiss of dismissal. "Thank you, Papa, but it is only a short walk down the Boulevard des Capucines. I need the air."

"Of course," said Meurthe. "Wherever you want to go." She wanted to go past the Café de la Paix.

Harding watched as Yvette went by. It was impossible not to. He had been a connoisseur of women once; painted them, made love to them, and appreciated them, clothed or unclothed.

Yvette's gown of water silk was as intimate as a good lover. It showed off every feature, from her high breasts to her famous dance-hall legs. Its frilly satin bottom shimmied back and forth along the pavement as she walked, making a rustling frou-frou sound that was almost hypnotic.

The way she kept her hand on it, pulling it up to tighten around her hips and thighs, was seductive in itself. Her hobble skirt made walking difficult, but emphasized those lovely feminine curves. Taking small steps, she seemed to glide, while her body undulated in a particularly sinuous way. As an artist it reminded him of a birch tree in an autumn breeze. But as a man, it was simply raw temptation.

As she passed, Yvette threw her head back just slightly and gave Alain a look—flaring green eyes that burned right through and came out the other side—the captivating look that a knowledgeable woman can give a man when she knows his eyes are upon her.

Harding saw everything. He saw Louise, her face wreathed in shadow but her eyes as watchful as a lookout. He saw pretty, naive Mary Ann, so in love with Alain, trying to hide her feelings.

And he saw Yvette. Oh yes, he saw Yvette. Everyone on the boulevard that night saw Yvette as she walked that walk.

And Harding knew that for one of these three women the story would have no happy ending.

thirteen

*A*LAIN'S SPEECH WAS A tripwire that set off an explosion.

It electrified Paris. By morning, all two million people had heard about it; everyone with his own flying machine conquering stars, immortal. The boule players, the brokers on the floor of the Bourse, even the men walking their dogs on Boulevard Saint-Michel could talk of nothing else. Alain was cheered wherever he went.

But some were not cheering. To the wealthy and powerful men all over Paris, Alain's ideas about flight smelled of anarchy. President Auguste Pouchet's phone began to ring before he awoke, and all the callers said the same thing. "Shut Chevrier up."

Pouchet wanted to roast Chevrier on a very hot spit. Twice this mere army captain had humiliated him. Captain? That was it. He called the minister of war, who called the general-in-chief, who called Alain's superior officer, Major Vitary, and ordered him to keep Chevrier quiet.

Major Vitary apologized profusely. He too hated Chevrier. But he reminded his superiors that they had ordered Alain to resign from the army when he entered the contest. That way, if he lost, there would be no disgrace to the French military; he had been a civilian all the time. If he won, the resignation would conveniently be forgotten. Pouchet, who had been trying to cover all bets, now found himself outpointed.

Very well, thought the president, there's another way. He called Henri Meurthe.

"Use your personal influence to silence him," Pouchet told Meurthe.

Meurthe shook his head at the angry voice in the knob-shaped receiver. "I only care if he flies, not what he says," Meurthe told Pouchet. Talking like a father to his son, Meurthe tried to calm the French president.

"Auguste," he said, "I can make no promises. He does not respect you and he hates me. But Alain Chevrier is also a patriot. He will fly . . . and he will win the prize."

"He'd better," shouted Pouchet. "If he fails, and the Germans win, the government could fall. You remember what happened last time? Barricades in the streets. The city in flames. All that will be on your head," his voice crackled over the phone. "On your head!"

Pouchet slammed down the receiver.

Henri Meurthe shook his head. He had never before seen his friend so near the breaking point, even during the dark days of the Dreyfus scandal. Pouchet had a reputation as a windbag who tried too hard to be liked. But he also had a hard edge.

A year ago, when the anarchists were setting off nail bombs all over Paris, he signed the orders executing two of them. Then he stood by the guillotine with Monsieur le Paris, the top-hatted executioner, and watched the blade come down. He was splashed by blood when their heads dropped into the basket, but never did he flinch.

ACROSS THE FIELD FROM Alain's workshop in Saint-Cloud was one of Paris's *pissotieres*, those ugly cast-iron green structures where men could stand and relieve themselves in a trough. The *pissotiere* reeked of acrid ammonia, but it was the one place that was truly democratic. As animals come to a truce at the water-hole, so do men at urinals.

Guillaume LeRond had just stepped up to the trough after finishing his day's work when his instincts warned him that something was about to happen. Two men came up to the urinal on either side of him. At first he felt fear, then he realized that he knew the one on the left. It was Fabian Bouchard, a wealthy member of the Aéro Club. The other was a striking-looking stranger.

"Guillaume," said Bouchard, "may we talk to you?"

LeRond was flattered. "Of course," he said. "I was only going back to my room."

"Then we would be honored to walk with you," said Bouchard.

They strolled through the city, three abreast, with the stranger on one side and Bouchard on the other, almost as if he were a fish in a net.

"We are very concerned about Chevrier," Bouchard said.

"As am I," LeRond admitted.

They walked on the grass that lined the middle of the Boulevard Richard-Lenoir. A legless *mutilé* on a cart pushed his way toward them and held out his tin cup. The stranger, annoyed at the interruption, casually gave the beggar a kick, spilling his cart and coins onto the street.

Bouchard paused. "If it becomes necessary to eliminate Chevrier—in one way or another—could you take over the project?"

Guillaume stared at them, open-mouthed. He never thought that such an opportunity would come along.

"Don't look so surprised, LeRond," said Bouchard. "We at the Aéro Club are aware of your work. We know how good it is. And we know how dangerous Chevrier can be. Show him," Bouchard ordered the other man.

They were walking along the Canal Saint-Martin now. The fishermen with their 15-foot poles watched them pass. Ducks bobbed in the water.

The stranger pulled a letter out of his pocket and handed it to Guillaume. "Wait until you see this," said Bouchard.

They were walking across one of the arched bridges over the canal and Guillaume paused at the top to read it. It was a letter from Chevrier to Émile Zola, the novelist who had done so much damage to the military—to everything Guillaume believed in—with his defense of the traitor, Dreyfus. Chevrier was offering to take his airship and use it to bomb Paris!

Chevrier a traitor? LeRond didn't like the man, but he couldn't believe . . . yet here were all sorts of details about the airship project that no one else could know: the number of gas cells, the amount of hydrogen, even the names of those involved, including his own! And Chevrier's signature at the bottom. Authentic! He had seen it many times.

The stranger took the letter gently from LeRond's shaking hands.

"Go home," Bouchard said softly, "and think about what we've said. But don't tell anyone else, especially not Chevrier."

LeRond walked off the bridge, trembling but proud. His talent had finally been recognized. And Chevrier, the one who had set himself up to be better than his fellow officers? Well, LeRond just hoped that he would be there when Bouchard and the others came to take Chevrier away.

Bouchard and the stranger waited at the top of the bridge until LeRond walked away into the night. Then Bouchard turned to his partner.

"Did we do well?" he asked.

"Very well," said Maximilian. "A good seduction must always be accomplished slowly and with infinite care. And I am grateful for the information about Chevrier's dirigible."

Then he took the letter and very slowly shredded it before throwing it into the water. He shook his head in wonder at his own brilliance. It was amazing what a little forgery could do.

fourteen

*G*OD, IT WAS UGLY, she thought.

The top of the boat had now been flattened out, and a device that looked like a Texas oil derrick had been installed in the back. On top of it was a huge lead weight, so heavy that it made the *Bethanie* stick up in front. It was part of the catapult, and when that weight dropped it would send the aeroplane down a 30-yard railroad track, fling it into the air 20 feet above the water, and it would fly.

Or so they hoped.

At the back end of the boat, what appeared to be a curved black cigar was sticking out at an odd angle. It was the exhaust pipe for the steam engine, which had been run from front to back inside the boat to avoid contact with the plane or catapult. But the connections were loose. The inside of the cabin was covered with black soot. Passersby, who looked at the *Bethanie* and shook their heads at the outside of the weird ship, should see the inside, she said to herself. It was 10 times worse. Here, in the heart of the most beautiful city in the world, they had created their own sweatshop, their own slum.

In the dirty bowels of the boat, they all worked and sweated and hated each other; Harding, Bishop, Mary Ann and two dockyard goons brought along by Bishop. They were still eating from the Limoges china that the French captain and his wife had left, but most of it had been smashed. The two hired men practiced throwing it at each other. The same was true with the furniture. Soon they would be eating on the floor, she thought.

As the aeroplane was built below deck, there was less and less room for them. Ever more space was taken up by the two sets of wings, the engine and propeller, struts, fuselage, and pontoons, so that in case the aeroplane fell into the Seine it would float and could be fished out.

Things got even tighter when Bishop decided the work was not going fast enough, and built an apartment for himself onboard, even though he already had a railroad car to live in just outside the Gare du Nord train station.

On the aeroplane the pilot would lie prone, facing forward in a harness with three leather straps tying him in at the chest, waist and legs. Which meant that his head would be the first to hit anything, she thought. And, if he was lucky enough not to knock himself unconscious, he'd have to undo the leather straps, one at a time, before he could escape.

"Who's going to fly this thing?" Harding asked Bishop.

Good question, thought Mary Ann. Bishop said that he had hired a professional jockey and stunt man named Jack Reece, who would arrive from England within a week. Then he went on and on about how great Reece was and how clever his plan was.

Actually, Bishop's plan did make some sense, she admitted to herself. The idea was to let the boat do most of the work. It would chug downriver to Pont d'Iéna, just a few hundred yards from the Eiffel Tower. Then the aeroplane would take off, and as long as it stayed above the ground until it got around the Tower, it didn't matter what happened next—to the pilot or the plane. At least that was Bishop's thinking.

But time and money were both against them. Time, because it was obvious Alain Chevrier could fly at any moment; he had already proven that the day he took Mary Ann on that now famous flight over the president's palace. He was only waiting until July 14, Bastille Day, when the contest would officially start.

And money, because it was increasingly clear that Neville Bishop was going broke.

Harding would go to Bishop's private railroad car at the Gare du Nord each day to pick up the mail. One day he brought back a half-opened letter, took Mary Ann to a local cafe and read it to her.

My Dear Sir:

The limitation on your line of credit has been exceeded again. We are aware of your explanation for the aforementioned difficulty and are sympathetic. However, at this point, all advances will have to cease.

Finally, we have been in contact with the other stockholders of the Bishop Air-Car Construction Syndicate and they informed us, to a man, that no further advances would be made on their part until there is word of definite results from Paris.

We hope this letter finds you well. We remain,

Very truly yours,
Thomas R. Sommers, Manager,
Morgan Bank

"It seems old snootface has empty pockets, doesn't it?" said Harding. "What's that mean for you and me? Do we jump ship, make our way across France, and hope someone takes us back to America? Or do we stay with Bishop?"

Mary Ann didn't know, but she stayed around the next day and the next. And, on that day, several things happened. First, Bishop told her to leave her hotel room and come live on the boat. She would have a "private" room, he promised.

And then the kindly old couple who owned the *Bethanie* came back to see how Bishop was treating it.

Mary Ann was on deck when they passed by early in the morning, arm in arm, not recognizing the boat as theirs. She waved, then was sorry for it, thinking that they might have passed by without ever knowing. But it wouldn't have made any difference. Their dog, chained to a post at the stern, also recognized them and started to bark.

At first they seemed stunned. The wife put her hand to her mouth. She was sobbing: "*Mon Dieu! Mon Dieu!*" The old captain's face turned red and he let out a string of rapid French that Mary Ann assumed was swearing. He was shaking his fist.

"Mr. Bishop!" Mary Ann called. "I think you should get up here."

Neville Bishop's head popped through a porthole. He was half-shaved and she could see that he was annoyed at being disturbed. The dog was barking, the woman was screaming, and the captain was storming up the gangplank, ready to take back his ship. The old man was in his 60s, but the muscles in his neck and shoulders were bulging and he looked ready to kill.

Bishop's two dockyard thugs appeared, seemingly out of nowhere, and were on him like dogs mauling a deer, one on either side, bearing down on him with all their weight. It was the first time Mary Ann had witnessed real violence in her life and it horrified her to see their knees banging against his groin, their thumbs gouging for his eyes and their fingers around his throat. But the captain kept on going, fueled by sheer strength and anger.

She sensed rather than saw Bishop coming up behind her, turned, and gasped. Bishop had his silver-headed cane back over his head, holding it with both hands like a club, ready to brain the old man.

"No!" she screamed and grabbed the cane just before he swung it.

Bishop turned toward her, the lather on his face making him look like a demented hydrophobe, and raised his hand to hit her. Then he stopped, and all the violence drained away as suddenly as it had started. The two thugs held the captain, one by each arm, and lifted him up by the elbows so that his heels were slightly off the ground. All he could do was squirm and yell and kick like a hanged man.

"I let you rent my boat," he spoke hoarsely in broken English, "not destroy it! You told me that you would take care of my *Bethanie*. You gave me your word."

"That is not dispositive," said Bishop, brandishing his silver-headed cane in the old man's face. "You read the lease . . . or should have. It gives me the purview to make whatever changes I see fit."

It was obvious from the captain's face that he didn't understand a single word of Bishop's speech. Just then Harding came on deck, looking bleary-eyed.

"Harding!" Bishop called out. "Explain to this French idiot what I just said."

Harding shrugged and turned to the captain. "He cheated you," he said in French, pointing at Bishop. Harding's words set off a new burst of violence.

The old captain must have known that the odds were against him, but he couldn't retreat, particularly in front of his wife. He made a last effort, wrenched his right arm free and grabbed for Bishop, who jumped back.

The bodyguard who still had a good hold swung him around efficiently—as if he were a drunken bum at the bar—while the other came up from behind and pushed. They may have wanted to send him down the gangplank, or perhaps they just didn't care. The old man went sprawling off the edge of the gangway. He hit so hard that the planking cracked and he fell headfirst into the water. Mary Ann heard the splash, and then more screams from his wife.

The two thugs didn't bother to see if he was alive. They went below deck. Bishop finished wiping his lather off, looked at Mary Ann's shocked face, and told her to get back to work. She saw with relief that the captain was wading up onto the quay, soaked and exhausted.

His wife was still on the quay, but now her chant had changed. She was moaning, "*Mon chien, mon chien.*"

Mary Ann looked where she was pointing and saw that the dog had leaped over the side and was being strangled by its collar. Harding walked over, broke off the stake, and the dog fell into the water. It swam to shore to join the captain and his wife. The three of them stood there, a portrait of the dispossessed. The fishermen on the quay sat with their long bamboo poles in the water. None of them moved a muscle. What must they think of us? said Mary Ann to herself.

fifteen

$\mathcal{A}$LTHOUGH SHE WOULDN'T ADMIT it to Harding, the reason Mary Ann wouldn't leave was that she wanted to finish the aeroplane. Every time she stretched a piece of varnished cotton over a wing, fitted a strut or tightened a belt on the motor, she remembered her father Samuel, and how they had laughed at him. Then she would look at Saint-Cloud. Win or lose, she wanted Alain to be proud of her.

As time went on, it was obvious that she had absorbed more wisdom from her father accidentally than Bishop had ever accumulated on purpose. Bishop knew only the mechanical things. His idea was to make everything big and put rivets in it; a large enough motor would push anything off the boat. But he didn't understand the subtleties of flight the way she did: the need for balance, the lightness of wings, and the energy of motion.

She knew, for example, that to raise their machine cleanly into the sky, the wings would have to be curved and set at exactly the right angle. That way the air rushing by above the wing would go faster than the air below, creating a vacuum above the wing and lifting it up. A Swiss had figured that out more than 100 years ago.

But she didn't know what that angle should be. She looked in her father's old logbooks. Many of the notes were in equations. Mathematical formulae were everywhere, along with jotted notes and, occasionally, exclamation points. She concentrated on these last.

Mary Ann had studied French in finishing school until she was 17 and it helped her survive in Paris. But, like most girls, she had been taught only the most basic math. She needed to know more. She rummaged through Samuel's papers until she saw what she was looking for: a letter from a French professor of mathematics at the Sorbonne that her father had kept all these years because he was so proud of it, a letter praising his work.

The Sorbonne was full of big, intimidating buildings with high columns and arches. She found the professor's office in a tower overlooking the flagstone courtyard of a walled medieval castle. She was so nervous that she didn't even knock, just waited outside the door until she saw him. Would he show her the meaning of those formulae?

"*Mais oui*," he said, smiling. He was an elderly man with pince-nez glasses and white mustache. He thought it enchanting that a woman, a mere slip of a girl really, would want to learn such things.

She sat and listened politely as he explained. She smiled whenever he looked up, nodded when she was supposed to, and left without knowing a thing more than when she came.

So she went back. This time he was less polite, but he explained it again as he rushed across the courtyard to class, followed by a covey of his students. He made a comment about how women's minds weren't meant for such things, and everyone, except Mary Ann, laughed. Once again she tried to do her father's equations for herself. Tried all night. And failed.

So she went back again.

This time the professor wasn't friendly at all. He rolled his eyes and called her "a little fool who would be better off having babies." But she stood stubbornly in the doorway.

Finally he took her to a classroom and scratched out her father's equations on an old blackboard. The chalk dust made her eyes water, but she wasn't going to give him the satisfaction of seeing any tears. He hurried through his explanation while she desperately scribbled notes. Then he told her not to bother him again and walked out.

But this time she got it. And that night, when she read and understood one of Samuel's formulae, she felt like a child who has spoken its first word.

With her new language she began to learn what Samuel had done. Most men were groundlings; scuttling moles who hurried from one meaningless place to another with their heads down. They understood life only in two dimensions. They were condemned to the flat earth.

But her father had comprehended it in three. Like Alain, he had envisioned a new world above them, a turbulent sea of tides, currents and eddies more expansive than the ocean, a world constantly in motion, constantly changing. To survive in that world either the wind flowed around you or you flowed through it. "In the air—as in life," Samuel had written, "one is condemned to go forward." She recalled those birds that lived in Alain's Region of Fire, the birds who flew forever, and now she understood. To stop was to fall. And to fall was to die.

With her new language Mary Ann began to see a different world, a world of relationships. The Eiffel Tower was an inverted bridge extending up into the sky, its struts and openness designed to both fight the wind and forgive it by letting it pass through. The windmills that churned throughout Paris were nothing more than big propellers. And riding a bicycle required the same sense of balance as flying would. It was all part of the Great Equation. Understanding that was her father's last, best gift to her.

She started explaining to the others how it had to be done. Bishop's two thugs didn't listen, but one day shortly after the fight with the captain they were gone. She suspected they left when the money ran out.

Harding would help when he was around, but he was often out at the bars, places with strange names like Men Without Women, The Lavatory Club, and The Wrath of God. He didn't seem to care anymore. Was it because he wasn't getting paid? Or was there another reason? she wondered.

Even Bishop seemed depressed, poring over his books, perhaps trying to calculate how much of the one million francs he would need to save himself.

That left it up to Mary Ann to find the perfect angle for the wings. Theory was one thing, but she needed to experiment. She needed a wind similar to the speed of the plane when it was traveling through the air. But where would you find such a wind in Paris?

Then one night the wind came to her.

On that night late in June, Mary Ann was sleeping an unsettled sleep when she felt the boat rocking. Then she heard the wind howling and the portholes rattling. A summer storm was attacking the city.

She struggled into her clothes and ran on deck. The aeroplane was almost completed now, with the wings ready to be set into place, but she needed two men to help her. Bishop was onboard. But where was Harding? Probably in that hole-in-the-wall room of his near the Panthéon.

She searched in vain for a fiacre to take her there. When one did come by, the driver ignored her outstretched arm, and instead whipped his horse and held his coat tight around him as he drove by in search of shelter. Then the rain hit, billowing her dress and blowing her hair back. Since it was only a few blocks away, she decided to run.

She dashed down the Boulevard Saint Germain past the empty, unlighted churches and through the maze of apartment buildings, ignoring the crack of lightning and the rain that drenched her, knowing that he had to come back to the boat while the wind was still high.

She ran into his building, past the concierge's apartment and up the stairs to what looked like Harding's door. Did she have the right one? She knocked, uncertain, and heard muffled noises, then Harding's voice. Good, he was there. She knocked again.

Harding answered the door in his nightshirt and told her to come in and get warm. She caught a glimpse of bare buttocks as he struggled with his long johns. He seemed groggy.

Then she heard a woman's voice say, "Who is it?"

The room had a strange musky odor. As Mary Ann came in, her dress plastered to her body, a big redhead was getting out of the bed, and she was nude. She pointed an accusing finger at Mary Ann.

"What is this thing?" she said. Her nipples jiggled as she pointed at Mary Ann, as if they were accusing her of something too.

"This, my dear Marquessa, is a friend of mine," said Harding. "She has asked me to perform a small service for her."

The woman loomed over Mary Ann, who was soaked and shivering.

"And what kind of 'service' does this little tramp, this piece of baggage, need?" she sneered.

Mary Ann saw a sudden flash of anger on Harding's face. "That is something that a *horizontale* such as yourself wouldn't understand. Now get out!"

The Marquessa tried to slap him, but Harding caught her arm in midswing. With his other hand he gathered up her silk dress, parasol, undergarments, boots and wrap, and pushed them at her. As she grabbed them, still naked, he shoved her out the door.

"Don't keep your husband waiting too long!" he yelled loudly enough so the whole building would hear. "He may be home from his mistress by now, although God knows why he'd come home to you. And one more thing . . ." He picked up her whalebone corset and threw it in her face. "Don't forget your bastion of modesty."

She turned toward him, face full of fury. "Bast . . ." she snarled, but Harding slammed the door and turned back to Mary Ann.

"I love making a scene," he grinned.

THE STORM WAS STILL in full force when they got back. They turned the boat and anchored it in the middle of the river so it faced the wind. Then Harding and Bishop stood on both sides of the aeroplane, each holding one end of the wing and facing one another, while Mary Ann made adjustments with a wrench, trying to find the angle at which it caught the wind. They had to dig in their heels to keep from being blown off the boat.

A bolt of lightning struck the river so near that the flash and crack came at the same time and a blue haze swept across the water to envelop the boat. It crept up her body and made it tingle. It formed a fierce halo around Bishop's unkempt hair. She could see fear cross Harding's face, perhaps more for her than for himself. A spark jumped from her upturned metal wrench to the frame of the aeroplane.

And then the miracle happened. The plane bounced up and down on its mounts, like a dog eager to obey her, jumping higher with every driven gust. Ready to fly, she thought. Ready to fly.

As quickly as it came, the storm rumbled off toward the hills to the east, as if it knew it had served its purpose. Neville Bishop offered no congratulations, and seemed annoyed at having been dragged from his cabin. Mary Ann wondered if he even knew what had happened. He ignored her, and went back down the hatch, rubbing his pince-nez on his shirt to clean them.

But Mary Ann could see from Harding's face that he understood, and was happy for her. "Congratulations!" he shouted, his voice strangely loud and hoarse now that the storm was over. "You know, the French call electricity 'white magic.' It feels like we've been touched by it just now. Maybe God or whatever power has mercy on lost souls wants us to win."

Then he grabbed her and, before she could stop him, kissed her. But she pushed him away, remembering the woman back at his apartment. It was too late to make amends, she decided. From now on she would ignore him, except when she needed him.

sixteen

*T*HE AEROPLANE MAY HAVE been ready to fly at the end of June, but Neville Bishop wasn't.

"Wait until Jack Reece gets here," he told them. "I've seen him. He can fly or ride anything. I can't take a chance on letting one of these Frenchmen . . . or anyone else (and his eyes slid over Harding and Mary Ann) fool around with it."

So they waited. First they heard that Reece was in London. Then in Cherbourg. Then he wanted another 100 dollars. The days turned into a week . . . and then two. Mary Ann fidgeted. Harding barely talked to her at all now. She wondered what other women he was seeing. And she wondered about Alain.

Then it was July 13, and that night the whole sky lit up. Fireworks were exploding at parks all over the city: from the Garden of Acclimization to the Tuileries, from the heights of the hills of Chaumont to the Luxembourg Garden, and even from all three levels of the Eiffel Tower. Red, white and blue flags— the French tricolor—fluttered from every window.

"What's going on?" asked Mary Ann, watching from the deck of their boat on the Seine.

"Tomorrow is Bastille Day, France's Independence Day. But for us it's the start of the contest," Harding reminded her. "And tonight, in case you've forgotten, the Aéro Club is having its annual ball, and one of us has to be there for the ceremony."

"Why?" she said skeptically.

He shrugged. "Orders from President Pouchet. To accept 'permission' to fly over the city. It has to do with that little escapade you and Alain pulled over his palace."

Mary Ann had forgotten about the ball, or perhaps did not want to remember. The idea of going out in "Society," of dancing, of a ceremony frightened her. But who would go? Bishop was down in the hold poring over his ledgers, trying to figure out a way to get Reece to come to Paris without paying him any more money. She didn't even want to talk to him.

"Go by yourself," she told Harding.

"But Alain will be there," said Harding with a half smile, as if he assumed that would change her mind.

It did. "What do we wear?" she asked. "We can't go dressed the way we are. And everything I have on this boat is covered with soot."

"Leave it to me," said Harding, "I know where I can rent some clothes."

What kind of clothes? She wondered if he would pull them off a clothesline somewhere, but she kept her doubts to herself.

Harding left and came back in an hour with a full outfit for himself—even including top hat—and an evening gown for Mary Ann. "A cab will be here in an hour," he said.

Mary Ann rushed to her cabin to try on her gown. It was

slightly too long, but it would have to do. She hitched it up at the waist and pinned the hem the way she had seen her mother do, wishing now that she had paid more attention. She washed up by drawing a bucket of water from the Seine, not the purest of water, she realized. Sometimes she would see dead cats and other refuse floating by. The clock kept ticking away the minutes.

Next, she pulled back her light hair into a bun and put on powder and rouge—or was it rouge and powder—which came first? Mary Ann realized that she knew more about greasing an engine than making up her face. She looked in the cracked mirror that had been left in the room. "You don't look too bad," she told herself, then turned away quickly, afraid the mirror would answer back.

Only 20 minutes left. Mary Ann laid out the pile of clothes: white stockings, knee-length pantaloons, petticoat, corset, cashet corset. All the clothes! Some of them had a funny smell, like cleaning fluid. To cover it, she found a bottle of perfume the French captain's wife had left, and splashed some on.

Now the whalebone corset. Try as she could, there was no way to reach the strings in back.

"Harding!" she called, angry at both herself and at him for seeing her undressed.

He came in, put his knee against her back and matter-of-factly tightened the corset, a little more roughly than necessary.

She slipped into the gown and found out that she needed him again; a hundred little satin buttons went down the side and back. She had heard women say that their lovers enjoyed playing with these buttons, but all she needed was to make sure that they were fastened.

Harding helped out again.

Then she tried to walk. Parisian fashion was famous for its tight slippers, unstable coiffures and hazardous headgear. The theory was that the more useless and hemmed in the wearer, the more genteel she must be. Mary Ann was wearing a dress that tightened to a sheath in midcalf, then spread out at the feet.

"Where did you get this thing?" she asked Harding as he lay on the bed with his arms folded, watching her struggle with it. She suspected he was enjoying himself.

"It's a copy of a design by a famous Paris couturier who boasted 'I liberate the bust but I hobble the legs,'" he said in a fake French accent. "You're looking very décolleté this evening."

She knew what he meant. Mary Ann had only a small bust to liberate and her legs were short, so the dress didn't fit well at either end. She tripped over the hem while going down the gangplank to the cab and nearly splashed into the Seine. Her stocking snagged at the same place on the planking where the French captain had fallen in, an unlucky omen.

Damn dress, she thought. She dreaded the ball. She wished that she was back on the mountaintop in Tennessee . . . wearing trousers.

As they got out of the cab at the opera house, Mary Ann gasped in surprise. Every window was lit, and it looked like a great gaudy sugar cube. Below the winged figures and gold crown, she could see the swirl of taffeta and bare sensuous shoulders in the huge second-floor windows, and hear the pop of champagne corks.

"Where did you get these clothes?" she asked.

"Monsieur Mouftant," said Harding. "He's right up the block."

"But isn't he the undertaker?" asked Mary Ann. "My God, who was wearing these before us?"

Harding didn't answer. Instead he took her arm and propelled her through the doors, where Henri Meurthe and his daughter Yvette were waiting to greet their guests.

Yvette had no problem with clothes, as Mary Ann saw immediately. Meurthe's daughter was delighted to show off her new Fortuny gown, a slate-gray velvet-and-brocade dress with a silver lace collar, V-neck and sweeping satin train in back. She wore a tiara on her high-set hair, one of the many gifts that she had received from a "secret" admirer. But her lovely face seemed troubled.

As they approached, she asked, "Have either of you seen Alain Chevrier?"

"No," said Mary Ann, "but I'm looking for him too."

"Alain seems to be in demand tonight," she heard Harding say dryly.

Then President Pouchet came in. He asked the same question.

Meurthe grimaced. "He is supposed to be here. He promised that he would come."

"Is he prepared to fly?"

"I understand that he is."

"Excellent, because I am told that the Germans are ready," warned Pouchet. "We had better be ready as well." He shook his head ominously and moved on.

"Tell me," Harding asked Meurthe, "why did you pick Chevrier for this contest? After all he's said about you? He even mispronounces your name as 'merde.'"

Meurthe gave a short laugh, as if this was a question he'd asked himself many times. "So he refers to me as 'shit,' does he? I don't deny that Alain Chevrier is impetuous, arrogant, insensitive, in short, a true Frenchman. I too am a son of France. In the end we will forget our differences in victory. For us, country is more important than pride."

"And the two of you, locked in this embrace? The practical capitalist and the socialist fanatic?"

"This lazy, self-indulgent nation needs a fanatic," said Meurthe grimly. "Soon we will be facing a far greater threat than socialists . . ."

He paused and glared as Maximilian von Hohenstauffen walked by. "And we'll need brave men to defend us, braver than the *flâneurs* that you see strutting around at this ball as if they had peacock feathers stuck up their rears."

MAXIMILIAN WAS UNDER NO illusion that Meurthe liked him. He had been invited only because he was a contestant. Fortunate for him because he had a second mission tonight. To make himself inconspicuous he wore elegant dark evening clothes with a black cravat and white gloves, rather than his gray German uniform. Decadent, he thought, but necessary.

Maximilian walked casually into the long bar called *le buffet* that ran down the right side of the opera house and strolled past Fabian Bouchard.

Bouchard gave no sign that he recognized Maximilian, but the German heard him whisper, "He's at the end."

Maximilian knew who "he" was.

Guillaume LeRond had a whole bottle of Veuve Clicquot in front of him and was gulping it, glass after glass. The bartender was eyeing him with disgust, but LeRond didn't care. He had convinced himself that he was invited only as an afterthought, in case the great Chevrier did not show. So the invitation was just another insult. To hell with it. He leaned over and dribbled saliva into a brass spittoon.

Maximilian walked up to join him. First, he thought, I'll give him one more barb to hook the fish. "So is Captain Chevrier here yet?" he asked the Frenchman cheerfully.

"Chevrier!" spat LeRond as if it was a curse. "The man has it all, and he pisses away what others would give their life's blood to get!"

The bartender and several people heard him.

Maximilian realized that he'd gone too far. He took LeRond's elbow and guided him like a rudderless ship around the corner to the Rotonde de Glacier. Its circular ceiling and tapestry-covered walls muffled sound. There he found a quiet, glass-enclosed alcove overlooking the street.

"It may soon be time to do something about Chevrier," said Maximilian. "You remember me, don't you?"

Guillaume struggled to recognize Maximilian. Then it came to him. "You were with Bouchard that day on the Canal Saint-Martin. But who are you?"

Maximilian gave LeRond his card. The Frenchman looked at it for a moment, blinking. "But you are German . . ."

"I am a patriot, like yourself. And someone who can offer you opportunities that you will never have anywhere else. Aren't you the man who has done most of the work on the dirigible?"

"Yes, but . . ."

"Then let's meet tomorrow," he patted Guillaume on the shoulder, "when you are sober and you can decide if your future lies with Chevrier or . . . somewhere else."

MARY ANN WANDERED AWAY from the ballroom. She didn't understand the dances, with strange names like the Consuelo and the Varsovienne. And the young mesdemoiselles who had been practicing them for weeks with a glass of water on their heads and could dance them like ballerinas intimidated her.

She joined a group of older women and tried to remain in the background, feeling more comfortable when the conversation turned to motorcars.

"I am upset about my automobile," said a woman in a stately black dress who proved to be a *comtesse*.

"You have a car?" asked Mary Ann.

"Of course. Doesn't everyone? Anyway . . . before I was interrupted . . . my chauffeur just killed a cyclist."

"Were you in the car at the time?" asked one of the other women. "It must have been dreadful!"

"Fortunately not, but I don't understand what happened. My chauffeur said the rear wheel barely touched him!"

"He was probably only waiting for a good chance to die," said a third woman.

"Moreover, my insurance company had to pay his family 25,000 francs," said the *comtesse*.

"That's a great deal for a man who only rode a bicycle," a fourth woman sympathized.

"My dear, are you American?" asked the *comtesse*.

"Yes, I am," said Mary Ann.

"You see them all over these days," said the *comtesse*. "Our country is Americanizing."

"Politics particularly," said another. "It has become the province of tawdry men who can do nothing else."

"Pouchet, for example. Why, that fat pretentious little man looks almost American."

"Do I detect the odor of cheap perfume?" said another

woman, looking at Mary Ann. "It smells like shop girl around here."

Mary Ann wanted to move away, but felt herself frozen to the floor, as if she were a butterfly pinned to a wall. She didn't want to turn her back on these women. Fortunately they chose another victim for their venom.

"Do you see the dress that Mademoiselle Meurthe is wearing?" asked the same woman.

"Whose design is it, a Worth . . . or a Paquin?" asked the second.

"Whatever it is, one has to admit it's beautiful, although rather daring," said a third.

"But one can be too chic!" said the *comtesse*.

There were titters of laughter, except for Mary Ann, whose blank stare betrayed her ignorance.

"My dear," said the *comtesse*, laying a hand on her shoulder. "It is well known that the best-dressed women in Paris are the courtesans and women of the night.

"And speaking of dresses," she added, "tell me, my little one. Where did you get that rag you're wearing?"

They might have continued to insult her, except one of them saw Alain Chevrier.

CHEVRIER HAD COME IN quietly through the servants' entrance, and escaped everyone's attention. He paused to clean his boots at one of the marble benches, leaving the mud where it lay. Then he saw Mary Ann across the room and started to walk toward her when she burst suddenly into tears and ran from the room.

"What happened to that lady?" he asked.

The *comtesse* recognized him. "Ah, Monsieur Chevrier," she said. "Let me introduce you to my friends. This is Alain

Chevrier, the aeronaut. They call him the Wild Man of Borneo because he was raised in Borneo, weren't you?"

"It was New Caledonia," Alain corrected. "And the natives, I assure you, were more civilized than the French."

"But didn't they have shrunken heads?" asked one of the women.

"Yes, and for that reason alone they would feel at home in your company. Let me ask you again, what did you do to that lady?"

"We got rid of her," said the *comtesse* defensively. "She was a nobody. It is a shame the kind of people that they're letting in here these days."

"But what is an even bigger shame," said Alain, "is how many well-born women of Paris—like yourself—have taken to sleeping with their goats."

He turned to walk away, and almost bumped into Yvette Meurthe.

"Hello, my secret admirer," she said. Her eyes were dancing as she flashed her famous smile at him.

Alain was puzzled. "Do we know each other?"

"Why, Monsieur Chevrier, how coy you are," said Yvette.

Alain started to look away, and then was caught and dragged back again by those measuring, challenging green eyes. "You're Meurthe's daughter, aren't you?"

"And you are the soon-to-be hero of France and giver of beautiful gifts," she said, touching her tiara.

Alain started to speak when Henri Meurthe rushed up.

"Father," she said proudly, "I have found Alain Chevrier."

"But now we have lost Mary Ann Pitman. Try to find her," he pleaded. "The occasion demands that she be present."

MARY ANN DIDN'T REMEMBER leaving the four women who had been ridiculing her. She didn't recall whether she ran or walked or simply stumbled away. Somehow she found the bathroom.

She didn't realize it at first. It was bigger than any room like it that she had ever seen. In the center was a gigantic pink marble urn with roses in it. Blue hydrangeas filled every corner. There were women's knickknacks spread all over the white marble countertop: powder, rouge, lipstick that anyone could use.

Then she saw the stalls, and ran inside the first one. They were Crappers, the new flush toilets named after their inventor, Sir Thomas Crapper. Each one had a box of water on the wall above, and a pull chain to flush it into the bowl.

I will not cry anymore, she told herself, and she didn't. But the effort cost her. She began to have hiccups—loud ones that echoed off the marble walls. To drown out the noise she reached up and pulled the metal chain attached to the box. A noisy geyser of water appeared in the porcelain bowl below. She kept hiccuping and flushing.

Then someone flung open the door. She turned and saw Yvette.

YVETTE HAD NEVER KNOWN anyone to do herself more damage than Mary Ann. White spots of powder had settled into her cheeks and red streaks ran down the sides of her nose. She was gasping for breath. She looked consumptive.

"Come," said Yvette, taking her hand. "Let us make you pretty again." She pulled harder.

Mary Ann was still holding onto the metal ring of the chain with her other hand and the toilet flushed once more.

"Come out," urged Yvette again. "There is no one here to see you."

Yvette led her to the sink. She found a handkerchief in her silver handbag, wet it and wiped Mary Ann's face clean. It was like taking care of a child.

Yvette shook her head: "The things I do for my father," she said to herself. She took what she needed from her silver réticule, and the rest from the counter. To Mary Ann, they might have been instruments on an operating table. Yvette was on intimate terms with them.

"Now tilt your head back," she ordered.

Mary Ann started to protest, but Yvette simply put her index finger under Mary Ann's jaw and raised it.

"I use charcoal to line the eyes, powder to whiten the face," she explained as she went.

She made Mary Ann smile when she applied the rouge and pucker up for the lipstick. Soon she stopped fighting. It was pleasant to be fussed over for the first time in years, and to have another woman around.

"What's that?" asked Mary Ann, caught off-guard as Yvette misted her hair with fragrance.

"An atomizer," Yvette answered. "Now look up! No blinking. I am doing your eyes."

Finally she finished. "There," she said with a smile, "look at yourself. My work of art."

Mary Ann looked, grudgingly at first, then again.

"You see," said Yvette, "you are pretty. You are what we French call a *gamine*."

In the mirror, for the first time in her life, Mary Ann caught a flash of her own beauty. Yvette had arranged her hair so it gave her an off-balance elegance, with nuances of face and form that had not existed a few moments ago: wide-set, almost Oriental brown eyes with subtle highlights, long lashes, high cheekbones. The little girl running her stick along the picket fence was suddenly transformed into a woman that men would kill—or die—for.

It scared her. It was like seeing a different person inside her skin taking possession of her. How could she handle this? She didn't want to. Gradually as she stared, the old Mary Ann came back, and it reassured her.

"See, life is full of tricks," said Yvette. "A small thing like rearranging your hair, and you are beautiful. Your eyes, for example. It is not with your body that you attract men, but with your eyes.

"When I was a little girl, I studied *La Joconde* . . ." she saw puzzlement on Mary Ann's face. "The Smiling One—you call her the Mona Lisa. I wondered: Why all the fuss? She was simply the wife of an upstart peasant who had gotten rich. But those eyes . . . those eyes that follow you everywhere. A woman is all in her eyes. They are her most powerful weapon."

"You talk as if men were the enemy," said Mary Ann.

"Aren't they? Our law, the Napoleonic code, gives them the right to buy and sell us."

"No!"

"I saw it happen in the village where Papa has his summer home. A farmer put his wife on the auction block. But she was fat and blubbering and no one would pay a sou for her. They just laughed. Do you have a man here in Paris?"

"I have someone that I love . . . like," said Mary Ann. "His name is Alain Chevrier."

"Really," Yvette smiled as if she didn't believe it. How could this dolt of a child even know Chevrier? "And did he give you any sign of his affection?"

"He gave me his ring," said Mary Ann. She fumbled in the pocket of her dress and pulled out the heavy St. Cyr ring.

If Mary Ann had looked up in that second, she would have seen a shadow pass between Yvette's face and the mirror.

"So what is this Chevrier like?" asked Yvette with cool nonchalance.

"Well," said Mary Ann, grateful for the chance to talk to a woman, "you can feel his presence across a room even before you see him. And when he's close you feel he's touching you even though he's not." She winced. Her whalebone corset— pulled too tight by Harding—was pinching her across the back.

"What do you do about these contraptions?" she asked.

"Do?" said Yvette. "I don't wear one."

"You don't?"

"It is as stupid as wearing a bustle. Most women wear the old-fashioned corset because they are fat. They lie in bed until noon, then drink tea and eat cookies all day with their friends. They think corsets make them beautiful by taking all their belly fat and rolling it up into their bosoms. Bound up in a corset, a woman cannot even button her own shoes.

"I wear a new garment called a brassière," said Yvette with just a hint of a smile. "It supports you from straps at the back of your arms. "Here, I will show you . . ." She dexterously reached around, unbuttoned herself and the front of her gown fell forward. Then she reached back and took off the brassière. She was nude to the waist.

In truth, Yvette hardly needed a brassière. The white V of her throat continued down her chest like an avenue that many men would love to travel. At symmetrical distances on both sides were two perfect hemispheres topped with apricot-colored nipples, breasts so firm that there was no perceptible line at the bottom to indicate where they stopped. Yvette wasn't just well endowed; she was perfect. Her body looked sculpted, rising from the folds of her dress like one of those statues of goddesses and nymphs that decorated the opera house.

And, at that moment, Alain walked in.

Yvette didn't move a muscle. "Monsieur Chevrier," she said. "This is a ladies' room."

"So I see," answered Alain. "I came to find out if Marianne is all right."

"She is fine," said Yvette, still not covering her nudity. "Go on now," she said to Mary Ann, but with her eyes still fixed on Alain, like a bullfighter waiting for the charge. "They are waiting for you."

As she walked out, Mary Ann once again tripped on the hem of her dress. Yvette shook her head. There was nothing more awkward than a woman wearing another woman's clothes, she thought. Alain started to follow, reluctantly.

"Monsieur Chevrier," she called to him. He turned. "You should be more careful to whom you give your jewelry."

He started to answer, but at that moment the door opened and the *comtesse* rushed in, muttering to herself. Then she looked up, saw Chevrier and Yvette together and cried "*Mon Dieu!*" She shut herself in a stall while they both laughed.

BACK IN THE MAIN ballroom, the ceremony had begun. The crowd hushed as President Auguste Pouchet mounted the dais between two ice sculptures of winged figures that had just been wheeled in.

Meurthe followed him. From the dais he looked out over the Grand Foyer. It was the most magnificent room in the Opéra, with candelabra glittering from its 60-foot ceiling. Now it was packed with people, most of them unforgiving people. He prayed silently for a quick ceremony with no problems.

The plan was for all of the contestants to come to the stage and receive certificates from the president allowing them to fly over the city. The certificates were not entirely ceremonial; they would—hopefully—prevent the kind of incident that Alain had caused at the Palais de l'Elysée. A clause in the certificate said, quite pointedly, that no one was allowed to fly over military installations or government property.

Things went well at first. Chevrier even gave the semblance of a bow when Pouchet handed him the certificate. No one except the president heard him say: "Next time I'll give you a 21-gun salute." There was loud applause.

Maximilian proved to be a superb gentleman. After accepting the certificate, he bent at the waist and kissed Yvette's hand. Ladies in the audience began to clap.

"So handsome," one sighed as he took his place next to Chevrier. "Hard to tell them apart. Such a German could well capture me!"

Then Mary Ann tried to mount the platform. She negotiated the first two steps, and missed her footing on the third. Unable to use her knees, she fell forward on the stage.

There were titters of laughter from the audience. "Can't walk—how can she fly?" shouted a heckler from the back.

Alain left his place on stage, walked over and lifted Mary Ann to her feet. He signaled to the orchestra. "Play!" he ordered.

"Play what?" asked the conductor.

"Play music!" Alain shouted.

The conductor's baton cut a curlicue, and the band launched into a waltz.

"May I have this dance, Marianne?" he asked.

"I don't dance," she said.

"I don't either," replied Alain. "But let's make the best of it."

He swept her across the floor and suddenly she was dancing, not knowing the steps, but as light on her feet as if she were in the air. She glimpsed people moving back, watching, some even applauding. The dress was no longer an obstacle. Alain held her so close that her feet barely touched the floor. She swirled back and forth across the Grand Foyer, the lights of the chandeliers glittering from above.

If I never know happiness again, she thought, I've had this. The opera house was beautiful and she was beautiful. And Alain had her in his arms.

Then, suddenly, it all went wrong.

AS THE DANCE ENDED, a waiter tapped Alain on the shoulder. "Monsieur Meurthe would like to see you in the small room over there," he said.

Alain's face betrayed not fear but concern. "What does 'Merde' want with me?"

"I don't know, sir," said the waiter. "Something to do with the *comtesse*, I believe."

Mary Ann followed Alain as he strode across the floor, but she couldn't keep up. He was heading toward a small chamber at the side of the ballroom that she had passed through earlier, when she marveled at how its circular ceiling was painted to look like the night sky. When Mary Ann reached the door, she could see Meurthe inside with his back to Alain. Meurthe seemed to be watching the painted owls, their wings spread as they floated up the ceiling, surrounded by stars and crescent moons.

"Shut the door," he ordered.

Alain slammed it. The closing door would have hit Mary Ann if Harding hadn't yanked her back.

"You have something unimportant to tell me?" Alain asked.

"I am told that you have been seen with my daughter in a compromising position," Meurthe answered, turning toward Alain with a look that would have made any other man cringe.

"What if it's true?" Alain retorted. He thought for just a second of giving an explanation, and then rejected the idea. Meurthe didn't deserve one. "Is she better than other women because she's your daughter?" he challenged. "Is she too good for me?"

"I want you to stay away from her. I forbid you to see her. I have put up with your petty insults and your pranks. I have shielded you from those who would have destroyed you. But I will not let you near my daughter."

"I know your kind," Alain sneered. "You treat your women the way you treat your dogs. You keep your bitches locked in the kennel because if they go into heat they might mate with a mongrel like me. People like me are useful to keep around, but only to do your dirty work, right?"

Meurthe shook his head. Suddenly he seemed sadder, and older. "Your problem, Alain, is that you are an all-knowing fool. You may be able to do trigonometry in your head, but you know nothing about people, and less than nothing about me."

"If I'm a fool, then find another fool to win your prize!"

Mary Ann could hear the shouting, but she couldn't tell what was being said. She started to open the door, and saw Meurthe and Chevrier standing nose to nose. Harding pulled her away.

"Stay out of there," he told her.

"But Alain's in there."

"And so is Meurthe. One of them will kill the other, and I'm not taking any bets."

Just then Alain stormed out, nearly knocking her over.

She heard Meurthe call after him: "You have a chance for glory—for yourself and for France—and you are throwing it away!"

"A chance for your glory," retorted Alain. "I'm not your altar boy . . . and you're far from being a priest!"

Waiters were still moving through the crowd, carrying champagne glasses on silver trays. With a bow, one offered a glass to Alain.

For Alain, who believed that all men were equal, it was the ultimate embarrassment. He upended the tray with one sweep of his hand, drenching the waiter. Then he stalked over to the grand piano at the far side of the room opposite the orchestra and began to hammer out "The Internationale," the song of the workers that Mary Ann had first heard that night at the Place de Grève.

The dancing stopped. Gowns ceased to swirl. Men shook their heads in amazement. The orchestra lost its place, flagged and stopped; flutes, clarinets and, lastly, cello.

Meurthe came out of the room with the owls and saw instantly how Alain had taken control. Meurthe walked across the ballroom, his jaw set. He spoke to the orchestra leader, pulled out his watch and gestured. The maestro nodded, raised his baton, and the band played:

Rise up, children of our country,
The day of glory has arrived.

It was "La Marseillaise," France's national anthem. Meurthe began to sing, and after him his friends, and then everyone. Alain's song was drowned out by their voices, for the clock had just struck 12, and this was Independence Day.

Alain rose from the piano.

From across the room, Mary Ann saw Meurthe make a short, graceful bow in Alain's direction. Was it a gesture of respect for a worthy adversary, she wondered, or just one of contempt for a beaten foe?

But there was no doubt about the way that Alain took it. He stared at Meurthe for a second, looking as if he would kill him, then strode out. Mary Ann heard his footsteps, sounding like a drumbeat on the double-sided marble stairway of the opera house.

Above on the balcony, Yvette watched as Alain, the only man who dared defy her father, stormed down the Grand Escalier toward the street. Then she ran after him quietly, her slippers making no noise as she followed him discretely down the other side of the stairway and through the front door.

Outside the noise and smoke were everywhere. Boys were throwing firecrackers under the carriage horses' feet and being chased away by the angry valets. Fireworks were still going off; lighting up the night sky with long bursts of red, yellow and blue that unfolded like flower petals in the darkness. Trailers made white flashes and whistling noises ended with hollow, reverberating booms that shook the air in her lungs. She came up behind him just as he reached the street.

"Monsieur Chevrier," she called. "Alain!"

He turned. "Well, Mademoiselle Meurthe," he said. "Aren't you afraid of your father, like everyone else?"

"I am afraid of no one," she said proudly.

He paused. "You know, I almost believe that."

"Will I see you again?"

Alain laughed. "Of course you'll see me. When I'm ready—in my time and not your father's—you and the rest of Paris will see me." He gestured toward the exploding sky. "I'll be up there." And he walked away into the night.

Yvette watched him go. "Oh, no, Monsieur Chevrier," she whispered to herself. "I'll see you much sooner than that."

seventeen

The City of Light—14 July

Now it begins. And, from the heights of Belleville to the Valley of Gold, the city waits. From Montmartre to Montparnasse, people go to their slender iron balconies, hoping for a glimpse of a balloon, an airship, or a more exotic flying machine, perhaps even one with wings? The poor, who can't afford balconies, prop open the small square windows of their steamy rooftop garrets and chase the children away so they can watch.

At the racetracks of Longchamp and Auteuil, more money is being wagered on the flyers than on the horses. The betting favors the Germans. At the Buffalo Bill Vélodrome, where lean cyclists sprint their laps around the hardwood oval, a spotter is placed on the roof where he has a clear view of the Tower.

The city waits. In the Bois de Boulogne, boys climb oak trees, listening for the pop-popping sound of a motor overhead. At the other side of the forest, kings and princes, counts and marquises take their wives and mistresses for the ritual 4 P.M. carriage ride, peering through their opera glasses at the "Tour Eiffel."

The city waits. Along the Canal Saint-Martin boatmen rest their weary mules and ask the fishermen for news of *les hommes oiseaux*, the "bird men." At Notre-Dame a mass is interrupted when a young boy rushes in and yells, "He's coming! He's overhead!" Everyone runs outside and in the crush of people the prankster escapes, with three priests in pursuit.

The city waits. One Parisian theater, famous for its spectacle, designs a fake dirigible held up only by wires, seeming to vanish into the sky. Dancing girls, dressed in gossamer, climb on board, singing, "When I Am in the Air," until they rise to the rafters. But the mechanism breaks and they come crashing to the stage, offering paying customers in the front row a good view of shapely legs and garter belts.

The city waits. And, in the presidential palace, behind his cordon of guards, President Pouchet waits too. More than any other, he has reason to fear. If the Germans win, it could doom his Republic. There are many who wish to replace him with a new Napoleon.

The German kaiser, that haunted man with a withered arm, sits far away in his dark palace at Potsdam and waits too, nursing his dreams. A great nation must show itself to the world, and Germany is a great nation—perhaps the greatest. But has he overstepped himself? Maximilian has told him he will win. So Maximilian must win.

And the Eiffel Tower waits too, like the pointer on a giant sundial, counting out the hours of a summer day. It is the tallest structure in the world, and nothing of this earth can rise above it. It is waiting for someone to measure himself against it.

ON THE *BETHANIE*, STILL moored at its dock on the Seine, Mary Ann waited too. Every last bolt had been tightened, every last wire strung, and now there was nothing to do but wait. The tension grew as the heat beat down on the plywood boards, making the boat's interior almost unbearable.

In late afternoon, Neville Bishop came back from his private rail car with the mail. He was waving a telegram and, for the first time in weeks, he looked happy. "Reece will be here on the 17th," he told Mary Ann.

He started to go below, then turned and stared at her.

"You saw the letter from my bank, didn't you? Don't deny it. I saw how it was ripped." He drew a deep breath, as if he were on the witness stand about to make a confession. "I have deep financial problems. Very deep."

Bishop held up his silver-headed riding crop. "Do you know what this is?" he said, pointing to the design.

"No, sir."

He regarded her contemptuously, as if she should have known. "It's a wolf. And do you know why I carry it?"

Mary Ann shook her head.

"I keep it to remind me that the wolf is always at the door. Those men who are backing me, Edison, Graham Bell, do you think that they are kind men?"

"I don't know."

Neville Bishop looked at her with disgust. "They are not. To the public they are legends, heroes. But they're wolves, like myself. Like me, they will not tolerate failure. To fail is to be torn apart by the other wolves . . ."

"Mr. Bishop, what happens if we don't win?" she asked.

"We must win!" And, for one moment, she caught a glimpse of the old Bishop, the arrogant, determined man who let nothing stand in his way. "If I can't go home a gentleman, with my debts paid, I won't go home at all . . ." Then, his voice trailed off and he looked at her as if he had just noticed her. "As for you, you'll have to fend for yourself."

Mary Ann started to speak, but Bishop silenced her with a raised hand. "Fortunately this stupid feud between Chevrier and Meurthe has bought us some time. We must make use of it."

Then he went ashore again.

Would Reece come in time? she wondered. Or would Meurthe and Chevrier settle their quarrel and would Alain fly? Part of her, she admitted, wanted Alain to win.

But what would happen to her and Harding if they lost? Would Bishop abandon them on the dock the way he had the barge captain and his wife? Leave them stranded in Paris? He was capable of that. And would Alain remember his promise that they work together when this was over?

Just then Harding came up the gangplank, carrying a rolled-up blue cylinder called a *petit bleu* that came through pneumatic tubes beneath the streets.

"It's a message from Meurthe," he said.

"What does he want?" she asked.

"Not Henri . . . Yvette," said Harding as he unrolled it.

"Yvette!" said Mary Ann. It was the first happy news that she'd had today. She remembered how Yvette had befriended her the night before. Perhaps she had been wrong to think Yvette a flirt.

"It's an invitation to a soiree, and it's tonight," said Harding as he read. "A famous Egyptologist is going to unwrap . . . a mummy. Do you want to go?" It was obvious by his tone that he hoped she'd say no.

"Yes, of course," she said.

"Mary Ann, this isn't your kind of party."

"And what is my kind of party? The kind of place where you hang out, bars like Cabinet of Assassins and The Devil's Revenge? And I'll need a dress, a real one, not that undertaker's thing."

"I'll find one," he said, grimacing. "I'll put it under 'petty expenses.'"

"Tell me," she asked, looking toward Neuilly where the Meurthes lived. "What do you think of Yvette? Isn't she beautiful?"

Harding stared at the far shore, stared hard before he answered:

"She is so beautiful one would never dare to love her."

AT THE GERMAN WORKSHOP in Montparnasse, Maximilian lectured his men as they worked on the skin of the huge dirigible. There would be no weekends, no time off until it was done, he told them, and they would eat on the job.

"A working man's week has seven days," he said. "A lazy man's, seven tomorrows."

"*Macht mir die eier kaput,*" ("You bust my balls") muttered a voice from the other end of the workshop.

Maximilian knew who it was. He lined up all the workmen for an inspection and walked down the line. When he reached that man, he simply pivoted on his left foot, not saying a word, and hit him between the eyes. The man fell on his back with a thump as his head hit the cement. Maximilian didn't even bother to see if he had killed him.

"Get back to work!" he barked.

"What do we do about him?" asked a sergeant.

"Leave him," ordered Maximilian. "He'll be an inspiration to the rest of you."

Then he left. He knew now what he would have to do.

AS THE HOLIDAY WORE on, crowds of sightseers passed by Alain's workshop in Saint-Cloud. Children would run up and peek through the huge double doors, open to catch the breeze. Their parents would yank them away and then look themselves, marveling at the blue aerodynamic shape floating 20 feet above the floor, ready now for the voyage to the Tower.

But was Alain ready? He stood in the open gun-metal colored cabin just below the balloon, checking and rechecking the wheel that steered the rudder at the back, and the crank that adjusted the weights along the keel that would move the airship up or down. He would stop occasionally to laugh at the children or wave at passersby. He's wasting time, Guillaume LeRond thought. But why?

The day grew more and more frustrating for Guillaume, who stood by Alain's side in the cabin. Guillaume could feel pools of sweat forming under his armpits, and he kept glancing at his pocket watch. He was due to meet Maximilian shortly, but he was worried that if he left now his absence would be noticed. He prayed that something would divert Alain's attention and allow him to slip away.

Then at noon his prayer was answered. Both of them heard the stuttering sound of a faulty car engine. Alain looked out from the cabin. "Well, I'll be damned," he said. "It's Yvette."

Most women of that era would not drive automobiles, although they were more than happy to ride in them. But Yvette was not most women. She liked to drive, and drive fast. Her hair was swept back by the wind and a small pair of square-framed dark glasses covered her famous green eyes. She was wearing a shimmering pink dress with a skin-tight bodice and a lace choke collar as she roared into the big barn.

As always, Yvette was well aware of the impression she was making. She stepped from the automobile, catching up the hem of her garment just enough to show a triangle of flounced underskirt. Work stopped as all the men turned to look. But her attention was on only one man, who stood in the cabin above her and ignored her.

"Monsieur Chevrier," she said. And repeated it, knowing that he had heard. Finally he looked down.

"I wish to apologize for my father . . ."

"You can go back to your father," Alain retorted, "and tell him to apologize for himself. Tell him to apologize for being who he is and for everything he has ever done."

They glared at each other for a moment. Then Yvette turned away. "I'm sorry that I bothered," she said. "I'll leave now."

She tried to start the car with her handcrank. It backfired and stalled. She tried again and it coughed and died. Finally she turned and looked up, helpless. "It won't start."

"I can see that."

"How shall I get home?"

"Why don't you take the Necro?" Alain shouted down.

The "Necro" was the nickname for the new metropolitan subway system. It was so badly ventilated that people believed you could suffocate riding it. The image of Yvette riding the Necro sent roars of laughter echoing through the workshop . . . until she started to sob.

Alain, for all his gruffness, was not about to leave a lady in distress. He turned to LeRond. "Well, Guillaume, if a man is going to be guillotined for a crime, he might as well commit it."

He jumped down from the airship, walked over and looked under the hood. Then he tightened two bolts with his hand. "The carburetor has shaken loose," he said. "It will start now."

"My father just bought this for me. How was I to know?"

"The rich girl can't get her toys to work," joked Alain, but his voice was not rough. "I will drive you home. I would not have your father accusing me of abducting you."

They traveled down the slopes of Saint-Cloud and across the Aqueduct Bridge in silence.

Finally Yvette spoke: "My father is not a bad man."

"Yes. I am sure that his dog loves him, too."

"I must tell you," she giggled, "you made him so mad when you came to the ball without a suit and tie."

"I don't wear ties," said Alain. "A tie is a symbol of slavery. In the Middle Ages, when the king captured a city, all the men had to come out wearing nooses around their necks to show that the king had the right to hang them. Also, a tie is a useless garment. What purpose does it serve? It is like underwear. It constricts the body for no reason."

"You do not wear underwear?" Yvette appeared shocked. She was silent for a moment. Then she asked, "Have you named any of your balloons?"

"I have named my favorite one after a woman."

"Oh," said Yvette. "Which woman? Evangeline, Liselle, perhaps Mary Ann . . ."

"I call her the *Bitch*," said Alain with a grin.

"Really, Monsieur Chevrier," Yvette retorted. "Is that the only kind of woman you know? You, who could have any woman you want?" She tossed her head to show the dark glow of her hair. "Well, almost any woman."

Alain was silent.

"So, do you have a woman?" she asked.

"No, I don't have a woman, nor does any woman have me. Slavery was abolished several years ago. It was in all the newspapers. No one has a claim to anyone else's life—or love."

"Then you believe in free love? I've heard that you anarchists do."

"Let's put it this way. I've never had to pay for it."

"I wonder what it would feel like to make love in a balloon," she mused, rolling her eyes toward the heavens. "So public, up there in the sky, and yet so alone. I am told that if you take a woman high enough, she loses all her inhibitions."

"That's all talk. However, if you go high enough, as some of our aeronauts have, your brain becomes starved for oxygen, and you act as if you were drunk. But who would want to make love in a balloon when there's so much to look at?"

"Pah!" she said. "You lack imagination."

"No, I don't. I just see things differently from you. You would go to a bourgeois play like *Romeo and Juliet* and say 'how marvelous.' I would see two cats, one on the balcony and the other in the alley below, howling at each other."

"Then what do you see?"

"I see the stars."

"Is it true that you see the stars in daylight?" she asked.

"Anyone can. You just have to look hard enough."

He stopped the car. "Look straight ahead of you and up." He

put his arm on her shoulder. "Over there where Orion stands. There is a legend that—when God comes—he will come from Orion. There is just the faintest glow."

Then he realized that he had touched her.

Yvette turned and looked at him over the top of her dark glasses. Their faces were only inches apart.

"Come," said Yvette, "we are going to the Eiffel Tower."

"I thought that I was taking you home."

"First I have a challenge for you. We will have a race."

When they arrived at the Tower, Yvette bolted for the elevator. Alain ran for the stairs and started up, leaping two and three at a time. Yvette took the trolley elevator where passengers sat 10 abreast, and when she arrived at the first level, he had already passed her.

The elevator from the top took its time coming down. She watched the pulleys as they spun like bobbins. Behind her waited a child waving a tin sword and a man holding his wife like a sack of potatoes. They all got on and the elevator started up with a lurch. Through the window she could see them gaining on Alain as he ran from landing to landing. She turned to the operator.

"Can you slow it down?"

He looked surprised. It was the first time that he had ever heard this request.

Yvette reached into her purse and handed him a 10-franc note. "Now can you slow it down?"

"But mademoiselle," he said, "the other passengers?"

She gave them all 10-franc notes.

She reached the top a few seconds after Chevrier. He was panting, but proud of his victory. "Man against machine! I've always wondered if I could win a race like that."

He pointed out. "Below on the river is the Americans' craft, almost ready to fly. That menacing building in Montparnasse is the Germans' huge barn. And up there, in Saint-Cloud, is where I will fly from . . ."

Yvette looked at him levelly. "And when will you fly?"

"When I'm ready."

"And could someone persuade you?"

"With what?" he said. "Something more than money?"

Yvette raised her right leg to the top of the railing like a ballet dancer to the barre and, oblivious to the stares, slowly rolled down her stocking. She had a red tulip embroidered into the stocking at the ankle, something nice girls normally didn't do. She gave Alain the stocking.

"Tie it to the lightning rod at the top of the Tower," she told him. "Then, when you fly around it, you can retrieve it and give it back to me. And afterward you'll be rewarded . . . with something more than money."

She smiled at him.

He took the stocking and climbed up the latticework that led to the roof.

When she heard his footsteps on the slippery brass sheathing above her, she realized what she had done. What if he fell? Then she considered it. What better for a woman's reputation than having a gallant young aeronaut make a leap of love from the Eiffel Tower?

Suddenly he was down again.

"Now, I think it is time for you to drive me home," she said.

They traveled back through the quiet, tree-lined streets of Neuilly with its secluded estates and high, spiked walls, and stopped in front of the wrought-iron gate of the Meurthes' mansion.

"Kindly slide the bolt on the gate," said Yvette, moving into the driver's seat. "I'll drive from here."

"All right," he said, a little put off by the way she had taken charge. "But be sure to get your automobile fixed. It still rattles."

She turned to him as he stood by the gate. "I have one more challenge for you, Alain. I'm having a soiree tonight and I want you to come."

"Why would I do that?" he scoffed.

"Perhaps because my father doesn't want you there . . ."

"A soiree? I'll think about it."

"Don't debate with yourself too long, Monsieur l'Anarchiste," Yvette laughed.

Again her face was only inches away from his, and he leaned in to kiss her. She threw the car into gear and sent it rattling through the gate, leaving him behind.

When Yvette had turned the corner of the building, she got out a wrench and flung up the hood. A quick adjustment and the rattle stopped; the engine ran smoothly. Men always believed that women were stupid about mechanical things. It was insulting, but it could also be turned to advantage, if one were clever enough. He will come, she thought. He is a man who needs to be challenged, and I can challenge him better than anyone else.

When she entered the house, the maid gave her a knowing look. "Send another invitation for the soiree tonight," Yvette ordered.

"For Captain Chevrier?" the maid asked.

"No," said Yvette. "Captain Chevrier needs no invitation. This one is for a mademoiselle . . . Pitman."

eighteen

*G*UIGNOL WAS ONE OF the most famous people in Paris. His house was in the center of the Garden of Luxembourg, near the pool where the children sailed their wooden boats. He was short, mean-spirited, stingy, long-nosed, hard of hearing and empty-headed. He beat his wife and drank too much, so he was very popular with everyone.

Now Guillaume LeRond was going to meet Guignol.

LeRond had been there before in happier times when he was young. One of the children fidgeting in the long line that snaked around the hedge and small cottage, he had pulled on Mama's hand, impatient to get in. The ritual never seemed to change; there was always a new generation that loved Guignol. But I have changed, he thought. Now he felt out of place, the only man there, and the only adult without a child. He looked around nervously to see if he'd been followed.

It didn't help when he got a strange quizzical look from the ticket-taker, who sat on a small stool next to the wooden gate outside Guignol's house. Guillaume pushed past him through the gate and entered the backyard enclosed by the hedge.

He saw rows and rows of wooden benches filled with a sea of small happy faces, all waiting for Guignol. Then, at the far back, he saw another face, scarred but handsome, waiting for him. Maximilian's long legs were stretched out in the dirt aisle and he patted the seat next to him. Guillaume moved carefully to the back and slid in beside him.

"Nougat?" said Maximilian, offering a bag of candy. "I'm sharing it with my little friends here."

Guillaume shook his head and glanced around before pulling out one of his Gauloise cigarettes. "Why are we meeting here?" he whispered. "Don't we stand out?"

Maximilian snapped a match with his thumb. The flame seemed to come right out of his fist. He held it steady for Guillaume, whose cigarette was trembling in his hand.

"Not at all," he said. "We look like a couple of bored fathers who brought the little darlings to see Guignol and then went back for a smoke. Do you see anyone here who might be a policeman or an informer? And how could they hear us even if they were?"

The red velvet curtain went up and the children screamed, "Guignol! Guignol!" He popped up on stage, seemingly out of nowhere. Guignol was a hand puppet with a long nose and a red stocking cap, like the French revolutionaries.

Guignol was having trouble again with his wife, Madelon. She was a bigger puppet than he was, so she beat and bullied him and the two had many good fights. He would come in late and she would catch him—just as he reached the edge of the stage—and hit him over the head with a pot.

The children loved the swift, jerky movements of the two puppets, and they particularly loved the way Guignol talked to them.
He would complain long and loudly about Madelon, not knowing
that she was coming up behind him. The children would giggle.
Then she would knock him down, his head hitting the floor with a
solid wooden thump, and he would run for the wings of the stage.

The children would try to warn Guignol whenever his wife
came closer. When Guignol didn't hear them they shouted louder,
jumping up as they tried to make themselves heard over the
other children who clustered at the fence in front of the stage.

In the back, Guillaume complained to Maximilian: "I have
given my time and sweat to the army for 20 years, and what do
I get? Guillaume go here, Guillaume do this. Guillaume, this is
your responsibility. But the glory is all Chevrier's. He gets it all!"

Maximilian nodded sympathetically. "I know. But the question is: what are you going to do about it?"

Guillaume was taken aback. "What can I do?"

"You can come with me to Germany."

"Do you mean that?"

"Would I be here watching this silly children's show if I didn't?"

"But how could this be arranged?" asked Guillaume. "And
what kind of prospects would I have in your country?"

Maximilian thought this would be easier than expected.
"When I saw you," he told Guillaume, "I said, 'There's the man
with the brains behind this project, a man Germany can use.'"

Guillaume laughed harshly and pulled out another cigarette
from his pocket. His movements were as jerky as those of the
puppets on stage. "Ha, you are forgetting, my friend. You are
German and I am French."

Maximilian looked straight at him. "In our new world, the

world in the sky, nationality is nothing. Ability is everything. The people who understand what it takes to get up in the heavens; the future is theirs, no matter what language they speak. Some day they may even have their own language."

For the first time, Guillaume lost his skeptical look. He wanted to believe. "You know what would happen if they caught me here with you? They shoot spies. Look what they did to Dreyfus, and he wasn't even guilty."

Maximilian shrugged. "Dreyfus is a Jew, and they are all part of a worldwide conspiracy. He deserved what he got."

ON THE SMALL STAGE, Guignol had declared that he would give anything to be rid of his troublesome wife. A figure in red with a mustache and pointed chin popped up behind him. The children screamed. They knew who he was. Their mothers and the priest had frightened them with him often enough, and many nights they had crawled deep under their blankets, hoping the tapping sound outside the window was not his knock.

But today, in the bright sunlight, they were not yet afraid. "Look behind you!" they cried. "No, to your left! Your right!" But their cries were useless. Every time Guignol turned to one side, the devil came up on the other. The message was clear. He would be seen only when he wanted to be seen.

Finally the devil shouted "Boo!" and Guignol's head popped up. The children giggled.

The devil was sympathetic to Guignol's problem. He asked Guignol if he would like to be rid of Madelon. Guignol nodded his head vigorously.

"Just promise me, old friend, that you'll give me a small reward later on," said the devil. "A very small reward, in your case."

Guignol agreed. His wife's booming voice was heard offstage calling him, and the devil ran off.

Maximilian recognized the plot. It was the classic Faust. Guignol little knew that he had struck a bargain with the devil and would have to give up his soul. Silly to think of a puppet having a soul . . . or even a man.

Now it was time to move his plot forward. Maximilian leaned over so close to Guillaume that their faces were only inches apart, and pretended to be lighting a cigarette from LeRond's.

"I am going to tell you something that even my subordinates don't know," he confided. "The kaiser is very interested in this project and has authorized me to do anything necessary to make it succeed. At any price," he emphasized. "And that includes citizenship and a handsome salary."

"How much money would I get?"

Maximilian wrote down a figure on a slip of paper and passed it to him.

Guillaume gasped. "That much?"

"Every year."

Guillaume's face showed his surprise. Suddenly he had value; far greater value to Maximilian than to Alain.

"But . . ." said Maximilian.

"But . . ." mouthed Guillaume after him, anticipating his next sentence.

"But first we must win the Meurthe Prize," said Maximilian. "What you get later depends on how well I do now."

Guignol's wife was in the kitchen, her trusty pot in hand, when the devil entered from the other wing and stole up behind her. Again the children screamed: "*Là-bas! Regardez là-bas!*"

("Over there! Look over there!") But Madelon might as well have been deaf. She went on mumbling about how much work she did and what a *clochard* was Guignol.

The devil grabbed her from behind. She whooped and hollered and battered the devil with her pot. But when he seized her by the feet and upended her, Madelon's head hit the stage with a crack, and the devil, chuckling, dragged her off.

Guillaume had no interest in the Guignol show. It was a distraction. His mind was racing ahead to future glories. What does it matter where I live? A wrench is a wrench and a bolt is a bolt, and no one can match them up as well as Guillaume. Maximilian sat there, letting the game play out, letting the fish have more line. Finally he spoke.

"How close is Chevrier to flying around the Tower?" Maximilian already knew the answer, but this test would allow him to see if Guillaume would tell the truth.

Guillaume stiffened, his reverie gone. "He could fly anytime. But he won't because of that feud between him and Meurthe. And now, to make matters worse, that little bird fluttering around our workshop distracts him."

Maximilian laughed. "You mean Yvette Meurthe?" Things were working out perfectly, he thought.

Now there was a tinge of steel in Maximilian's voice. "If he does decide to fly, we must do something to insure that he doesn't win."

"What do you mean?" Guillaume was apprehensive again.

"What is the word you French use? The one where you throw your wooden shoes in the machines?"

"Sabotage," said Guillaume softly, and for a second Maximilian thought he had lost him. Guillaume started to rise and Maximilian grabbed his arm.

"All we're talking about is something simple, something that would delay Chevrier for a day and could never be found out.

"Look, you know your future is not with Chevrier. He doesn't respect you. If he flies, all the glory will go to him, not to the men who did the work. The new Germany, the Germany we're creating, isn't like that. It's a partnership between the workers and the employers. That's why our technology is so superior. That's why we win our wars."

Guillaume was silent for a moment. Then he shrugged with resignation. "What do you want me to do?"

"I have a simple device, only two inches square, that you attach at the front of the balloon. You push a button. Inside is acid. The acid eats a hole in the balloon. The balloon deflates and then settles to the ground."

"And the device?"

"It falls off when the job is done. It is also eaten away by the acid and looks like a piece of the airship's skin. Here, I will show it to you."

Maximilian reached inside the sack next to him. The package was the same bright blue as Alain's airship—an exact match.

Guillaume did not want to touch it. He kept his hands at his sides.

"What's in the package? Candy?"

Guillaume looked up in horror. A small, dark-haired boy with bangs over his eyes was watching them.

Maximilian smiled. "It's a present. Would you like to see it?" He gave it to the boy. "One must never hide things from children," he told Guillaume. "It makes them suspicious."

"It's heavy," said the boy. "May I open it?"

"No," answered Maximilian. "It is a gift for this man. It is going to make him rich." He took the package from the boy and placed it very carefully in Guillaume's shaking hands. Then he patted the boy's head.

"I love children," said Maximilian after the boy had turned away. "Someday your children and mine will be sitting together at a show like this. By the way, you should disable Chevrier's other balloon as well. Rip a seam or something."

"And what about the Americans?"

"They are awaiting their pilot. And we have provided him with enough whores to keep him occupied for a long time."

ON STAGE GUIGNOL SAT in a big red chair, smoking a pipe. He was telling the children how comfortable life was without his wife and how he wished that it would go on forever. Just then there was a sound like the wind coming through the trees. "What's that?" said Guignol, sitting up in his chair.

The noise became louder and turned into a voice, the devil's voice. "Guignol," it moaned, "it is time to collect my reward. Come along."

But Guignol wasn't going, at least not willingly. He tucked himself back into the chair and wrapped the arms around him. "Later," he called. "I'll come later. Not now."

Then, with a twist of the head that had remained tucked into the chair like that of a sleeping bird, the children saw the red chair was actually the devil himself. They shouted and screamed and tried to explain it to Guignol, but he would only yell, "Go away! All of you! Leave me alone!"

Most of the children were standing at the fence that separated them from the stage or jumping on the benches. The small dark-haired boy was crying because he could not see. Maximilian reached down and swung the child up on his shoulders.

Guillaume was weighing the package in his hand. "This device will not hurt anyone?"

"Guillaume, I give you my word," said Maximilian, bouncing the boy on his shoulders. "In a few days we will both be in Germany. Be sure you follow the instructions. Then burn them."

Guillaume nodded.

Maximilian watched his face carefully. He had misgivings. Guillaume was a weak vessel, a blunt instrument to set against someone as strong and determined as Chevrier. But even a blunt instrument could kill. Maximilian knew that from experience.

THE CHILDREN SQUEALED WITH fear as the devil seized Guignol, carried him off-stage and tossed him into hell. A fan underneath the stage blew orange ribbons that symbolized flames, and Guignol danced across them.

"Oh, ow, ouch! It's hot down here," he told the children. "But at least there's one good thing. I'm alone."

And that was the signal for his wife, Madelon, to come out, still waving her pot, and beat him over the head. She was even madder now, because her stupid husband had condemned them both to this place.

The older children were laughing, but many of the younger ones cried, their faces buried in their mothers' dresses. The mothers tried to explain that this was only a puppet show; Guignol would be back next week. And when you are older you will like it. See how happy the big children are?

Especially the tall man in back with the blond hair. He had the broadest smile of all.

nineteen

*T*HAT NIGHT ALAIN CLIMBED onto the seat of his smaller airship, the one he called the *Bitch*, and started the engine. The little dirigible looked like a racing car, and was perfect for what he wanted; so light it could cut through the air like a knife, and so agile it could dart down an alley or up into the clouds. It was the ship in which he had flown with Mary Ann the day they taunted President Pouchet.

Tonight, though, as the propeller churned the air behind him and the airship rose from its hangar, he wasn't thinking about Mary Ann, or flying to the Eiffel Tower. He could fly to the Eiffel Tower anytime. Tonight he was flying for fun, to avenge an insult by Henri Meurthe and to kiss a beautiful woman.

It could not have been a more perfect night. The moon was full and the sky as bright as if a friendly God had lighted a street lamp above his head. The shadow of his craft was a luminous, swift-moving ghost on the boulevard below. With no wind the little airship was easy to handle. Passing over the avenues at treetop level, he waved at everyone, then seemed surprised when everyone waved back.

Then he spotted a corner cafe on the Champs-Elysées where he knew the tavern keeper. He reached overhead and slid the coiled drag rope forward. Instantly the little torpedo-shaped balloon responded to the change in ballast, and he brought it to rest between two outdoor tables, hovering just above the sidewalk.

Three pretty young ladies begged him to share an apéritif. Alain shook his head; he had too much to do, but he bought a bottle of wine for them. Then he slid the drag rope to the back and sent the airship spiraling skyward, its engine roaring, startling a flock of pigeons who couldn't believe they had competition for the night sky. One flapped its wings and clucked at him only a hairsbreadth from his nose, scolding him for invading their domain.

Alain slowed as he reached the upper floors of the six-story mansions that lined the street, turned his handlebars gently and glided past the long floor-to-ceiling windows. He paused to pick flowers from a window box and scattered them over the people on the street below, who dashed beneath him to catch every one. Farther up the block, women ran to their windows to throw their undergarments at him. Some of them undressed to do it. Children ran from roof to roof, leaping over the parapets between attached houses like rabbits, trying to keep up with him.

It was the most beautiful flight of his life.

HARDING HAD FINALLY GOTTEN Mary Ann a dress that fit, a flowing white gown with golden leaves woven into the cloth. Alain liked white, she remembered. She bought a bottle of perfume, the same kind she had smelled on Yvette, and set her hair the way Yvette had shown her, even painting her face, a little, just under the cheekbones. Dress, camisole, chemise, translucent slip. She felt a glow that seemed to rise up from deep inside her at the thought of the masquerade she was putting on.

Harding came in a rented black landau with chrome handles that glowed in the dark, and a leather roof that swung back to reveal the starry night sky. She noticed that his suit was clean—for a change—but he seemed distracted. On the way to Meurthe's he sang a song popular in America:

This life's a hollow bubble, don't you know?
Just a painted piece of trouble, don't you know?
We come to earth to cry,
We grow older and we sigh,
Older still and then we die,
Don't you know?

"I liked your pig song better," she grumbled. "By the way, how did you get old snootface Bishop to pay for this gown?"

"I didn't. I paid for it. Remember that little hole-in-the-wall where I lived? Well, I don't live there anymore."

After that they didn't talk for another mile. Finally she made herself say it: "I'm sorry. I know that place had memories." They were nearly there.

"Don't be," answered Harding, "it's too late for me anyhow. Look, I hope everything works out for you tonight. I hope you see Alain and he dances with you again, and he and Meurthe end their feud, and this damn pilot shows up and we win the prize. But I have a bad feeling." And he started to sing again, "This life's a hollow bubble . . ."

Mary Ann tried to distract him. "Oh, look! There's a full moon out and it's floating right over the Meurthes' house." She could see the second-story balcony surrounded by tall shrubbery and ivy. As she watched, a second, smaller moon came in and hovered at arm's length just beyond the edge of the balcony. It was Alain's airship.

She paused, unable to move or even breathe as she watched what happened next. Then she screamed as if she'd been bitten by a snake, threw herself on Harding's shoulder, and started to cry.

FOR HENRI MEURTHE, IT was another night, another one of those infernal parties. This one was of even less interest to him than the others were, because it fell in the realm of pseudoscience. A man he despised was doing a thing he despised even more.

His daughter Yvette had invited the Egyptologist, Professor Belique Trivard, to do a mummy unraveling, which was all the rage this year. A crowd of more than 100 guests in evening clothes had gathered at the foot of his marble staircase where a trestle had been set up. The cloth-wrapped corpse that lay on it—surrounded by surgical instruments—was the guest of honor.

What was this morbid fascination with the dead? Meurthe wondered. He remembered how some of these same people had poked their canes and umbrellas under the rubber sheets after the Bazaar de la Charité fire had left 200 poor souls dead, gawking at the mangled remains of people they knew.

Meurthe turned away from the door when he saw Professor Trivard come in and hand his cane and gloves to a butler. Trivard had a reputation for liking young boys more than he should, a thought that turned Meurthe's stomach. In Meurthe's opinion, Trivard's trips to Egypt were just an excuse to indulge his passions for hashish and pedophilia.

Meurthe almost stepped on a live turtle that crawled around the floor with jewels stuck to its back. He hoped the jewels were fake. At one side of the room was a long cylinder that looked like a gas tank. On top was a pressure gauge and—coming out at another angle—a hose that led to a nose and mouthpiece. Some fool has brought ether, he thought. Soon all the other fools will be inhaling it, and then staggering around like drunkards. He hoped that no one put a candle next to the tank and blew them all up.

As he watched, Professor Trivard began his lecture next to the mummy, talking about how he had made his way back from the Valley of the Dead in the lower reaches of the Nile after all the other members of his expedition had died. Accidental deaths, of course, but the treasures that Trivard had brought home had made him a wealthy man, Meurthe remembered.

And now the famous Egyptologist with the perpetual leer took surgical scissors and cut through the resin membrane that had kept the wrapped corpse airtight for long centuries. Meurthe felt violated, as if it were his body lying on the trestle. There was a hissing sound as the dry air of the Middle East collided with the humid Parisian summer night, and then the smells of ancient Egypt, frankincense and myrrh, permeated the house. There were screams from the audience. One woman appeared to faint, falling backward into the waiting arms of her paramour.

Trivard, using a crochet needle, explained how the embalmed brain was pulled out of the skull through the nose and placed in the earthen jar that sat in the crotch of the mummy. When he passed the jar around, one of the ladies dropped and broke it, and the others kicked the brain back and forth, shrieking as the desiccated organ touched their shoes.

"That's enough!" Meurthe said out loud, although no one heard him. Disgusted, he pushed his way through the crowd and headed for the peace of his outside garden and a good cigar. It was a warm night, and the doors that opened onto the promenade were already wide apart. He stepped outside and drew a long breath.

Then he too looked up at his daughter's balcony.

"Get my car!" he roared at his servants. "Get me my car!"

YVETTE'S MAID WAS THE first to notice him. She ran to get Yvette. "You should greet your guest," she said, smiling.

"I will be down when I am ready," Yvette snapped.

The maid shook her head. "He's not down," she corrected. "He's up."

Yvette was puzzled for a second; then she understood. She dashed to the balcony. The full moon seemed to engulf the whole sky. Alain was waiting on the seat of his airship just beyond the balcony's edge. Yvette slowed herself to a walk (Never look too eager, she thought) and came to the edge of the railing.

"So you came, Monsieur Chevrier," she said quietly, as if greeting an ordinary guest downstairs.

"Yes, I've met my part of the bargain. And what of your promise?"

"I will keep mine, too," she said, and leaned over, one leg up behind her like a ballet dancer.

When two people—even experienced men and women—take their first kiss, it is a finding, fumbling process. Much worse when one of them is on a bicycle seat on a tiny airship and the other is trying to balance like a tightrope walker. The first time they collided with their noses and missed each other's lips entirely—grazing cheeks in a parody of the traditional French fashion of greeting one another.

"One would think we were cousins," said Yvette, laughing.

They tried again, more successfully. Her mouth was deep. The third time she gave him a touch of her tongue, just a taste, running it across his lips and then retreating. Then she broke it off.

"Tomorrow night, Alain, after you fly to the Tower." And she ran inside.

HARDING HELD MARY ANN with one hand while he clasped the reins with the other as they rode back to the *Bethanie*. She was sobbing uncontrollably and, for the first time since they had met on the mountaintop, he was afraid of what she might do to herself. Two blocks away from Meurthe's house, fierce white acetylene lights framed them and he heard the roar of a motorcar behind him. He saw the angry flash of Meurthe's taut white face as the car sped past, rocking the carriage with its speed.

He's headed for Saint-Cloud, Harding thought, and the final confrontation with Chevrier.

When they reached the *Bethanie*, Harding helped Mary Ann up the gangplank and down to her cabin. For once, she was unresisting. She lay on the bed, still sobbing softly, mumbling how she would never forget the sight of Alain and Yvette kissing, framed by the full moon, the damned moon. Even the moon had betrayed her.

"I thought that he loved me," she blurted out. "I'm a fool. I've been a fool ever since this started."

Harding cradled her gently in his arms.

"Maybe he does love you. I know that he cares about you. But he's a different kind of person than you or me. Alain can see things you and I never will. He can see distant stars, even in daylight. But he can't see people the way they really are. He can't understand the way you feel. He doesn't know you the way I do. He doesn't care about you the way . . ." and he stopped.

Mary Ann opened her eyes wide and looked at him. She could see, suddenly and quite clearly, how Harding felt about her, how much of her own pain he was willing to share, and it shocked her out of her own misery.

Then the door to her cabin burst open and Neville Bishop walked in without knocking. So much for privacy, she thought. But she realized that his mind was elsewhere. His hair and beard were limp and stringy and he wore a nightgown so baggy that he resembled a washerwoman. He looked bleak and defeated.

"I have just received an invitation," he mumbled. "Alain Chevrier will be flying to the Eiffel Tower tomorrow at 5 A.M. We have been invited by Henri Meurthe to observe—from the reviewing stand at the Tower."

twenty

*F*IVE A.M. THE DUELING hour. Paris was already awake. By now everyone in the city knew that Alain Chevrier would make his flight to the Eiffel Tower this morning.

And most were positioning themselves to see it. Outside the giant workshop in Saint-Cloud, a crowd had gathered in the gray light before dawn. Billowy dresses swept the grass. A company of bicycle riders, volunteers in blue uniforms from the post office, waited to take up stations along the route.

Alain was inside looking at a map and making final preparations with Guillaume LeRond. Alain looked drained; it was apparent that he hadn't slept. His usual confidence was absent from his face. His dark hair was uncombed and his eyes were like empty headlight sockets.

"I will follow the line of the aqueduct down to the first crossing of the Seine . . ." he said. Then he stopped as he saw the pain in Guillaume's face. For a moment the two studied each other. The depths of despair in Guillaume's eyes might have warned another man of danger.

What do I tell him, Guillaume thought. That I have betrayed him? He started to speak, to say something, anything that would stop what was going to happen . . . but Alain silenced him with an upraised hand.

"Don't worry, old friend," he told Guillaume. "I'm not afraid to go up there today. It's something else that's bothering me. I'd rather be up there than down here among people. I'm used to that kind of danger. I enjoy it. This is the moment that I've spent my whole life training for. All I need is to 'Have a little courage.'"

Alain turned and sprang into the metal gondola of the airship like a cat leaping from floor to table, an unconscious display. He gave a sign to two of his mechanics who turned the big windmill sails of his propeller until they started to beat the air like kettle-drums. Guillaume's last words were swallowed by the backwash.

IT WAS A HOT, muggy morning, and the mist was rolling off the Seine when Mary Ann and Harding arrived at the Eiffel Tower. The reviewing stand, where the Aéro Club, the generals and the nobility would watch Alain's flight, had been set up near the Pont d'Iéna bridge so that they would have a full view of the top of the Tower. Mary Ann saw that the bottom of the grandstand was packed with uniforms and dark suits, but at the top, Henri Meurthe had a place all to himself. Well, almost to himself. Yvette stood beside him.

Yvette looked the way she always did: cool, beautiful; if anything, more confident than usual. She was watching through a pair of opera glasses hung on a jeweled chain around her neck, and, like a good actress, she had a magnificent backdrop, the frame of the Eiffel Tower. Behind the reviewing stand were the rockets and fireworks that would explode once Alain had triumphed.

Mary Ann hesitated when she saw Yvette. Then Harding pushed her forward.

"I don't want to go," she'd told Harding earlier.

"And let Yvette know that she's won?" he goaded her.

He was right, she knew. Alain had made her no promises. He hadn't led her on. He had been nothing but kind to her. Now she was going to be there to see him win. She would smile through her pain, and Yvette could go to hell.

But she almost panicked when she saw the Meurthes. They looked so unapproachable. Then Henri Meurthe glanced down and flashed a smile. So did Yvette, but it was a different kind of smile. Meurthe motioned them to come up.

Mary Ann recoiled.

"Come on," said Harding softly, nudging her. "You've got to face her. You're fighting for your self-respect now."

Then, fortunately, another man brushed by them and pushed his way through the nobles and generals to the top, where he stood next to Meurthe. It was the German, Maximilian von Hohenstauffen.

"No false modesty there," whispered Harding, as he and Mary Ann followed in his wake.

"So glad you could join us," said Meurthe, running his eyes over the two of them, and then fixing them on Maximilian. "I thought you would like to see this."

"I assure you, nothing will give me more pleasure than to witness this," said von Hohenstauffen. "A great event. A triumph for Man no matter who achieves it. I wish him all the best."

Meurthe shrugged, as if he didn't trust Maximilian's sentiments and, what's more, didn't care. But von Hohenstauffen didn't seem to notice the small discourtesy. "There!" he said.

"Chevrier's airship has started to rise. Would you like to look through my German-made glasses?"

"Mine is French, and just as good," retorted Meurthe, putting a telescope to his right eye. Both of them watched the distant hills of Saint-Cloud.

Maximilian scrutinized the balloon with his powerful binoculars. It was impossible to tell at this distance if the device was attached. After all, it was supposed to be invisible.

"Is that a dueling scar on the left side of your face?" asked Meurthe. "I have fought duels myself."

"So have I," said Maximilian, "and always won."

"Yet someone managed to cut you a bit, didn't he?"

Von Hohenstauffen laughed. "Oh, no. When you are a German officer, it is almost 'de rigueur'—how I love your French words!—to have a dueling scar. But no one could manage to touch me, not even my instructors. No, I did this myself—with a scalpel."

"Interesting," said Meurthe. "It took God to mark Cain, but you have conveniently done the job yourself. If I were younger, I would be delighted to duel with you."

"Perhaps we already are," said Maximilian.

"The trip has begun well," said Meurthe, turning away from him and talking directly to Mary Ann. "Chevrier is making his journey across the Bois de Boulogne past the little gatehouse in the park. There is a huge crowd at the racetrack at Longchamp cheering him on. Now he is past the Auteuil racetrack and coming over the city. He has reached the Seine below our replica of the Statue of Liberty. Both sides of the river are lined with people . . ."

Mary Ann listened to Meurthe's voice, soothing and instructive, but in the background she could sense Maximilian. The German seemed to be pacing, even though he was standing still. Something was wrong, she sensed.

She turned away and found herself facing Yvette. Cool, gray-green eyes looked Mary Ann up and down. Strange how life—and love—had become a battlefield, thought Mary Ann. She set her jaw, determined to endure whatever happened. Harding spoke first.

"Sorry we couldn't come to your party last night," he said.

"That's all right," said Yvette, equally the poker player. "It was a bore. The real excitement is here today." She motioned with one gloved hand to the top of the Tower where her stocking floated.

"Do you see that? Alain and I made a private bet yesterday just before he came to our house for the soiree. When he passes the top of the Tower, he will remove my stocking and bring it back to me."

Mary Ann lost what little composure she had left. Her eyes welled with tears. Then she felt Harding's hand gripping hers and forced herself to focus on the sky, where Alain's blue dirigible was drawing closer.

Yvette saw the pain in Mary Ann's face. And enjoyed it. So she thinks she is the wronged woman? thought Yvette. I have wronged many women. They do not frighten me. Eventually they go away.

"Oh, that reminds me," said Meurthe to his daughter. "Chevrier gave me a note for you last night."

She opened it, holding it close so no one else could see, not sure what she would find. It said:

Yvette:

We must never see each other again.

Alain Chevrier

She looked up at her father, anger and despair in her eyes. What had he done? Why did he want to hurt her like this? Henri Meurthe looked away, following the flight.

And Alain! Sending her this smug note! Dismissing her. Today he would be a hero of France, and she would be . . .

"I hate you," she said to the distant figure floating through the sky. "I hope you die up there."

The dirigible was 500 feet above the Seine when the phosphorous bomb went off and the back end of the balloon burst into flame. Alain had been standing up at the edge of the railing, and the sudden lurch nearly sent him overboard. He caught himself on the edge of the metal frame.

Then, in a supreme act of courage, he pulled himself hand over hand back into the cockpit, where the flames drew closer every second. At the back of the dirigible the cells exploded one by one. Mary Ann saw Alain slide the ballast weight forward and put the airship into a dive. Then he set his hands on the wheel and headed up the Seine.

She couldn't stand it anymore. She had to do something. Yvette had turned away, the opera glasses still around her neck. Mary Ann reached over and grabbed them, snapping the jeweled chain. Yvette glared at her, but Mary Ann hardly noticed as she focused on the dying ship and its doomed captain.

"Jump! Why doesn't he jump?" yelled the crowd on the reviewing stand as the dirigible fell from the sky.

But Mary Ann knew why. Alain had seen the spectators, many of them children, on the banks of the river. He would not let the flaming mass of dirigible crash down on them, so he was steering it directly into the Seine, but at a terrible cost to himself.

Suddenly she was bumped from behind and saw Maximilian pushing his way down from the top of the reviewing stand. He looked angry.

Maximilian was annoyed. He had told Guillaume to place the device at the bottom front of the balloon. That way, if Chevrier put his craft into a dive, the flames would have blown back into his face. But Guillaume had placed the bomb at the back of the airship. Could it be Guillaume knew all the time that it was a bomb?

Alain was not concerned with his own life, as Mary Ann saw through her borrowed glasses. Behind him the flames had become a blowtorch. The frame was bright orange where the fire had burned everything but metal. He was holding onto the wheel with both hands even as it scorched his flesh. He could barely see ahead. He's steering by instinct, she thought with a shudder, the way an animal senses its way to water.

Alain's last flight was beautiful and desperate, a fireball come to earth, a miniature sun. Mary Ann watched it all, saw it plunge toward the Pont d'Iéna bridge in front of her, heard the people on the bridge scream and start to run. She felt someone's hand grip her shoulder. It was Henri Meurthe. His face looked ashen, as if he'd suffered a heart attack.

Just before his airship hit the bridge, the flames reached the gas tank behind Alain, and it exploded with a white flash. The airship went into the river like a galleon into the deep, and the rasp and groan of the suddenly cooling metal structure sounded like the death throes of a mythical beast.

Her last sight of Alain was as intense as her first; wrapped first in fire and then in water, his hands clutching the wheel. A cloud of steam rose from where the flaming wreck had struck the water. It was as if a curtain had dropped on the last act of a tragedy, and she waited for him to appear from behind the curtain. He was Alain Chevrier, larger than life, invincible. He had to come back!

FOR ONLY A MOMENT, but what seemed like an eternity, no one moved or made a sound. Then Mary Ann heard a collective sigh of despair as the crowd started to breathe again. She became aware of the scratch-scratch of an artist's pencil as he sketched the scene; the living forced to confront their own mortality.

Yvette burst out crying. For Mary Ann, it went beyond crying. She felt empty, as if all her tears and feelings had been stolen from her, and she was with Alain somewhere under the water.

The one who seemed most affected was Henri Meurthe. He staggered from the reviewing stand onto the grass, holding his head in his hands.

And then she saw him sway, as if a wave had crashed over him. He tried to sit down. But because of his stiff leg, he simply fell over backward, as if he'd been hit. Perhaps he had, she thought.

People walked by him, in no hurry now. "Who is that stupid man sitting in the grass?" asked one woman.

"Don't you know? That's Henri Meurthe, the one who started this foolishness," said her husband.

"That's him? Why, he should be shot!"

"I agree. And it may happen soon enough."

twenty-one

*T*HE NEXT MORNING WHEN Harding came back with the newspapers it was obvious that Henri Meurthe had reaped the whirlwind. One tabloid had run Alain's and Meurthe's pictures side by side. "Chevrier . . . And His Killer!" screamed the caption. A cartoon in a second paper showed Meurthe with a bloody sword, standing over Chevrier's body, while a third paper claimed it had proof that Meurthe was part of a shadowy "Syndicate" that was out to destroy France. Mary Ann kept reading them, one after another, all full of lies, insults and humiliation.

"Look at this one," said Harding. "I guess this ends it. *Le Petit Journal* is saying that President Auguste Pouchet has scratched the contest—and canceled the million-franc prize."

They were sitting on the *Bethanie*, their floating slum, with their backs up against the strange winged machine that they had built. Occasionally children would come by and point and giggle, and then their mothers would pull them away. Mary Ann was struck by the absurdity of it all. They had come all this way, labored so long and hard, suffered through the storms and heat of a Parisian summer, been sinned against in so many ways, and now, to see it end here, like this.

"Do you think it's true?" she asked Harding, wondering if he would give her hope.

"I always believe what I read in the newspapers," he said sarcastically.

"Well, I'm going to find out." She stormed off the boat.

At first Mary Ann had no destination in mind. She didn't want to go to Meurthe's house—couldn't even if she wanted to—remembering Yvette would be there. Then she thought for a moment. Meurthe had an office at the Corn Exchange, near the Church of Saint-Eustache. Would he be there? Or would he be in hiding somewhere? No, it wasn't like Henri Meurthe to hide.

Mary Ann arrived at the height of midafternoon trading. Through windows inside the second and third story of the huge round building, she saw merchants come out of their offices and make hand signals to tell the traders on the floor to buy or sell. The noise was deafening, echoing off the rotunda above them where murals of iceboats, tropic steamers and trains explored the world. She started to walk onto the floor when a guard took her arm.

"Mademoiselle," he said politely, "women are not allowed here."

"But I must see Henri Meurthe." She strained to look over his shoulder at the bustling floor, searching for the tall, distinguished-looking man.

Then, instead of seeing him, she heard him. His voice, engaged in argument, came at her from behind a pair of nearby closed doors. The guard heard him too, and glanced in that direction. She took advantage of his momentary distraction, pushed past him, and rushed through the double doors.

There, on either side of her, were two identical circular staircases. She didn't have to decide which one to take. She could hear his voice—and Pouchet's. They were coming down opposite stairways, shouting across at each other. Obviously their friendship was over.

"I am ending this contest," roared the French president.

"That is not your decision to make, Auguste!" retorted Meurthe.

"I will not countenance any further loss of life."

She heard Meurthe's harsh laugh. "When did politicians ever care about people's lives! I saw thousands sacrificed uselessly when I fought in the war. Why don't you just admit you're afraid the Germans will win."

"And if they do? There will be riots. Possibly another war. Do you remember what happened in the last one? You should. You suffered as much as any."

"I cannot control who wins."

"But what if the explosion was sabotage?"

"What do you mean?" asked Meurthe. She could hear uncertainty in his voice.

"We suspect Guillaume LeRond, Chevrier's assistant. He has disappeared. When we find him, we will find the answer."

"Then I doubt you will find him," said Meurthe in a voice laced with sarcasm.

"I have been patient," shouted Pouchet. "I have been reasonable. I have endured insult and embarrassment. But now the decision is out of your hands, do you hear me? Out of your hands!"

Mary Ann watched Pouchet hurry down the final steps and out the door. Meurthe came down, too, but when she looked at his face, she knew better than to bother him.

He shuffled across the floor of the Exchange, a shambling, stooped figure. She remembered how he had run down the stairs of the Eiffel Tower. Was that only two months ago? The traders and brokers cleared a path for him, as if his misfortune were contagious. Faces closed when he looked at them. Eyes averted. Smiles vanished. The noise of trading hushed. Meurthe had always been envied. Now it had turned to hate, and worse— to contempt.

Mary Ann followed at a distance as Meurthe limped across the square and into Saint-Eustache. Inside, the world's noises— the sounds of the little Teuf-Teuf autobikes, the jangle of harnesses, the yells of the vendors—were hushed. There was only candle smoke and fading light. And peace. Old women dressed all in black—in spite of the summer heat—came, knelt, bowed their heads and departed. The little wickerwork chairs were in place for the next mass. Meurthe took one and sat, propping his bad leg up on another.

Day edged into twilight and still he didn't move. Light through the stained glass windows made painted shadows on the floor. Finally she steeled herself to approach him. He looked up when he saw her standing there, and smiled as if he were glad to see her.

"I finally understand why people like churches," he said. "They are like our *petit zincs*, or what you Americans would call 'saloons.' They're where you go when you can't go home. I dread going home. A hundred reporters are waiting outside my door to badger me with their questions." He patted a wicker chair. "Sit with me for a moment."

"I was just looking at the windows," he pointed to the stained glass. "Did you know that each pane tells a story? There is Susanna being raped by the Elders, and then the devil with a face on his belly, and finally Cowardice as a knight being defeated by a rabbit. And that one over there," he added, "is Abraham on the rock, about to sacrifice Isaac. That is my story. Mine and Alain's."

For a second she was confused. Then, looking at his face in the dim light, with the votive candles guttering, she understood, and wondered why she had never seen it before.

It was Alain's face, 30 years older.

"Do you see now?" he said.

She nodded. "How did it happen?"

"In the War of 1870 I was a cavalry officer, a brave and stupid one like Alain. In the battle of Sedan they ordered us to charge the German guns, time after time, until there were none of us left. In the final charge my horse fell on me. I was sent back to a Paris hospital to die.

"Louise was a nurse there. She refused to let me die. I was not an easy patient. I knew that our country was beaten and I did not want to live under the Germans. But she was then, as now, defiant. She brought me back from death. 'You will live to fight again,' she told me. And she was right.

"There was never anyone like her before or since. She could make me so angry one minute and happy the next. We had so little in common—but it didn't matter. The Germans were attacking Paris and we would all be dead soon anyway. We did what so many did at that time. We leaped over the fire. Do you know what that means?"

"Yes," said Mary Ann.

"When I was able to limp around, they put me to work. We were planning an offensive against the German lines around Paris. If the forces outside the city knew, we could attack at the same time and crush the Germans.

"The message had to be memorized and delivered by someone who understood military strategy. I spent hours with Louise, studying the plans, learning each detail so I could recite it all when I got out."

"But you could hardly walk . . ."

"One does not have to walk when one can fly," said Meurthe. "We began to send balloons out of Paris, hoping they would reach areas of the country that were still free. In the balloons we put homing pigeons, which would fly back to the city, carrying microdots—coded messages in capsules taped to their legs.

"In late November, I was ordered to fly out. By that time daylight flights had become too dangerous. The Prussian cannonmaker Krupp had built guns that would shoot straight up at us, so balloons had to be sent off at night.

"I can still remember that evening when Louise and I arrived at the train yard where they housed the balloons. It was an eerie world of glare and shadow. All around us, the huge lights of the trains no longer in use had been set up. The Germans were firing their guns and one shell hit the corner of the station roof, sending pieces of slate pelting down on us.

"When they brought the balloon out, it was stiff with frost and riddled with small holes; even the mice in our city were hungry. So Louise and I took pieces of her petticoats and, with our cold hands, glued patches on the balloon.

"Then we waited for the signal. Three o'clock came, then four o'clock. We had received our mail and provisions. The balloon was inflated from a nearby gas line. The basket of pigeons with a blanket to protect them from the cold, was hung from the ropes above our heads. I could hear them cooing to each other.

"We stood there. We said our good-byes—anxious to get the pain of leaving over with. I told her that her nose had turned red. She said mine had turned blue. A moment later our crew received the order to board. I climbed in and they cast off the lines. As we started to rise she looked up at me from below and said very softly, 'I am having your baby.' And then, before I could say or do anything, we were a thousand feet in the air and I was looking down at Paris through the clouds.

"The two islands in the Seine, the Île de la Cité and the Île Saint-Louis, looked from that height like twin ships, their pointed prows just grazing each other. No one who ever left this city was more torn. I could not stay, and I could not go, and the wind carried me onward."

He paused. "You know the rest of the story. My balloon ended up on a mountaintop in Norway; all of our messages were lost, the carrier pigeons were lost. Our city was lost. Louise thought that I was dead. Before I could return, Paris had revolted, and the Communards were crushed.

"By the time I got back, my father told me that Louise and all her family had been shot at the Traitor's Wall at Père-Lachaise cemetery. I don't know how long I stood at that wall . . . until someone came and got me, I suppose.

"Then I fell into a loveless marriage and, years later, I saw Louise on the street when she came back from New Caledonia."

"What did she say?" asked Mary Ann.

"What could either of us say? I was married. And my father, I learned, was the one who had ordered her family shot. So that is the way it remained for all these years. We are two forgotten casualties of war, *mutilés* whose wounds don't show, except to each other. But I followed my son's career every step of the way: through school, through military college, in the army. When stupid officers stood in his way, I used my influence to remove them. I planned this contest to bring him glory. Instead, I brought him death."

"Alain . . . and Yvette . . . didn't know?" she said.

"Alain didn't know until the night before he died."

"And that's why he agreed to fly, when you told him the truth?"

"I had to. The thing with Alain and Yvette would have been a transient affair, like so many of my daughter's. Yet for their sakes, I could not allow it to run its course. As for Yvette, she will never know."

"Why are you telling me all this?"

Meurthe looked at her, as if the reason was obvious. "Because I think that Alain loved you. I heard him call you Marianne."

"But what does that mean? He knew my name was Mary Ann."

Meurthe smiled gently. "Of course he knew. But it was his secret code for you. You see, Marianne is our national symbol, a flowing-haired peasant girl who represents Liberty. Each year in all our towns and villages there is a special ceremony where the most beautiful woman is chosen to be Marianne."

He paused. "Come now, Marianne, you did not follow me here so you could hear an old man reminisce."

"I heard Pouchet tell you that the contest is over."

"And you want it to continue . . ."

"If we don't win, we won't get home again. Bishop is bankrupt."

"Do you need money?"

She shook her head. He reached out, cupped his hand under her chin and stared into her eyes. "No," he said, "you are like Alain. You don't need money. You need to prove something, to yourself and to the world."

She could see him do a quick calculation in his head. "I cannot guarantee you much time," he said. "But I know the Germans will not be ready tomorrow, the day of Alain's funeral. Can you fly then?"

"I don't . . . yes," she said. "Yes, we'll fly."

Suddenly Meurthe looked 10 years younger. He sprang out of the wicker chair, almost knocking it over. "Then I know what I must do," he said. He walked to the door of the church and looked back.

"You will fly, Marianne," he promised, his voice echoing through the darkness. "You will fly even if the whole world stands against you."

twenty-two

*F*OR HIS PLAN TO work, Henri Meurthe had to talk to Louise Chevrier. He knew where he would find her that evening. She would be with her son. Alain's body was lying in state at the Arc de Triomphe.

Meurthe left the Church of Saint-Eustache and walked past the Tuileries, along one of the 12 wide avenues that came together at the Arch at Place de l'Etoile, or "Place of the Star." At first he thought that the city was deserted; tables and chairs had been left out at sidewalk cafes, but they were empty. Shops were still open, with pots and brooms hanging outside, but with a simple sign on the door—"Gone to the Arch."

As he drew closer, he saw little knots of people, many of them families, hurrying down the street. As they got closer the rivulets became a river and Meurthe was swept up with the human tide, stunned at the power of a doomed man to draw a whole city to him.

Up ahead was the Arc de Triomphe, tall as 30 men and massive as a mountain cliff, a monument to battle. There were purple draperies everywhere he looked: at the top of the Arch, obscuring the names of Napoleon's many victories; at the sides, surrounding the women warriors sculpted into each pillar; and blanketing the base of the coffin itself.

Alain's body lay in the mammoth bronze coffin at the center of the Arch, hung between heaven and earth by a catafalque so high that it made the bayoneted guards who stood shoulder to shoulder at its edge look like a picket fence around a house. The top was open and, under a glass case, Meurthe could see the white face of the corpse—all that remained of his son.

President Pouchet and the French military had spared no expense. The body was dressed in the full regalia of a major; Alain had been promoted posthumously. Lying next to the casket, winking out from the purple draperies, was another star, the 10-pointed Legion of Honor that made Alain a chevalier, a knight of France. A bitter irony, Meurthe thought. Alain had always made jokes about his name: "I'm a Chevrier—a goatherd—not a chevalier." But he was now.

Meurthe shook his head grimly. He hated the cult of death, which minimized a person's importance while he was alive, then glorified it afterward. But what was one to do? he thought with resignation. We have so little choice over what is done to us in life, even less in death. He searched the crowd for Louise without finding her.

Pouchet and the politicians were standing in a group, admiring their handiwork. The president pointedly ignored Meurthe, as did the others, taking their cue from Pouchet.

Meurthe searched in another direction. He saw orphan girls, tied together by a rope whose end was around the waist of an old nun, being pulled along like Alpine climbers. It would almost be funny, he thought, if his son wasn't lying dead in the middle of this circus. He moved to the edge of the crowd, searching the shadows, and startled couples who were kissing and groping, seemingly excited by death. All emotions were burning this night, he thought.

He felt his stomach churn. So many people, all moving, all in darkness. He panicked; overwhelmed by the crowd, he was convinced that he would never find her. His plan—and Mary Ann's hopes—would fall apart if he failed.

Control yourself, he thought. You've always survived by your wits, they won't fail you now. She must be here.

He turned back toward the Arch. Huge torches on each pillar ignited the night, their flaring light reflecting on the red flowers at the peak of the Arch and the scrolling that encircled its edges, as well as the waxen figure inside the coffin. Where the pillars did not obscure the flames, they spread light in four distinct spokes. He told himself to search each one of those shafts of light. Sooner or later she would have to pass through one of them.

Then, in the faint light of one of those spokes, Meurthe spied a tall woman in a black dress, regal in her isolation, like a statue in a lonely square. He knew instinctively that it was Louise. What would she say to him? "You killed my son with your foolishness," perhaps? Or worse. The churning in his stomach got worse. He could barely make his feet move forward.

Then she saw him and, surprisingly, she smiled.

"Hello, Louise," he said, still not sure what she would say.

"Hello, Henri. I've been expecting you. Many friends have come up to me tonight, but you're the only one I truly wanted to see."

"Thank you for saying that," he answered.

His words came out in a gasp, and with them, all the fear that he had held inside. For a few moments they silently watched the milling crowd—Alain's army of homage—as it moved, counter-clockwise, around the points of the great Star. The alternation of light and shadow coming from the Arch was hypnotic, Meurthe thought. If you weren't careful you could be swept along, marching around and around until you dropped from exhaustion.

Fathers would hold their sons over their heads, promising them ice cream if they wouldn't squirm. "And now you can say that you've seen the Great Chevrier," Meurthe heard one man tell a boy.

Louise winced. "The Great Chevrier," she repeated. "No one would have taken a second look at Alain two months ago. But he was alive then, wasn't he?"

"Do you blame me for what happened, Louise? For the contest. And for all the folly that led up to this?"

"No. I'm as much to blame as you are. Even when he was a little boy I encouraged him to climb the rocks on our island in the South Pacific. I knew he could fall, but I couldn't bring myself to stop him. And now he has fallen, hasn't he?"

Meurthe drew a long breath and searched for something to say. He wanted to tell her that at least she had known Alain as a child, at least she had that. But it would hurt them both if he did. "You know he was still holding that wheel when the divers found him?" he said finally. "He wasn't afraid to die, Louise. And neither of us is to blame for making him a man."

"I blame them, though," she said, pointing to where Pouchet stood, surrounded now by a squadron of cavalry in their ceremonial breastplates and helmets. "They have turned my son into a mannequin." Her voice choked.

"Yes, it is quite a show, isn't it?" said Meurthe.

"Actresses are swooning for him beside his coffin. One even bared her breasts and pretended to commit suicide—with a nail file—to get in the papers. All the famous demimondaines of Paris are claiming that they slept with him. And—after he is dead—they give him the Legion of Honor!" She looked like she was about to cry, and Meurthe reached over to hold her. But she forced herself upright, putting one hand on his shoulder for support.

"Did you know that they would not let me sit with him? They sent a special train to bring in a famous mortician from Vienna. He acted like a chef in his kitchen: 'No one can stay while I work!' They pushed me out of the room. They took away my last moment with my son."

"Do not blame them too much, Louise. All this pomp and pride is only to hide the fact that they are afraid. Their hero has died—now who will fight for them? That is what is really being mourned here."

As she turned toward him, Meurthe studied her face. People had always thought he was invincible. But he knew that without Louise he would have died in that hospital 30 years ago. He remembered, too, how beautiful she had been. And still was.

"I heard that you killed a man in a duel," she said.

"Yes, he insulted a lady's honor."

"Henri . . . always the brave one." She touched his face with her hand. It was a reminder of what might have been, if things had been different.

"You know my wife is dead?" he said.

Louise said nothing.

"Do you remember when I was going up in that balloon and you said . . ."

She smiled. "Yes. 'I'm having your baby.' It was my best trick on you."

"It's too late for us, isn't it?"

Louise nodded.

Meurthe sighed. "I have lived 58 years, and sometimes I think that I have learned nothing."

And then, as if this single, small confession was more than she could take, Louise broke down and cried. She turned and buried her head in his shoulder, and Meurthe did what he had wanted to do for so long. He held her.

"What shall we do, Henri?" she sobbed. "Shall we let it end this way, with children running up on a bet to touch his coffin? With taxicabs selling rooftop seats for five francs so people can see him dead?"

"I know what Alain would have wanted," said Meurthe.

She studied his face. "Tell me."

"Then it would be difficult and dangerous for both of us," he warned.

Louise's eyes were full of tears, not all of them for her son. "Why are the men in my life always lost to me?" she asked herself. "First my father and brother, then you, and now, my son. And why is it no loss ever prepares us for the next? Each time it hurts more."

Now, looking at him in the flaring light, she could see death in Meurthe's face, and she knew, however hard she tried, that he would be lost to her again.

twenty-three

*G*UILLAUME LEROND ENTERED THROUGH the private door in the alley off Denfert-Rochereau, and went down the long winding stairway that took him sixty feet underground. He lit his lamp and looked at the directions. "Go right and take the first left," he mumbled to himself. The limestone was slippery under his boots. Water dripped from the ceiling, cobwebs caught in his hair.

Then he made a wrong turn, and came upon the remains of a moldering body. He scurried back onto the main path and rushed under a huge arch, now pitted with the smallpox of decay, and passed the well at the foot of a staircase. The still green water below him was silent, without a ripple. He nervously threw a sou in the well—good luck to erase the bad luck of seeing the body. It made a loud splash, and disappeared beyond where his eye could see. He shivered. A body would sink forever in this well.

He walked on, passing between the white pillars with the black crosses on them and under the sign that said: STOP! THIS IS THE EMPIRE OF DEATH.

Why did Maximilian want to meet here? Guillaume wondered.

Is he playing cat-and-mouse with me? If he is, Guillaume had an answer. He carried a pistol in one coat pocket, a spring-loaded knife in the other. And he would use them, if necessary.

Guillaume was now in the ossuary, still following Maximilian's directions. Here lay row on row, pile on pile, of skulls. In Paris, land had become too valuable for the dead. The city dug up its cemeteries and put the bones underground, stacking them neatly in platforms of interlaced thighbones, calf bones, femurs and tibias.

Some of the groupings had skulls laid out in the shape of a cross. Others had symbols that reminded Guillaume of the flag of a pirate ship. Each church had put up a tablet with inscriptions in Latin to mark the section that housed its bones. One of them said: IT IS SOMETIMES MORE ADVANTAGEOUS TO BE DEAD THAN ALIVE. Did anyone really believe that? Guillaume wondered.

The bones were brown with age. The skulls showed the strange stitched design where the three pieces joined together and, in the case of those who died young, a hole in the center where the junction never formed. There were other bones; soldiers of the Commune who were hunted to their death, victims of gangland stranglings whose bodies were dumped in the catacombs, even stray animals who couldn't find their way out. The remains of more than six million creatures lay beneath the city.

Guillaume heard a whistle from one of the small corridors. He put down his lamp, opened a metal gate, and peered inside.

Maximilian was in the far corner. He lit a match with his fingernail. It flared to life with a hiss of sound and light. Guillaume saw skull after skull and then . . . Maximilian's face. His eyes were bituminous—dark and shining. He is like a chameleon, Guillaume thought, he can take on the color of his surroundings. And he was smiling; the secure, self-satisfied smile of someone who is never in doubt, who always knows what will happen.

The match flared out, and Guillaume's lamp gave barely enough light to see by. Instinctively he reached for the gun in his coat pocket.

"Welcome to our little kingdom," said Maximilian. He chose two skulls from a nearby pile and juggled them as he spoke.

"Why did you want to meet here?" Guillaume demanded. "It is cold and damp . . ."

"And it reminds you of death, doesn't it," Maximilian finished. "Well, I like these catacombs. At night I sometimes walk down here. It is safer for a German among the dead than up there among the living. Your problem is that you don't trust me."

"I trust you."

Maximilian eyed Guillaume's hand clutched around the pistol in his coat pocket. "And that's why you keep that gun pointed at me? You have never trusted me, have you? Yet trust is everything. Without it, we would be no better than wild beasts."

Guillaume took the pistol out of his pocket—it was no secret anyway—but kept it pointed at the ground, waiting to hear what Maximilian would say.

"But should I still trust you?" the German asked. "You betrayed your superior officer and your friend!" Then Maximilian's tone softened. "Yet I do. And I am here to tell you that you will be traveling to Berlin, where you will meet the kaiser himself."

"No joke?"

"Do I look like I'm joking? Standing here among these skulls like Hamlet himself, do you think I'm joking? Trust someone for a change!"

Guillaume snorted. "You almost sound like Chevrier."

Maximilian laughed. It sounded hollow inside the limestone caves.

"You know, Guillaume, we did him a favor, you and I. In life he was an arrogant son of a bitch. But in death he is a national hero. Your people have immortalized him as if he were Christ himself." He threw one of the skulls across the room, where it shattered against the wall.

Guillaume winced. "I think he knew that he was going to die."

"Why do you say that?" Maximilian looked surprised.

"Because, just before he went up, he said he needed to 'Have a little courage.'"

Maximilian shrugged. "So . . ."

"Those are the last words they say to a man who is about to be guillotined! I tell you, he knew!"

Maximilian put his hand on LeRond's shoulder. Guillaume flinched.

"You still don't trust me, do you?" Maximilian asked. "Well, let me try to convince you. If I had wanted to betray you, I could have. 'Jealous subordinate plants bomb,' the headlines would have read, and a swift execution would have followed. Don't you think Pouchet would love to find a scapegoat like you?"

Guillaume said nothing. He brushed off the cobwebs that clung to his shirt.

"Or I could have had a few of my men meet you down here and you would have joined your ancestors. Plenty of bodies in these caverns—one more would never be noticed."

Maximilian gripped him by the arms. "Guillaume, Guillaume, Germany wants you. Wants your skills, your knowledge. We need to create new and better flying machines. You are the man who can do that. You and no one else. So take your hand off the gun."

Maximilian took the gun out of Guillaume's hand and threw it into the pile of bones. All right, I will trust you, Guillaume thought. But I still have my knife.

They walked past the little well that went down so deep.

"Take a look down there, Guillaume," said Maximilian. "That pool flows forever. All water is linked— thousands of feet underground. Did you ever look at a map and try to decide where one ocean ends and another begins?"

Maximilian's eyes grew misty for a second. "Someday humanity will be like that. There will be only one nation. You and I may not live to see it, but our children will. Come on, I will show you something."

Guillaume hesitated. It was dark in that direction. Maximilian laughed. "All right, I will walk in front."

They went single-file down the narrow passageway. For a moment Guillaume lost sight of Maximilian. He panicked. Was Maximilian behind him? Then he heard the German's voice above him say: "Up here."

Guillaume climbed a high set of circular stairs, staying far enough behind so that Maximilian couldn't push him. When he reached the top, Guillaume was puffing.

"Do you see what I mean?" said Maximilian with a smile. "It's like exploring the woods at night in the dark. Now watch this." He pushed open a door. Suddenly they were in a brightly lit subway station. "See, it's the Necro."

In the lighted tunnel, Maximilian looked more human, and acted like it. He studied Guillaume's anxious face.

"You were worried about being questioned, weren't you?" he asked. "Well, you're safe now. Take the Necro to the Gare du Nord and look for a train with only one car, just outside the station. Knock twice on the door. You'll be the only passenger."

In the distance they could hear the rumble of the Necro coming into the station. Maximilian stood with his back to the track, only a few inches away and, for just a second, Guillaume was tempted to push him over the edge just to see the shock on his arrogant face when he fell under the wheels of the train.

Then Maximilian surprised him. He held out his hand in a gesture of friendship. "And now," said Maximilian, "I wish you a good trip. I will see you in Germany."

Guillaume took his hand and shook it. Maximilian mumbled something. Guillaume leaned closer. "What did you say?" he asked.

"I said 'Have a little courage!'"

Still holding his hand, Maximilian yanked Guillaume forward and then twisted and let go. Trying to catch himself, Guillaume fell flailing off the platform and landed on his hands and knees on the metal tracks. He looked up just in time to see the panicked face of the motorman . . . and the front of the train rushing at him, its brakes shrieking.

MAXIMILIAN WATCHED FOR A moment after the blood-spattered train came to a stop. Guillaume's body was still moving, but he knew they were death spasms. No one could survive wounds like those.

A cluster of the curious had gathered on both sides of the tracks, gawking at the corpse. Maximilian joined them for a moment, seeking safety in numbers. No one would remember him. Then he eased away. As he walked up the steps to the street, he thought, *the Necro has claimed its first victim.*

He went upstairs and headed toward the Seine. He still had more work to do tonight.

twenty-four

*T*HE SHORT, WIRY MAN walked up to the gangplank. "'Allo," he called out. "'Allo the boat."

Mary Ann was the only one awake. She had been up most of the night, wondering if she should have persuaded Henri Meurthe to let them fly. What if the pilot didn't show up today? Why hadn't she just taken his money and gone back to America?

"'Allo," he called again. "Is this decrepit tub the *Bethanie*?"

"Yes," she answered, "and who are you?"

"Jack Reece. At your lovely service."

Her first reaction was relief. Then came anger.

"You're days late. In fact, you're weeks late."

"I was kept occupied," he said with a snicker. "Christ, is this it?"

"Yes," she replied, looking at the aeroplane as it rocked gently on the deck. "And it will fly."

But Reece wasn't looking at the aeroplane. He was eyeing her. She felt uneasy.

"Mr. Bishop!" she called. "Harding! He's here."

"Not so fast," he said, coming closer. "Not so fast. I'd like to talk to you first."

Mary Ann watched him suspiciously. He was a shade over five and a half feet, with pinched nose, pointed chin and a balding scalp that flaked dandruff. He was pigeon-chested but had muscles like bridge cable, and he made swift little movements with his head, like a snake about to strike.

"I'm a Cockney, no 'arm in that, is there," he said. He didn't wait for an answer. "Some snooty people look down on Cockneys, but I always say you got to be what you are, no changin' it.

"I was a bicycle racer once, and when me legs gave out I was a jockey. That's why they call me 'Ride-Anything Reece.' And then I became the human cannonball. I'd play a trick on the rubes. I'd go up underneath a balloon nestled in a long piece o' pipe that looked like a cannon. Then I'd touch off a charge at the top, so people would think I'd been shot out. Then while they was watchin' all that smoke and noise, I'd slide out the bottom and go down in me chute. Pretty smart, eh?"

Why is he telling me all this? thought Mary Ann.

Reece moved in even closer, almost touching her. "I'm a trained athlete. You know, some athletes say sex makes your legs weak. Why, they even ice themselves down the night before a race to avoid a nocturnal emission. But me, I think sex is good for you anytime at all, Missy. Don't you agree?"

"Reece!" she heard Bishop call from below. "Come here. Now!"

He winked at her and went downstairs.

She heard the three of them talking in the cabin, first softly, then louder. There was a dispute over money, with Bishop telling

Reece that he'd be paid when he flew, and Reece demanding it now, before he risked his life on that "fool contraption."

"I could take it out in trade," she heard him say. "That warm bit upstairs might persuade me to stay."

It took Mary Ann a moment to realize that *she* was the "warm bit."

"She's not for sale." That was Harding's voice.

And then Bishop: "Wait a second. Why don't we let her decide? She wants to go back to America, doesn't she? Tell her that the only way she'll ever see it again is if we win the million francs."

There were more words between Harding and Bishop. She heard Reece say something like "'ore." Then a bottle smashed, and there was a crash and a thump as something heavy hit the floor. The last of the captain's furniture, she thought.

She heard someone running up the steps, and suddenly Reece came crashing out holding his left eye. He saw her with his good eye, recoiled and took off down the gangplank. Then he stopped and turned around.

"You're barmy, the 'ole bleedin' lot of you!" he screamed. "Bloody lunatics! You've got about as much chance of flyin' your bloody tub of a boat as you do that machine."

He might have gone on, but he saw Harding come out of the pilothouse and took off, still holding his eye. There was a long gash on Harding's cheek that was oozing blood.

"I'm leaving," he said quietly.

"What about Bishop?"

"I decked him. He was trying to hold my arms while that little snake cut me with a bottle."

"What are you going to do?" She realized, suddenly, that he was carrying his carpetbag, the same one that she had seen the first day on the hill at Jericho.

"Well, I'm not going to collect my pay. Who knows? Maybe I'll join the Wandering People again. Roam Europe with a guitar on my back. Wanta' come?"

It was more than an invitation. He expected her to say yes.

"No," she said.

He looked at her closely. "You know what you're saying? You're going to stay on the *Bounty* with Captain Bligh? I won't be here to protect you from people like Reece anymore."

"I'm staying," she said. "My life is wrapped up in this. It was my father's dream and Alain's dream. They didn't find their place in the sky, but they knew that they belonged there, knew it in spite of all the people that told them they couldn't. I'm going to find that place."

Harding shook his head as if she were a child who had just said something stupid. "Mary Ann, you're tied to two dead men and they're like anchors. They're going to drag you and Bishop and this boat and that stupid machine so far down that you'll never ever come up again." He hoisted his worn carpetbag and trudged down the gangplank.

She might have said more. She might have told him that she had been waiting all her life, through all those lonely days and nights on the mountaintop, for this hour to come, and she wasn't going to let it pass her by. But she could see that he wasn't listening. He was trudging away, that stupid carpetbag on his back so threadbare that she could see a shirt peeking out. So she just stared at him as he left.

And in the distance, the Eiffel Tower stared back down at her, cold and hard and higher than she had ever imagined. And now she knew who would have to fly—if anyone could.

twenty-five

*T*HE DAY BEGAN WITH the hazy light that comes just before it rains, when the sun is barely able to shine through thickening clouds and all the color seems to emerge from the earth itself. Thunder rumbled in the distance. Everyone's eyes were on the slate-colored sky. Would it stop the funeral march?

The companies lined up: brightly-colored Zouaves with red breeches and shakos, stocky soldiers from the Vendee, four military bands. Then cavalry sabers flashed. Hussars and lancers trotted up and took their positions, scarlet saddle blankets embroidered with gold. They were followed by the cuirassiers, the heavy cavalry, in metal breastplates, knee-high leather boots and silver helmets. The black-creped carriages of government officials and nobility formed behind. Meurthe was not among them.

The coffin slid down from the catafalque onto the waiting gun carriage. It looked like a dark gondola. Twelve black-plumed horses stood waiting. A single soldier, picked especially for the honor, held a purple cushion. He would march with

Alain's Legion of Honor medal all the way to Notre-Dame, where the funeral would be held.

The parade began down the Champs-Elysées. Every beat of the drum sounded like a heartbeat. Troops representing all parts of France's empire were there, from huge dark Senegalese to small yellow Annamites. The boulevard was awash with turbans, plumes, kepis, pith helmets and rows and rows of lances.

The gardens of the Bagatelle had been stripped to provide flowers for the parade; asters of all colors, Jacob's trumpets, roses were scattered in the street. The statues were covered with black bunting, but the children waved red banners— oriflammes—as the soldiers marched by.

Every lamppost had a boy on it. People were hanging from the peaks of iron gates. Poor farmers, their pockets bulging with radishes for their midday meal, had come to town just to see the coffin pass by.

At Place de la Concorde a little girl was caught out in front of the marching band.

"Halt! Knees up!" the leader shouted. The band marched in place, with the drum keeping time, while someone in the front row of spectators grabbed her. Then she was passed hand over hand above the crowd to her mother.

Maximilian stood on the Notre-Dame bridge as the parade came across. He lit a match with his thumb and started a cigar. The cigar tasted bad. As a company of light infantry went by he flicked his cigar among the marchers. It bounced off one soldier's cheek with a flash of sparks. The trooper didn't miss cadence. Very impressive, Maximilian said to himself. They can march, but can they fight? He didn't think so.

The procession continued across the bridge. All of the troops lined up on both sides of the square in front of the looming towers of the cathedral, marching in place to the beat of a single drum.

Then, precisely at noon, the bronze doors of Notre-Dame swung open. Sixteen husky soldiers in dress blue carried the coffin, placed it just below the altar and solemnly draped the French flag over it. The honorary pall bearers followed: President Pouchet, the French premier, the head of the Chamber of Deputies, the secretary of war, all the leading generals. They knelt before the coffin, blessed themselves and took their seats in the front row. Meurthe was not among them.

The members of the Aéro Club and other dignitaries entered, bowed their heads and took their seats. Meurthe was not with them either.

Then Louise Chevrier came forward alone, wearing a black dress as though she were born to it, and took her seat in the front row. She sat alone. She needed no arm to lean on and no shoulder to give her comfort. She was no stranger to sorrow.

The church filled. The ever-present reporters jammed in, wedging themselves against the walls. The doors were propped open so the common people, left outside, could hear what was said.

But the rain would hold back no longer. With a series of thunderclaps it rolled into the square and over it, drenching the soldiers resting on their arms outside the church, drenching the huddled crowd, drenching the patiently waiting horses. The sound of Berlioz's "Requiem" on the organ inside blended with the sky's own percussion.

The bishop with his gold miter and crosier led the mass; the choir sang, prayers were said in Latin. Then, as the mass reached its height, Auguste Pouchet stood to deliver the final eulogy.

"Stop!"

Louise Chevrier had risen from her seat. "I claim a Mother's Right," her voice rang out. "I do not want this man speaking for my son."

Pouchet turned to face her, contempt oozing from his voice. "Sit down, woman!" he shouted. "You are distraught."

But Louise remained standing, defying the French president.

"Not so distraught that I can't see through you," she said to his face. "The honor of speaking the last words over my son goes to the one of my choosing, and I choose . . . Henri Meurthe."

And Meurthe came forward.

Pouchet looked startled as he saw Meurthe approaching the coffin. Now he realized that he faced a serious challenge.

"Take him out of here!" he ordered the burly soldiers who stood nearby. Blue uniforms swirled around Meurthe as he stood next to the coffin.

Then the bishop spoke, his voice echoing off the stone walls so that the whole church could hear him: "*Monsieur le President*. She has that Right."

The bishop's voice froze everyone in place, like a tableau. No one could challenge him in his own church, not even the president of France.

No one moved, except Henri Meurthe. He took Pouchet's place, pushing him gently aside.

"Sit down, Auguste," he said quietly. "I promise you that this will be a short speech, unlike so many of your own."

The word spread out from the front of the church like a ripple turning into a wave.

Up until now everything had gone according to ritual, and ritual is man's best defense against the unknown. But things had changed. Louise Chevrier looked around. You could almost see the sawdust leaking out of the stuffed shirts sitting in the front row, she thought. How Alain would have enjoyed this if he were here! Then she remembered; Alain was here. And she almost cried, holding desperately onto her tears in the sudden silence that engulfed the whole church.

And then Meurthe spoke.

"I come here to read you something that Alain Chevrier wrote just before he died," Meurthe said quietly. "It is this:

> We cannot hope that a single flight will lead us to the sky. But each trial will show at least one fatal error, into which others might fall. So, by recording the wreckage of the first, we buoy out a channel that leads us to the heavens.

And here Meurthe's voice—still quoting Chevrier—gathered strength.

> We must not each work for our own selfish interests, but all have at heart the common cause. And even if each of us does only a little, then soon will come the day when we no longer grope in utter blindness and the path to true flight is marked out.

Meurthe paused for a moment, and then continued:

"Alain Chevrier knew what lay before him. He knew that he faced death each time he went into the air. And he also knew that it is by death that we are tested. Our glory is not that we live—futilely—but that we die nobly.

"The fight against death we can never win. But the struggle for life, we can challenge every day. And while we are yet living, we fight the battle Alain fought. When we fall, others will fight in our place. The spirit of Man, Alain's spirit, is unconquerable.

"The battle to win the air will go on. For we tilt not against windmills, but against the wind itself. Like Don Quixote, we raise our lances to the sky and give challenge: That nothing of earth, air, or fire is unconquerable to Man.

"And, yes, our bones can be broken. We are not angels, blessed with eternal life. More heroes like Alain will die in our quest for the sky. But each such loss takes us higher. It is not death but fear that confounds us, that brings us back to earth.

"So we can mourn Alain Chevrier. But we cannot linger over a grave. We are in the arms of the wind, suspended between heaven and earth, and there is no stopping-place."

THEN MEURTHE TURNED TO face Pouchet, who was still standing, clutching the stone railing with both hands as if he could put marks in the marble. Silence once again fell like a blanket over the entire church.

Meurthe raised the medal of the winged man above his head.

"I have been told to end this contest. I will not do it. The prize I offered still stands. I do not expect to convince you of my reasons. But every man must choose a time and place to stand his ground, and this is mine."

He walked down the two steps to where the draped coffin lay in state, then reached out and took the edge of the coffin in his hand.

"In this place," he thundered, "where so many have confessed their faith in God, I proclaim my faith in Man. I will not betray this man. We may die for our dreams, but we cannot be defeated. And I . . . WILL . . . NOT . . . END . . . THIS . . . CONTEST!"

Meurthe heard a crash as Pouchet knocked over a chair on his way out. His aides and guards rushed after him. At the doorway, as he stepped out into the rain and thunder, he turned back to look at Meurthe, a look seething with anger and frustration.

"You cannot dictate to France, and I am France," he shouted. "This travesty is over and so is your contest. And I will ruin you!"

Meurthe, standing beside the body of his son, felt his knees start to buckle as if he were facing the guillotine. For once Pouchet will be a man of his word, he thought to himself. Then he remembered Mary Ann . . . and his promise to her. *Fly quickly, little bird, before you are put in a cage.*

twenty-six

*T*HE PRESIDENT WASTED NO time. Within minutes soldiers fanned out across the city. They invaded the Corn Exchange. Fistfights broke out as they pushed Meurthe's traders off the floor. Pouchet had canceled all government contracts with Meurthe's company.

An entire company of hussars, led by a marshal of France so bulky that he could barely sit on a horse, delivered a notice of deportation to Maximilian von Hohenstauffen at the German workshop in Montparnasse. Maximilian read it . . . and laughed in the fat marshal's face. Then he pulled out his certificate allowing him to fly over the city, signed by Pouchet himself. The marshal seized it, pretended to read it, and called it "a worthless piece of paper."

"Just like the one you have," retorted Maximilian. "Among men like ourselves, the only thing that counts is force. Are you prepared to use it?"

The marshal hesitated. Through the doorway and all of the windows he could see men with rifles. His orders had been to move the Germans out, not start a war, particularly not one in which he himself would be killed.

"Stupid politicians," he muttered. "They talk out of both sides of their mouths." He stormed away.

Maximilian now had his reprieve. He could tie the deportation up in red tape, at least until tomorrow. And he would fly tomorrow.

AT THE *BETHANIE*, Mary Ann inspected the aeroplane once more, giving the propeller a swing and watching its blades rotate in the sunlight. The storm that had broken over Paris at noon had blown away, leaving clear skies and only a mild breeze. The hour that she had awaited—and dreaded—was here. She would finally fly.

Mary Ann went below and put on her overalls with the patched knees, the ones she hadn't worn since . . . since Harding had found her at Jericho. She remembered it was against the law for women to wear trousers in Paris, ever since the Commune was overthrown, so she tucked her hair under a cloth cap and then put on a cork lifesaving vest. There were pontoons under the wings of the aeroplane to keep it afloat, but it was better to be safe.

Back on deck Bishop was waiting, but he looked dazed, confused, almost suicidal. He had a welt on his cheekbone where Harding had hit him, and his hazel eyes were empty. Not the best person to send you off in flight, she thought.

Without hesitation, she told him to start the boat engine. Here she was, giving orders to a captain of industry; a man who had given orders all his life. She almost felt sorry for Neville Bishop. He had spent his whole career destroying other people and taking their money. Now it was happening to him.

Then she saw the three soldiers, a major, a sergeant and a corporal, coming toward the boat. The major looked vaguely familiar as he walked up the gangplank. Trouble, she thought, as she went to head him off before he got on board.

"I am Major Vitary, in command at the Parc de Chalais Aeronautical Institute," he announced pompously. "I have a message for Neville Bishop from Auguste Pouchet, the president of France."

"You're Major Vitary?" She remembered how they'd laughed that day when Alain had fired off his flare gun at the presidential palace and Vitary had hidden behind a tree. Well, Alain was dead, and Vitary didn't look so funny now.

"I'll take the message," she said.

Vitary looked her up and down. She knew what he saw—a greasy little woman wearing men's clothes. "Who are you?" he sneered.

"Marianne." The sound of the name threw him off balance. She didn't give him a chance to react. She grabbed the letter from his hands.

When she had read it her hands started to tremble. She looked up. That son of a bitch with his twirling mustache was watching her, smiling. So this is how it ends. First they were thrown out of Harvard, then burned out of Tennessee, and now the president of the Third Republic himself has evicted them from France.

"My subordinates," said Vitary, gesturing to the two soldiers behind him, "would be happy to help you and Monsieur Bishop collect your few possessions and leave immediately." He used the familiar pronoun for "you," an obvious insult.

Mary Ann brought herself under control and faced him as he

stood on the gangplank. "What would make me happy," she said, "is if you would get your ugly face off my boat!"

Behind him Vitary heard coarse chuckles from his men. He searched for something devastating to say. Wasn't this strange American woman rumored to be Chevrier's mistress? Finally he pointed to her clothes.

"There are rules in this city against women dressing as you do. Would you like me to have you arrested for wearing pants?"

"What! Half the damn women in this town are selling what they sit on and you're going to arrest me for wearing pants? Haul your fancy butt out of here."

Vitary did not move. "I do not have to take this abuse," he sneered, "particularly from a soiled dove like yourself . . . Chevrier's whore!"

She hit him. Mary Ann had never learned how to slap anyone, so she punched him right from the shoulder. He was twice her size, but the blow staggered him back two steps. His face flushed.

Vitary looked behind him. The sergeant and corporal who had accompanied him were staring discreetly into middle distance. He could tame this wildcat, he decided, but was it worth it?

While he thought, Mary Ann acted. She cast off the only line that held the boat to the dock. The gangplank slid into the water, nearly taking Vitary with it as he jumped for shore.

"Now," she shouted across the widening gulf, "if you want to stop us, you'll have to blow us out of the water!"

TIME. TIME WAS RUNNING out. The incident with Vitary had shaken her. She hadn't eaten all day and she felt hungry. Eat later, she said to herself. If there is a later.

She told Bishop to steer the boat downstream past the Pont d'Iéna bridge and then bring it around, heading into the current and the wind. The boat's motor would keep it steady for a few seconds while Bishop came up and cut the cable that would send the aeroplane off. No preliminaries. No champagne, like the kind they carry on balloon flights. Just cut the cable and we're off, she thought.

As they chugged down river she watched the crowd. Boys were riding bicycles, trying to keep up, and threading their way between the people who lined the banks. She looked for Harding. She missed Harding. All right, she needed Harding. He was part of her life, and win or lose, she wanted to share this with him. But he was nowhere to be seen.

Then she caught a glimpse of Henri Meurthe. He was standing in the prow of a rowboat, one foot on the gunwales. He tipped his top hat to her and she waved back.

Well, she thought, at least I didn't let you down. Not yet, anyway.

They passed under the bridge with its winged figure at the center. She hoped that it was a lucky sign. Bishop turned the boat around, clumsily, just below the Tower and lashed the wheel. It was time.

The aeroplane rested tight against the derrick at the back end of the boat. She seized the crank and slowly ratcheted the huge weight to the top. When it came down it would catapult the aeroplane forward.

Then she climbed aboard. The wings, like broad shallow gutters turned upside down, sloped down toward the center of the frame. Behind the propeller was a cradle for Mary Ann to lie in, facing forward.

She scrambled in among the wires that supported the frame and kept it taut. It felt like climbing into a too-small birdcage. She buckled the three straps that would hold her in the makeshift harness. With her arms outstretched, she could reach the two levers that controlled the craft, one for the rudder in back, the other for that strange wing-warping that would control the side-to-side motion, which she had told Bishop about so confidently a few months ago. She wiggled the levers. They worked perfectly . . . on the ground.

Bishop dumped a gallon of naphtha into the tank over her head. A hose ran down past her face to the engine, where the fuel dripped onto a hot plate and vaporized. The acrid odor drifted into her nostrils and stung them.

A breeze came at her, making her shiver. People thought Paris was hot in summer, but it could be cold as hell. Bishop turned the propeller and the engine kicked over, a spitting, snarling chunk of steel. It sounded like two rabid dogs in a fight. The propeller sent a draft to slap her in the face. Now it was really cold. Drops of hot oil came flying back from the engine and spattered her.

Time was up. She wished once more for Harding.

"Let's go," she said.

She felt a sharp jerk that snapped her neck back and then she was in motion. The scenery blurred on both sides. Then another jerk. This one snapped her head forward.

Is this what it feels like to be hanged? she thought.

Her senses told her the sky was below her; the water plunging at her from above. But that couldn't be. Then it hit her. It was water! She was sinking. The machine, what was left of it, was sinking around her.

She had to get out of the harness, had to. She ripped off the three straps. Still tied in. It was as though someone were holding her there, wanting her to die. Her mouth tasted like tin. It was the taste of fear.

The cork jacket—it was caught! She struggled out of it, popping the buttons. Now to find air. But which way? She saw oil and gas seeping upward. That way.

Then, coming down at her, like the hand of a ghost, was the white fabric of the wing. It surrounded her, pressing her down. No, not now! Not after all this. She panicked. She thrashed. She breathed in water. She clawed at the sheet, bunching it, pulling it down below her. In that moment she realized that she was crying.

And then she felt someone's arms reaching out to her, pulling her up, freeing her from the ghost. She kicked as hard as she could. Her head broke free of the water and she gulped air. There was Harding, hanging onto her.

"Oh, my God!" she heard him yell. "The boat! Breathe! Breathe and go under!"

She saw the black prow of the *Bethanie* coming straight at her. It was still moving forward.

She took a breath just as Harding pushed her head under. Then the black shadow went over her, crushing what was left of the aeroplane under its prow. Harding was still holding onto her. She had no sense of direction, only a desire for air, for an end to that black shape overhead.

And then it was gone, and they rose through the water to see the sky again. She looked through the waves.

The *Bethanie* was still chugging upstream and Harding was screaming, "Stop the boat, Bishop! Lower the anchor!"

But the boat kept going as waves smashed her in the face

every time that she tried to breathe. Harding was cursing Bishop and she was dizzy and starting to slide away into the depths of the Seine.

Then the *Bethanie* stopped, reversed course and came back. She saw Henri Meurthe's face above the stern railing. The anchor chain lowered just enough for Harding to grab onto it. Then the chain clanked back upward, carrying them toward the deck. Meurthe's hands reached out and pulled them aboard.

She lay there, with Harding still holding her. She threw up all over him but he didn't seem to mind. When she finally looked up she saw Neville Bishop sitting on the deck, just sitting, looking at the destruction in the river, not moving, not doing anything. His silver-headed cane lay by his side.

She knew then what had happened. Meurthe had come aboard and taken control. And Harding had saved her.

"Come on," said Harding, helping her up as they steamed into the dock. "We'll get you off this tub. And you'll never have to look at it again."

"Harding," Meurthe called him back. He pointed to the runway for the catapult. At the far end, just before the aeroplane left on its flight, a two-inch bolt had sheared off while another was bent over. "Imagine the force that took?"

"Enough force to flip the plane," answered Harding, as if he was reading Meurthe's mind. "Someone raised these bolts so they would catch the aeroplane as it came forward and tip it over. It must have happened last night. I checked the whole apparatus yesterday. Who could have done this?"

"I think I know," Meurthe shook his head grimly. "Harding, it is time for me to fight my last duel."

twenty-seven

*F*ABIAN BOUCHARD FELT COMFORTABLE at Maxim's restaurant. The most beautiful and exciting women of Paris came here to face off, counting each other's carats and admiring themselves in the huge flower-etched wall mirrors that reflected their images across the room and back at them. Spanish dancers wearing emeralds on their toes—and nothing else—did the flamenco on its tables. The restaurant had a wicked and sensual reputation. And so did he.

Fabian's demimondaine, a pretty, painted 14-year-old, was feeding him oysters, pulling them out of their shells with her teeth and putting them between his lips as he slumped down on the cushions. His brocade vest and shirt were open and she was rubbing his bulging belly. Oysters were love food, and Bouchard could feel himself becoming aroused. Soon he would take the girl upstairs to a private room.

Suddenly Henri Meurthe loomed over him. Meurthe sat down opposite him at the narrow table without an invitation or greeting of any kind.

"Send your *horizontale* away, Fabian," he ordered. "You do not want her to see this."

Fabian was ready to argue. The girl was angry at being called a common prostitute. Then he looked at Meurthe's face, with its crag of a nose and blazing eyes. What was it people said about him? "When Meurthe gets angry, the weak give way." And Fabian was not a strong man. He pushed the pouting girl off his lap and told her to go amuse herself.

"Now," Meurthe demanded, "tell me everything that you know about the Germans, von Hohenstauffen, and that building you put up for them in Montparnasse."

Fabian started to protest. His involvement with the German was a well-kept secret; the only man who had seen him with Maximilian was LeRond, and he had been eliminated. The workshop in Montparnasse—how could Meurthe know about that? Just deny . . . deny.

"I . . . I don't know what you're talking about." But the words rattled out of him. He sounded, even to himself, like a bad actor.

Meurthe shook his head; a schoolmaster correcting an erring pupil. "Do not try to bluff, Fabian. I have played cards with you, and you're not that good. My time is short. Here is something that may help your memory."

Underneath the table Fabian heard a click as the catch on a sword cane was released. Then, looking down, he saw its point at his navel, working its way slowly toward his crotch. It marked its trail with a thin line of blood, as if Meurthe were a surgeon planning a much deeper cut.

The small table masked the blade from the others, but both Meurthe and Fabian could see its point as it crept lower down his belly. Fabian sucked in his breath, tightening his stomach, and then was sorry for it. Meurthe pressed the tip of the sword even closer and now Fabian couldn't breathe at all. The worst part, Fabian thought, was the way the bastard was smiling.

Then, casually, the sword began to flick the buttons off his pants. One! Two! Bouchard remembered: Meurthe had killed a man in a duel.

"During the war," Meurthe said in an easygoing voice, "I saw men after their intestines were perforated. Their excrement entered the bloodstream and they died in agony." Three! Four!

Then he paused for a second.

"Fabian," he said softly. "This is your last button . . . and your last chance."

Fabian talked. It got easier as he babbled on, like confessing to a priest. He sensed that Meurthe knew most of what he was saying, but there was some piece of information he needed. And, if it would save his life, Bouchard was going to give it to him.

Then Meurthe raised his left hand as if he were bored with all this.

"Enough, Fabian."

As he rose, the three-foot steel blade took the narrow table and flipped it out of the way. Flowers, fine crystal and wine flew. Women screamed and nearby waiters jumped back. The rapier was visible now and Meurthe brought the point up to dance in front of Fabian's nose.

"Fabian"—the blade flashed back—"I have killed so many better people than you"—and forward again.

There was a blinding explosion in Bouchard's brain. He thought he was dead. Then he realized: Meurthe had driven the sword into the wooden pillar next to the wattles of his neck, pinning his collar and hooking him like a fish.

"—that you are simply not worth it," Meurthe finished. A second later, he was gone.

No one moved. The other diners averted their eyes from Bouchard's half-undressed body and chalky face, but Maxim's flowered mirrors reflected it all—back and forth and back again. Fabian was shaking as if he had palsy. He shook so hard that his collar came loose and he was free.

"Get away from me!" he shouted at the cluster of waiters. "Get my carriage. I'm leaving!"

But one waiter approached him anyway, holding a spritzer bottle and a pile of napkins. "Monsieur," he whispered politely, "you have soiled yourself."

MEURTHE WALKED THROUGH THE dark streets. He knew where he was going, and when he got there his life would be over. There was no need to rush.

While he walked, he dreamed that he was back in the balloon during the worst days of the war, flying out of Paris with the messages that would save his country. A dark mist of clouds surrounded him, and then, suddenly, the balloon rose and broke through to the brightest, most beautiful sunlight that he had ever seen, so brilliant that it hurt his eyes. The pigeons were cooing like music, and far below the clouds mingled with mountain peaks.

Across from him in the basket was Alain, who reached out to him and said, "We have found it!"

"What?" he asked.

His son smiled at him and answered, "the Region of Fire."

Then the vision vanished, and Meurthe was back on the silent streets again.

"Alain, my son," he spoke as he walked into the darkness, "you were right to believe Man could fly. But you were wrong to believe in Man—so wrong. Men may ascend the skies like living angels, but their natures do not change."

twenty-eight

THAT EVENING WAS THE most magical of Mary Ann's life. Despite all that had happened, she was alive. The city was alive. And Harding was back.

"Come on, let's do the town," he said to her.

"But we don't have any money."

"Yes, we do," he said with a sheepish grin. "I took Neville Bishop's silver-headed cane and pawned it."

For the first time she understood what Paris was like for Harding when he'd been here before. He bought her a frock, a beautiful shimmering turquoise dress with a narrow waist and pearl buttons down the back. Then they rented a Teuf-Teuf, one of the little motorcycles with a sidecar that made a strange coughing sound, and explored places like Fishing Cat Street, Prideful Mountain Street, and the Street of the Four Winds.

They traveled up the hills of Montmartre where grapevines still lined the streets, and ate charcuterie in the backyard of a little inn. There they met shaggy-looking artists Harding knew who showed them paintings full of wild animals and huge splashes of green. He posed Mary Ann in front of them. She heard the artists discussing her as a model, and then saw Harding laugh and shake his head.

Then they went to the big red windmill where two bands were playing noisy disjointed melodies at opposite ends of the dance floor and joined the whirl of high-kickers doing the can-can. They danced until their legs gave out. She rode a wooden horse named Clovis on the double-decker merry-go-round just below Sacré-Coeur.

Afterward they found an outdoor table at a corner cafe, fed each other strawberries and champagne, and chattered away; all the things that they had both been too angry or shy to say before. She remembered how she had passed people like this, lovers by candlelight, and been jealous. Now it was her turn. And it was all so simple.

"Who's your favorite painter?" she giggled. "I mean, besides yourself."

"Leonardo da Vinci."

"Do you like his 'Last Supper' or those beautiful etchings of the flying machines that he wanted to build?"

"No," said Harding, "what I love about Leonardo is what he did for the birds. In Milan, where he lived, they used to catch wild birds in nets and sell them to children. The children would tie the birds to strings on their wrists and walk around the city. The birds would flap and flutter until they died."

"So what did Leonardo do?"

"He'd run through the town like a crazy old man and whenever he saw a bird on a string, he'd take a pocketful of coins and buy it from the child."

"Must have gotten expensive. How many birds did he buy?"

Harding shrugged. "Probably hundreds."

"So what did he do with them all?" In her mind, she saw one of those famous pictures where a multitude of birds in harness swept you up into the sky.

Harding paused. She sensed in his silence that he was wary, unsure of where the things that he was saying would lead—or if he wanted to take her there with him.

"Are you still thinking about him?" he asked.

"Sometimes," she admitted. "But not in a bad way. And you? Have you come to terms with your memories about what happened the last time you were in Paris?"

"I think so. Maybe it was seeing you nearly drown. Maybe I redeemed myself today, at least a little, for what I did to my wife."

She nodded. Instinctively she reached out and took his hand, touching his fingers one by one and then putting his hand against her face. But they were interrupted when a street carnival pushed its way past them; children with painted faces riding on donkeys, goats, even pigs.

Harding stopped a vendor and bought her a little pot of heather and they climbed on board *l'impériale*, the open-top deck of one of the horse-drawn buses. They rode through the summer night, looking at the moon and the way its light flooded the city streets. And then he kissed her.

The first time surprised her. The second time, she slid her hand into his and drew him closer. The kiss never seemed to end, and when it did, another one started. She could feel herself responding, almost losing her breath in the giddiness of the moment, and then she pulled away.

"You told me that you were never going to kiss me again after that time in your room," she reminded him.

"But this time you kissed me back," he smiled.

"We're in a public place, you know."

"Do you want to go somewhere?"

"Where? I can't go back to that boat. I just can't. And neither of us has a place to live anymore. Things have changed."

"Yeah," he said. "I lost my job, and you lost Alain."

"I never had Alain. But I always had you."

"Yes. You always had me."

Harding thought for a second.

"I know. Bishop's railroad car. The old fool is probably still on the *Bethanie*, staring at the water."

They jumped off at the Gare du Nord. Harding told her that Bishop's railway car had been placed on a siding just outside the station, so they walked through the terminal beneath the 100-foot-high glass ceilings that looked like huge honeycombs. It was empty except for two pimps who stood under the gold clock, smoking and waiting for the young Breton girls to arrive from the country so that they could seduce them. They stared at Mary Ann—until Harding stared back.

"There it is," he said, pointing outside and down the tracks past the shed where the round red-and-gray sign signaled the next train.

Neville Bishop's private car was easy to find even in the darkness. It was a specially lengthened Pullman with heavy purple drapes in the windows, a gilded wrought-iron railing and a gold-striped awning that extended three feet beyond the back of the car.

It was locked.

"Give me a piece of your shirt," said Mary Ann.

"What?"

She reached out, her boldness surprising even to herself, and pulled his worn, bleached-out shirt from the front of his trousers. She ripped off a piece, wrapped it around her hand, and smashed a windowpane.

"All property is theft," she laughed as she reached through the broken window and unlocked the door from the inside.

He stared at her as if seeing her for the first time.

"You've changed," he said, following her inside.

She had. She didn't know exactly how, but Alain's death had somehow freed her, made her stronger. The pain of it had taken her to a new place in her life, like those levels that Alain had talked about, the ones in the sky. She wasn't a little schoolgirl with a crush anymore. She was a woman. There were a million romantic poems about females who had cast themselves out of windows after their lovers had died or deserted them. Well, she wasn't one of them. There was a life force in her that needed to be touched and molded and reformed. And tonight, perhaps, it would happen.

She gasped when she saw the interior: a fireplace lit by bottled gas, a high mahogany bar framed by crystal goblets that caught the glow of the fire, a wine rack full of rows and rows of bottles.

"My God!" she said.

"Keep going. It gets better."

In the center of the car was a dressing room with racks of suits. Mingled among them were women's clothes, gowns, slips, silk nighties that spoke of sybaritic sex and jaded appetites.

Harding watched as Mary Ann posed with one of them in front of her dress. Above them, built into the ceiling, was an observation deck with windows on all four sides surrounding a huge marble bathtub.

"So Bishop could sit back and scrub his ass while he watched the world go by," said Harding, looking up.

"I thought that he was broke," said Mary Ann.

"Some things you just don't give up."

"Back here," he heard Mary Ann call.

The bedroom was only dimly lit from the light outside and the corners were dark, but Harding could see Mary Ann in the center. Her shoes were off and she was bouncing up and down on the 12-foot bed. She was pointing and giggling. All around the top of the walls were oak carvings of nymphs and satyrs making love in all sorts of positions. And directly above the bed, on the ceiling, was a curved mirror.

Mary Ann sat on the bed; her wide eyes focused on him in the near dark. Harding could see her bosom rising and falling. He put his hand over her breast and felt her heart thumping. Darkness unleashed other senses, too. He breathed in the woman-smell of her, unmasked by complicated scents. It was erotic.

For a second he was reminded of when he had first met her at the church, and she had taken flight. Even then he had wanted her. Slowly he reached behind her neck to loosen the dress, button by sensuous button, starting at the down of her silky neck and moving toward the swell of her hips. Each time he touched her bare skin she shivered. Dress, chemise, petticoats, boots and stockings seemed to fall off her and land in a pile on the polished hardwood floor.

He began to kiss her. She watched in the overhead mirror as he explored her with his mouth; the secret hollows, the gentle slopes, the peaks of her nipples. Soon she was kissing him back, almost in a frenzy, pulling his clothes off to join hers on the floor. They were rolling over and over on the endless bed. Then Harding raised himself on his elbows above her.

"I want to remember this moment," he whispered.

"Me too."

A train pulled in on the next track, rocking the walls of their personal world, its monster eye of a headlight shining through their windows for just a second. But in that second, something in her inner ear told her that things weren't right. She tensed and turned away.

Harding reacted to the change in her. She felt his body tighten, pull back, grow angry before he said anything.

"It's Alain, isn't it? You're still thinking of Alain. He's still here, isn't he!" His voice rose with each syllable.

"Quiet!"

She strained her eyes as the darkness in the corner took shape. It wasn't Alain, but someone was there. They were not alone.

Then the gunshot. At first she thought that it was inside her head, it was so loud. Then that it was next to her head. Then she realized that it was inside the room.

She waited, still under him as if his body could protect her from all evil. Her right hand felt wet. She knew instinctively that this was a shot that had killed someone.

Harding drew a breath and she started to sob. At least he was still alive. He put his hand over her mouth.

Would the darkness and silence protect them? She didn't know. She waited for another shot. It didn't come. The flash of the gun had blinded her, but she could hear a dripping sound, like water, coming from the corner.

Harding got up. He nearly fell. The floor was slippery beneath his bare feet. He lit a lamp.

Then Mary Ann stopped sobbing and started to scream.

In the corner sat Neville Bishop. He had been there all the time, watching them from his vantage point where the darkness was especially dense.

But he was watching no longer. He had put a gun to the side of his head, a big .45-caliber revolver, and fired. The pressure of the soft-nosed slug inside his skull had forced his left eyeball out of its socket and left a huge hole in his forehead. Gouts of brain and clots of blood were scattered like dark seed as far as the bed.

Mary Ann now knew why her hand was wet. The dripping sound had been blood running down his arm and onto the floor.

Harding recovered first. He tore the sheet off the bed and threw it over her. Then he grabbed what he could of their clothes. She was still screaming as he pulled her out of the room, through the car, and out onto the railroad tracks.

"Calm down," he ordered. "You've got to stop. Someone's going to see us."

"Didn't anyone hear the gunshot?"

Just then came a white light from the other side of the city, followed by the sound of an explosion. Then an even greater light, illuminating the parallel lines of endless track and the two small figures who huddled half-naked in the vast train yard. It was as if someone had taken one of those gunpowder flash pictures—but of the whole world. They braced themselves as the inevitable "KAA . . . RRUMPH!" came at them, upending the whole city. The earth itself shook.

"No," said Harding, as the light faded. "I don't think anyone noticed our little problem."

"What happened? What was that?"

He stared at the far end of Paris, toward Montparnasse. "I'm afraid I know."

twenty-nine

Tragedy at Montparnasse—STILL LATER THAT EVENING

---

*A*T ONE TIME, MONTPARNASSE had been a quarry. Because it was a hole in the ground, people tried to fill it up with trash: cans, bottles, the remains of torn-down buildings. Gradually the mountain of trash grew; home to weeds, stray cats and the students of the Latin Quarter, who would sometimes paint themselves and parade naked in the streets. As a joke, the students named it Mount Parnassus, the Greek peak that was home to Dionysius, god of wine.

Then Fabian Bouchard bought an entire city block of Montparnasse under an assumed name, and put up the biggest building in Paris. At first, people asked questions. But then the Germans came, and there were no more questions.

Maximilian loved the way that his building towered over the slums around it. He thought of it as a cathedral. All the other cathedrals of Paris were monuments to dead gods and unimportant saints. This one was meant for a living God, and that God was already inside.

A sentry stopped him. The sentry had seen him a hundred

times before, but made a point of asking for his credentials each time to prove that he was doing his job. Maximilian was annoyed, but tried not to show it. He could not reprimand a soldier for being alert—particularly tonight. Tomorrow the kaiser would come in on a special train to watch him humiliate the French. To watch him fly.

Maximilian remembered how vast the workshop had looked before the airship was built—like a cavern. Now the dirigible, in its full height, took up the entire building. In daylight, illumination came from skylights in the roof, but this evening electric lights, powered by a generator, glowed dimly. There were no oil lamps or gaslights. Hydrogen, oxygen and flame were an explosive combination.

Maximilian approached the airship from the front. It was awesome—steel gray and ominous—like walking down the barrel of a gun toward the bullet inside, but it held no fear for him. He knew where he was going. Inside, at the far back, was a captain's chair where he could sit, and be at peace, on this final night. Its high arms made him feel as if he were on a throne. Perhaps some day he would be.

He walked up the passageway at the bottom of the airship and into its belly. A guard should have been posted at this entrance, too. Then he paused for a second. There was a strange sound that he couldn't identify.

The inside was even more eerie. Only a few weak overhead electric lights illuminated the central spine that ran all the way from tail fin to front. Maximilian could see the ribs coming out of the spine. They divided the dirigible up into 17 cells from front to back. The covering of the cells was like an elephant's skin, gray and baggy. Because they had been partially filled with hydrogen, they sucked in and puffed out without making a sound. It was like being inside the belly of a great beast.

Maximilian moved up the walkway of the central spine toward the far end, his eyes adjusting to the dim light as he went. Then he heard a voice say "Hello."

There was no echo. In a place as vast as this, there should have been an echo. But the walls muffled the sound. So there was only one "hello," and it came from Henri Meurthe. He was sitting in Maximilian's chair 40 feet away at the end of the airship. Because the dirigible curved up at the back, he was about 10 feet higher than Maximilian, a slight but strategic advantage.

Maximilian was surprised, but he recovered quickly. "Monsieur Meurthe," he said, "so happy to entertain you. I would have thought that the guards at the door or here at the dirigible would have announced you."

"I came in through one of our famous Paris sewer lines, which conveniently runs under your building," said Meurthe, "a method suggested by your colleague, Fabian Bouchard."

"Really. Thank you for that information. I will have to plug that rathole—and eliminate the rat—tomorrow . . ."

"If there is a tomorrow," Meurthe broke in. "As for your guards, you can see for yourself; they are no longer guarding."

Meurthe pointed to the foot of the catwalk. Two of the German soldiers lay there, their throats cut.

How the hell did he do that? Maximilian wondered.

His fingers tightened into fists and he recognized the classic signs of fear in himself: shortness of breath, trembling, sweat. For the first time since he had come to Paris he was frightened; he felt like the man in that legend who was racing over the ice while it cracked under his feet. And what was that sound? A hissing.

Then Meurthe spoke: "Your friend Fabian Bouchard has told me everything. How you sabotaged the aeroplane, how you bankrupted Bishop, that little romantic farce you played with my daughter, how LeRond planted the explosive that killed my son . . ."

"Your son?" Maximilian tried to keep the surprise from showing in his voice, but failed. He factored that new information into his equation of personalities. It was his best skill, he reminded himself. He realized quickly that it made Meurthe infinitely more dangerous. But what was that hissing?

I need a plan, Maximilian thought. First, get control of yourself. Keep him talking. Then get close enough to kill him. He walked up the gangplank, slowly, a step at a time, so as not to alert Meurthe.

"So why did you come here?" he asked. *Step.* "Do you plan to punch a few holes in our balloon? They can be easily patched." *Step.* "Kill a few soldiers? They can be easily replaced."

Meurthe ignored his questions. "Do you like Wagner? I suppose it's unpatriotic, but I've always admired your German composer. What is that famous piece of his, the one where the world ends in fire?"

"*Gotterdammerung.*" *Step.* Keep him talking. "I am pleased to hear it. It proves that you are not as prejudiced and provincial as most French idiots." Only 30 feet away now. Humor him.

Meurthe rose. "I said that you and I would some day fight a duel. Now that time has come. Listen."

Maximilian listened. And then he realized what the sound, like an angry snake, really meant. Meurthe had opened the valves to all the hydrogen tanks. It was seeping out, mixing with the oxygen, creating a bomb. *Step. Another step.*

"You know," said Meurthe, "there is not much about you to like, but I have always been impressed by the way you can flip a match with your thumbnail. I've tried and tried, but I don't seem to have the coordination . . . or my nails are too short. However, if you'll allow me to take the liberty . . ." and he pulled out a cigar and match.

"No, you fool!" shouted Maximilian. *Run,* he told himself. But his arms and legs were too heavy. He felt as if he were in a dream, where things move too slowly. He saw Meurthe flick the match once and then again with his fingernail. No spark.

Meurthe's failure gave him hope. Perhaps there was time. Maximilian ran up the catwalk, praying, trying not to stumble. Twenty feet. Ten feet.

Meurthe flicked the match again . . . and again. Still no spark. Now his face seemed worried.

Faster.

Maximilian was only five feet away now. Perhaps even if a flame did start he could smother it.

Then he saw Meurthe smile. And he knew that Meurthe had been toying with him, that Meurthe could have flicked the match all along, and that he was . . .

Holding the match up high, Meurthe flicked it for the last time. It sparked.

For Maximilian it was a last, wonderful sight—which he did not fully appreciate. Vapor trails of flame went out in 12 different directions and ignited in a pool over their heads like an enormous halo.

Because the hydrogen and oxygen inside the airship had already mixed, it was a bomb inside a bomb. The core blew the hydrogen in the cells apart. They exploded the hydrogen stored in the tanks around the dirigible, turning them into glowing fireballs. It was as though a monstrous torch had been ignited from underneath the ground.

"No . . ." screamed Maximilian. But his last word was cut short.

STRANGE THINGS HAPPEN IN an explosion. Windows shattered a mile away and shingles tumbled to the ground like snowflakes. One otherwise respectable woman had her clothes blown off and had to run into a nearby *maison de tolérance* for some garments. A couple making love in a third-floor apartment suddenly found themselves in the middle of a party on the second floor.

The blast even flattened the green cast-iron sides of the nearby *pissotiere*. Men in various states of undress came flying out of the collapsing structure.

At the German workshop, the walls held out for a few seconds longer than the roof. The walls acted like the muzzle of a cannon, sending the debris of the dirigible hurling upward. Aluminum girders went pinwheeling across the night sky, sinking deep when they landed. One plunged 20 feet into an asphalt road.

But a huge section of the skin of the balloon remained intact, and was thrust up hundreds of feet by the ignited air. When it reached the cold night sky, it spread out like a giant bat and blocked the moon. Then what remained of the German airship went on its first and final flight, moving like a dark cloud over Paris until it fell.

As for the building, by morning there was nothing left. The junkyard of Montparnasse was a junkyard again.

The city had reclaimed its own.

thirty

MARY ANN SAT ON the edge of the river across from the cathedral of Notre-Dame, watching the water, waiting for dawn. The boats below her were huddled together like birds plumped up against the cold. Under the great spans that arched the Seine, the midnight fires of the clochards were burning out. Some still hugged their bottles for the warmth of the liquor in them; occasionally, one would stagger over to the corner of the bridge to relieve himself.

Mary Ann had gone back to the *Bethanie* to get her clothes. But she couldn't bring herself to stay, even for one night. When she went downstairs to her cabin, she stumbled because there was no light. Then she heard a crunch under her foot. She picked up a pair of Bishop's broken reading glasses and started to cry. No matter who he was, he didn't deserve to end up that way.

Now there was nothing to do and nowhere to go. Time drifted. Harding had stayed at the railroad car to talk to the police. He had been gone for hours. She worried that he might have been arrested. She felt like a soul in limbo, uncertain of passage to heaven or hell. What was the French word for it? *Le cafard.* The despair. She remembered a song from one of the Parisian musicals, a song about suicide:

> *The atmosphere's filthy with sleaze,*
> *The boulevards fill me with pain.*
> *I've done all the bridges and quays,*
> *All that's left to do now is the Seine.*

In the back of her mind a tinny voice kept rasping: "Do the Seine, do the Seine." It would be so easy to slip into the water . . .

A foot nudged her and she looked up. It was Harding. And he was drunk.

"What happened?" she asked, not sure she wanted to know.

Harding sat down on the wharf. Fell down was more like it.

"You mean after I got done cleaning up the remains of our former boss? I went over to the Aéro Club to tell them what had happened. Hell, why lie? I went to have a drink. Or two. I figured that you weren't waiting for me with open arms—unless my name is Chevrier."

"It wasn't like that . . ." she started to say.

But he interrupted. "Wasn't even a doorman there. Club's lost the old cachet. Everyone was sitting at the bar getting sloshed and feeling guilty, trying not to look at each other. I felt right at home. Then I went to that room—the one with pictures of the dead aviators. They've got a new one on the wall. You know who it is, don't you?"

She nodded, and he heard her sob. He wrenched her shoulders around to face him. "Take some advice. Not for me or for us, because there is no us. Just for yourself: Forget about him."

"What do you mean?"

"What do you think I mean? The great Chevrier. The noble Chevrier. The courageous and now deceased Chevrier. The one true flame you keep kindled in your heart. You still think that he loved you, don't you?"

"I don't know if he loved me," she said, staring at the water. "I guess I'll never know. But he gave me something I never had. I'm not afraid of life anymore."

"So you're not afraid?" said Harding. He made it sound like a joke. "Well, maybe you should be." He pulled a bottle out of his coat pocket. "Before I left the Aéro Club, I snagged some of their best cognac. All property is theft, right? Isn't that what the Great Man said? Have a drink?"

She shook her head.

"Just as well. Almost gone anyway." He drained the bottle and threw it into the water with a splash.

A dog started to bark at the noise. They heard a voice shout, "*Arrête! Tais-toi!*" and then the sound of a smack. The dog yelped once and was silent.

"Have you ever noticed how people train a dog to warn them when he hears something?" mused Harding. "Then when he barks, they hit him. Hell, it's getting so you can't even be an honest dog anymore."

He hesitated for a second. "And that's what Alain was when you get right down to it. He was an honest dog who barked too much. So they shut him up."

It took a moment for his words to register, but when they did it was as if an earthquake had rumbled under her and left her reeling. She grabbed his arm. "What do you mean, 'they'?" she demanded.

"The same thing that they did to you. You don't think flipping the plane was an accident. The bolts on the runway were turned up. Meurthe saw that before I did."

"Why didn't you tell me?"

"What was the point? Ever since we came here, we've been in one of those moving pictures where all the action is speeded up and we're three scenes behind. The villain has already tied Little Nell to the railroad tracks, and we're still figuring out how she's going to pay the rent. It's time to go home to America where we belong. I just can't figure out how."

"Meurthe will help if we need it. He told me that he would."

"Henri Meurthe is dead," said Harding flatly. "When I last saw him, he was going off to get revenge for what happened to you and Alain. Then I heard that the German building blew up."

"Oh, my God! That was the explosion we saw."

"Took half of Montparnasse with it," said Harding. "That's all right, nothing in Montparnasse but students, rats and low-life artists like me. But Meurthe died too. I saw it in his face. He didn't want to live any more.

"So there goes our last friend and our last chance of getting home," he finished. "As my old football coach used to say every time that we'd go out and lose: 'Cheer up, boys, 'cause there ain't no hope.'"

He started to get up, steadying himself with both hands as he rose. She didn't want to look at him. A few hours ago he had been her friend, her rescuer, her almost-lover, and Paris had been theirs. Now death was once again everywhere around her, and hands were reaching up to pull her into the grave: Bishop's, Meurthe's, yes, even Alain's. And Harding? Harding had found his own kind of death—in a bottle.

Harding finished the long climb to his feet. "There's nothing more that I can do here, for you or anyone else. The fairy tale has ended. As for me, I'm going to see if there's another drink in this town." He started to sing: "Oh . . . You can tell a man who boozes by the company he chooses . . ."

She looked at him levelly. "And the Pig got up and slowly walked away," she finished.

She was sorry the moment she said it, knew that she shouldn't have said it, knew that she had hurt this beautiful and damaged man beyond any hope of making it up, knew that she had lost him.

But she couldn't take it back. She saw the look on Harding's face. Then she saw his back as it vanished into the remains of the night. He was gone. And now, for the first time since she had met Harding, she knew that she was absolutely alone.

For a few moments it was quiet, as if nature itself was willing to observe a suitable period of mourning. A *horizontale*, traveling home from her night's work, stopped at the cathedral across the river. She paused to put on her spectacles, then genuflected in front of the church and blessed herself, seeking mercy from the old stone.

Mary Ann felt a chill start at the base of her spine and work its way up until her shoulders were shaking. Was she looking at her own future?

"Come on," said the tinny voice from the musical. "Do the Seine. Do the Seine." It's *le cafard*, she thought. The despair.

But then the birds began to stir in the back courtyard of Notre-Dame, and the cacophony of morningsong began. Streetlights winked out avenue by avenue as someone shut off the gas. The sky was barely as gray as an old man's head, but the ever-frugal French were already turning off the lights.

And now she saw the sun, coming from the east, reach the skyline. It paused to bless the high clouds, then touch the flared Gothic peak of the church. It moved on to the huge square towers where Quasimodo had rung his famous bells, and edged down the gray slate roof to where bronze saints, clad in green, marched in lockstep toward the sky. It reached the gargoyles and brought them to life, snarling. And then, stone by stone, it illuminated the great shrine until it passed through the flying arches at its feet.

"Yes, you're alone," she said to herself, answering *le cafard*. "But you've been alone before. You were alone on the mountaintop after your father died. And you survived. You strapped on those wings. You even learned to fly."

Then she saw the pigeons, waking long before the lazy roosters, pop from their holes in front of the church and set forth— fluttering—to scavenge another meal. It was as clear a sign as she could ever hope for. Morning had come.

And with it, a plan.

thirty-one

$\mathcal{I}$T WAS MIDAFTERNOON BEFORE she had the courage to do it, and even then it was a long walk up the slopes to Saint-Cloud. She kept thinking as she took each step up those winding stair-streets: Was she crazy?

She remembered the first time she had come up here and had seen Alain riding on top of his magnificent blue airship, the master of the world. Look what had happened to him. Just as Harding had said; they had destroyed him. And here she was, a nobody, setting out to do something that no one had ever done before.

The doors at both ends of the hangar were wide open, and there was a feeling of hollowness inside. She walked in, trying to look inconspicuous. She was wearing trousers again, and with her hair tucked under a snap-brim cap, she hoped that no one would recognize her, or even notice her.

As she walked through the hangar, she realized why it felt so empty. Alain's big airship was gone, lost at the bottom of the Seine. And Alain, who could have filled up the room just by being there, was gone with it. There was almost complete silence in the place. No soldiers or workmen were around, except for a small group playing boule in one corner. She could hear the metal balls clanking on the concrete. As she walked by quickly, Mary Ann recognized the sergeant and corporal who had been with Major Vitary yesterday. They didn't look up.

At the far end of the workshop was Alain's small dirigible with the bicycle frame, the one that he had lovingly called the *Bitch*. It looked like a dog waiting at the doorstep for its master. She walked over and patted its side. "He's not coming home," she whispered, as if it could understand. "But I'm here."

She had watched Alain fly that day over the Seine, and it was burned into her memory: the day that he went up into the sky with her, for her, treating her as an equal, explaining each step to her. She remembered every word he had said to her that day. First you had to fully inflate the balloon with hydrogen. The tanks were right next to it. She looked around. No one was paying any attention. She added hydrogen until the skin was tight.

Check the gas and oil. Full. The rest of it seemed to be in good shape, too. Now unhook the ropes. Then jump aboard and pedal to start the motor. They would hear her then. But if she moved quickly enough, they wouldn't have time to stop her. The whirling propeller would keep them back. That was the plan. There was only one way to find out.

"Halt!"

She froze.

"Halt!" the unseen voice ordered. "Not another move."

She turned. It was Major Vitary, coming straight at her, his right arm outstretched, holding one of those big nine-shot French revolvers. She could see the large hole at the end of the muzzle, the loaded chambers, and then beyond that his face, the waxy ends of his mustache and his narrow black eyes. She felt as if her legs were going to give way and send her crashing to the cement floor.

From somewhere far away she heard Alain's voice. Or perhaps she only imagined it. The voice said, "Have a little courage."

Then she heard her own voice, so calm that she almost didn't know it was hers. "Major Vitary," she said casually. "So nice to see you. I am planning to go to the Tower today."

"I should send you to Hell."

Looking at his face, she realized how furious she had made him yesterday by striking him in front of his subordinates. A mere woman, and a foreigner at that, had humiliated him. Now she was in his realm, a trespasser, and he had every right to kill her. Behind him, she saw, the other soldiers had gathered. She played the only card she had left.

"Major Vitary, you would not shoot a woman, would you?"

She saw fear and anger collide in his eyes. Fear of being remembered as the man who shot a woman in cold blood; anger at the humiliation that he had already endured from her. Anger was winning as his finger slowly tightened on the trigger.

I am going to die, she thought. Will I see the flash, hear the gun, feel the pain? Or does it just happen?

Then the sergeant came up and took the pistol from Vitary's hand. "No, mademoiselle," the sergeant said, "he would not shoot a woman."

Vitary glared at the sergeant for a second. Then he turned and walked, stiff-legged, back toward his office.

The sergeant and corporal helped her cast off the ropes and climb aboard. It was a good thing, too. Mary Ann was shaking so badly that she couldn't even get the rope off the hook.

"I'm sorry," she said.

"It's all right," the sergeant smiled. "Alain was a friend of ours. But go quickly now, before Vitary finds his courage . . . or another gun."

Then she was in the seat and moving forward, through the doors of the workshop. She realized that the drag rope had come uncoiled, and that 300 feet of it was snaking along the ground beneath her. No time to worry now. Just go up fast, before it gets snarled on anything. She shoved the rope all the way to the back, as Alain had taught her, the nose tilted up, and suddenly there was nothing but open sky in front of her.

LOUISE CHEVRIER WAS BUSY at the family bakery, making the icings for the next day's *religieux*—black-and-white pastries that looked like a nun's habit. Two little neighborhood boys, both out of breath, came running in to tell her that Alain Chevrier was flying to the Eiffel Tower.

"Alain Chevrier is dead," she reminded them sharply. "You were at his funeral."

"But it is his airship," said the older boy. "We've seen it flying through the streets."

She looked surprised for a moment. Was it possible? Who was flying? "Here," she said, giving them each a bowl of icing and a paddle. "If what you say is true, you have earned it." She ran outside, shielding her eyes against the late-day sun.

YVETTE WAS IN HER bedroom in Neuilly, trying hard to forget. When she was a child and played with dolls, she would be absolutely devoted to one. Then eventually she would tire of it, become so sick of it that she couldn't stand to look at its painted face anymore. So she would smash it, throw it out the window, or tell the maid to dispose of it.

One time she took a doll all the way to the Pont Neuf bridge on the Seine in winter, propped it on the snow-covered parapet, and pushed it in, watching as it sank. Yvette had told her friends that the doll had drowned herself over a lost love, and her friends had promptly done the same thing with their dolls.

Now Alain was gone, gone into the Seine, just like her doll. But Alain was gone even before that. He had rejected her. He had pushed her off the bridge.

And her father was gone. She could always depend on her father to save her from whatever she'd gotten into. But now his problems were greater than hers were, if, in fact, he was even alive. She heard that he had gone berserk last night and attacked Fabian Bouchard at Maxim's. Then he didn't come home.

The maid knocked on her door, but Yvette ignored it. The knocking grew louder and then, surprisingly, the maid opened it, unbidden. Yvette looked up, angry.

"Mademoiselle," said the maid, "you must come down."

"I don't want to," said Yvette, dismissing her with a wave.

But the maid stood her ground. "You have no choice, mademoiselle. The president of France is here to see you."

Pouchet was fidgeting in the living room, walking back and forth. Did the man ever do anything but fidget? Yvette wondered as she came down the stairs. "Monsieur le President," she said brightly, "so happy to see you, and I'm sure that my father would be overjoyed too, but he is not here."

The sarcasm was lost on Pouchet. "Meurthe not here?" He seized her hand. "Then you must come with us."

She shrank back. "I am not well," she protested.

"No matter. You must come. It is for the glory of France. Where are your father's papers? The prize, the medal?"

She pointed to the Kingswood desk in Meurthe's study. "Why do you need them? What's happening?"

"Don't ask questions," said Pouchet. "Assist me!"

Both of them rummaged through the desk. There was a time when she had loved that round, sculpted desk with its candlesticks at both sides and its little porthole at the top where her father used to hide her candy. She reached into that porthole. Out fell her father's pocket watch, the big one that he used to call his "turnip." Opposite the clock face was a picture of Alain Chevrier. Chevrier! What was Chevrier's picture doing where her picture should have been? She threw the watch against the wall so hard that it broke and the springs popped out.

Pouchet didn't even notice. "Here," he said, holding up an envelope. "It's the bank draft and the medal. Come!"

Two soldiers escorted her outside. There, waiting in the back seat of the big Mors touring car, was Fabian Bouchard. She knew that her father hated Bouchard for some reason. What was it?

"So glad you could come," said Bouchard with an unctuous leer. "You have played as much a role in this as anyone. You should see how it turns out."

Pouchet came running to the car. He pushed her into the back seat between them. "To the Eiffel Tower," he ordered. "The other members of the Aéro Club will meet us there."

"Listen," he told her, "if your father is not back, you will have to stand in for him and give the award."

"Award?" said Yvette. "You mean someone is flying to the Tower? But who?"

"We don't know," said Bouchard, "but at least it's not one of the filthy Germans." He glanced about nervously, then added, "They're all dead."

"And a Frenchman will win the medal, one of our own beloved people," said Pouchet.

"Faster!" he yelled at the chauffeur as the big Mors, with its hood as long as a coffin, roared through the crowded city. Suddenly the touring car screeched to a halt, throwing the three of them against the front seat. One of the mounted police escorts had collided with a boy on a bicycle, who fell in front of the car.

"Get out of the way, you little turd!" shouted Pouchet.

"God," thought Yvette. "To be trapped in a car with these two hypocrites. No, three hypocrites. Include yourself."

AS SHE ROSE HIGHER, Mary Ann was thinking of when she was a little girl at the cottage on Long Island. Her father used to read western novels to her and her brother, and then they would act them out. Behind every door was an outlaw waiting to be shot down. They would charge across the fields, wooden swords waving, to face the wild Indians. They would climb trees to spy on enemy fortifications.

Then they got older, and she was excluded from his games. The stories changed too. Now they were about boy inventors who built electric trains that could travel 100 miles an hour, or an air cannon that could shoot a rocket halfway around the world or, yes, even a flying machine that would be the toast of Paris.

But they were about boys and for boys. So, at night, Mary Ann would sneak into her brother's room, steal his books and read them in her bed, pretending that she was the hero.

Suddenly, she felt a jerk, as if she'd been lassoed in one of those cowboy stories. The tug from behind almost threw her out of the bicycle seat. She looked back and saw the taut line of the drag rope caught on the top of the square tower at Auteuil, the city's steeplechase racetrack far below her. A race had started, but the sound of the noisy, popping motor of the airship overhead brought the crowd to its feet with a shout. She saw flowered hats and white upturned faces and everyone waving at her. Startled horses reared their heads and three dumped their jockeys.

"Don't daydream," she warned herself. But what could she do? She throttled the 16-horsepower engine all the way to its maximum, feeling every cord and line in the airship tighten as it tried to break free. Flames shot out of the exhaust just behind her. If the flames got close enough to the hydrogen in the balloon . . .

Then with a jerk, the rope came free. Go higher, she thought. Get above the range of anything that can snare that rope.

She gave herself more orders as she went, improvising, talking her way through it. She reached forward to turn down the carburetor, trying to keep the engine exhaust from spewing out those flames. She maneuvered the handlebars back and forth as each gust of wind jostled her from behind and bounced the airship off course. The breeze was helping her move forward now, but she knew that it would be in her face, an enemy, on the trip back.

Below her was the half circle of the Trocadéro, looking like a Mississippi riverboat, its minarets looming like smokestacks.

Almost there, she thought. Just across the river.

And now, as she rose toward the Eiffel Tower, she realized this was *her* story. It was in her hands to succeed or fail. And it was a simple story. There was no compromise, no one to answer to, no halfway solutions. She was like one of those birds in the Region of Fire. No feet, no claws. To stop was to fall, and to fall was to die. But whatever happened was between her—and the sky.

LOUISE WALKED DOWN THE block, trying to get a better look. Mobs of people were running into the already crowded streets. Everyone was drawn to the figure in the sky. All Paris seemed to be pouring out of its offices and shops, cheering, bumping into each other—and her. Factories were shutting down. Looms were left running. Men were hanging from gables and steeples.

In the distance the little airship looked like a cylinder with two pointed cones, its white balloon glowing against a backdrop of red clouds lit by the evening sun. It was sailing with the wind, moving like a clipper ship. Who is flying? she wondered. Then it passed out of sight beyond her roof.

"L-L-Louise, up h-h-here!" she heard a voice call. It was her neighbor, his stammer more aggravated than usual by his excitement. He was sitting at the peak of his six-story building, looking as if he were perched on a cliff, and waving her to come up.

She climbed the inside steps and came out the garret window that opened directly onto the street. Below her the road seemed to jump up at her and then fall back as if it were daring her to climb out. Unlike both Henri and Alain, Louise was deathly afraid of heights. She took a breath, knowing that if she stopped to take another, she would be frozen to the spot.

But she had to know who was flying in Alain's place. Whoever it was, he wasn't afraid, was he? Before she could give herself time to think, she scrambled out, her feet hitting the gutter and her hands clutching the outside corners of the window frame to pull herself up. Panting with fear, her fingernails scratching the slippery black slate roof, she scrambled up to the peak.

But the sight was worth it. Below her the streets were filled with a motionless throng, a sea of humanity. Traffic had stopped. Boys trying to follow the progress of the airship tripped on the hems of women's skirts and went sprawling.

The Seine near the Tower was crowded with small boats, jammed to the gunwales. The docks and wharves were, too. She watched a man fall almost casually off the railing of the Pont de Grenelle bridge into the river, where he floated downstream, waving at the shoreline and waiting to be rescued. No one noticed him. Every eye was on the figure above.

She watched, amazed. Chattering across the sunset sky, up in the air, and moving toward the Tower. She wished that Henri were there to see it too. Perhaps he was.

But who was flying? It looked like a boy. No, it was that woman; the one that Alain had called Marianne. She strained so hard to see that she nearly slipped off the edge.

Her neighbor caught her. "Are y-y-you all right?" he asked.

"Never better," she said, blinking back the tears. "Never better."

MUSIC. ABOVE THE SOUND of the engine Mary Ann heard music. Was she crazy? No. In the plaza just below the Tower a makeshift military band had formed and was pounding out a march. Two men were struggling up the last set of steps to the top with their heavy motion picture cameras and tripods on their backs.

The elevators were jammed and teenagers were scaling the girders. The Tour Eiffel had never been so crowded. It looked as if it would tip over. Those at the top held their places; those coming up pushed their way to the front. There were accidents, shoving matches, fistfights. One man leaned too far over and almost fell from the second level. He hung on by an arm and was pulled back up. But top hats, purses and papers all spilled into the void below.

As Mary Ann got closer, she heard the cheering. Then a sudden gust of wind blew off her hat and her long hair floated in the breeze. There was a gasp.

"C'est un femme!" shouted someone.

Then there was an even louder cheer, heard all over the city. The shutter of every camera clicked. She ducked as a shower of hats was thrown at her from the third level. Men leaned out to blow her kisses.

Now higher, higher. Up above the roof. To win the contest, it was enough simply to fly around the Tower. But for Mary Ann, one more thing had to be done for Alain, and herself. She throttled back until she could drift with the wind, and yanked the rudder to the left.

Her course took her directly over the roof. She stretched her hand out toward the very top, barely grazing it. Then she reached for the lightning rod.

POUCHET'S CAR WITH YVETTE and Bouchard in it thundered across the Pont d'Iéna bridge toward the Tower, and past the reviewing stand. Even with police escorts on galloping horses clearing the way, they barely arrived in time. The Mors swerved around a double line of iron pipes facing straight up like infantry on parade. It took Yvette a second to realize that they were the rockets that had been ready to welcome Alain Chevrier when he flew around the Tower. Had that been only three days ago? It felt like a lifetime.

But Pouchet didn't hesitate. "Fire the rockets!" he shouted to the soldiers as they roared on.

"How many?" she heard one yell.

"All of them!" he yelled back. The fireworks went off with a deafening roar just as the car jerked to a stop.

"Is he there yet?" Pouchet asked Bouchard. "I have lost my pince-nez."

"Almost," said Bouchard. "And 'he' is a 'she.'"

"A woman?" said Pouchet. "Is it that American? That Marianne?"

"Mary Ann," Yvette corrected him.

"No matter. It is Chevrier's airship. We can still claim the victory."

Above them the dirigible made a tight circle around the Tower. There was a second when it was lost to view, and then it reemerged like the sun from a cloud.

"Wait a second. What's she doing?" said Pouchet, standing up in the car.

Mary Ann reached over and snatched something that was flying from the lightning rod.

"What is it?"

Yvette looked up. Mary Ann was waving Yvette's stocking over her head. Then she crumpled it into a ball, and tossed it away. It came floating down like a rag in the wind, and was blown off toward the Champ-de-Mars to the south.

"Why don't you ask Mademoiselle Meurthe?" said Bouchard.

Yvette looked at him. He was smirking. So was the chauffeur in the front seat.

"You may turn around, driver," said Pouchet. "Get us to the reviewing stand. We've seen enough."

"Yes," said Yvette, so quietly that she could barely hear herself. "We've seen enough."

LOUISE HEARD A RAGGED cheer rise from the street. "What's happening now?" she said, pulling at her neighbor's shoulder as they sat on the roof. He had focused on the airship with his telescope.

"She's p-p-passed the Tower," he said. "But now she's hitting the wind head-on, and the b-b-balloon is seesawing back and forth, as if it's being hit by a b-b-boxer no one can see."

Then a moan came floating up from the crowd.

"And now," she said, shaking him, forgetting that they were both six stories above the street. "What now?"

"The balloon's l-l-losing elevation," he stammered, trying to stay focused on it. "It looks like it's leaking. When the f-f-front rises, the gas swells it full and the stern crumples, but when the front dips, the stern fills up and the b-b-bow sags like a wet towel. Wait a second . . ."

"What!" She strained to see through her own eyes, wishing that she had brought her spectacles and cursing her vanity for never wearing them.

"It's fluttering and flopping now, still m-m-moving, but s-s-staggering like a runner who's out of . . . No, it's . . . it's doubled up. She's going down like a b-b-bird that's been shot. She's done for!"

WHEN MARY ANN TURNED the Tower and started back, the first thing she noticed was sluggishness. Alain's airship had handled easily, even in the wind. But now the force of the 10-mile-an-hour gust that had helped get her there suddenly hit her—and her ship—head on. And the seam that Guillaume LeRond had ripped the night before Alain's flight had opened.

She looked back. The sharp steel edge of the Tower, like a sword, was still close behind her. The wind would drag her back into it, raking her across the cutting edge, unless she fought it.

"Got to keep going," she said out loud. She squeezed the throttle open, squeezing as hard as she could. The motor barked and backfired again and again. The explosions sounded like pistol shots. Flames spurted from the exhaust, much too close to the hydrogen inside her balloon.

And now she could feel the balloon above her lose its tautness and start to sag. The handlebars didn't want to turn. She craned her head to the right and saw the seam breaking loose, forming a pouting mouth, spewing out the precious gas that kept her from falling. The balloon started to wilt. Wrinkles and pouches formed like skin that had suddenly aged. She looked back, thinking that things couldn't get worse. But they were. The rudder was jammed.

Stop it. Stop the panic. Think about what's going on. Just because you're 1,000 feet in the air doesn't mean you can't think.

When she was in trouble as a child, her father used to tell her: "Step back and see it as someone else would." She tried. She saw the cylinder shape of Alain's balloon as it would look in the distance, doubled in the middle, leaving the two pointed ends high in the air. The rudder, at the back end, had become snarled in the piano wire that connected the bamboo keel to the balloon above it.

Only one thing to do. Go and free it. Easier said than done. You've got to go up there and do it. Take a breath, a deep breath, maybe your last. No, fight that! Put one foot on the bicycle seat, and hoist yourself to the rigging. Don't look down. Everything is so dangerously small. It will get bigger in a hurry, won't it? Now, up!

With the keel in both hands, she lifted her feet until they were wrapped around it, and started to inch her way, hand by hand, out the slender spar toward the rudder.

It seemed everlasting. The dirigible made a huge lazy circle that brought it closer to the Tower. In a few moments it would be over the Seine once more. She recognized the spot where Alain had fallen just as she reached the tangled wire.

She jerked it loose, and the rudder was free. Then she realized that she was almost upside down, her head facing toward the ground. Her weight at the back end of the airship had acted as ballast, sending the airship up at a dangerous angle. It was strange to be falling and rising at the same time, disorienting, like doing an endless cartwheel.

Stop it! That way lies madness. Inch your way back toward the center.

She moved slowly, trying not to kick any of the piano wire supports with her feet as she moved backward. Finally she reached the spot directly above the seat, now terribly far below her.

At that moment the engine gave one last pneumatic cough and died. The airship had leveled out, and was starting to sink fast. She heard a ripping sound overhead as the seam split completely. The floor of the city was rushing toward her.

She saw the two pins that kept the bicycle frame and engine attached to the keel, one on either side of her. Instinctively she reached out with her feet, angry now at this thing that was killing her, and kicked at one of them. It came loose, and she realized that Alain must have thought of the same thing. Without the extra weight, the balloon could stay aloft longer.

She kicked at the other one. It held. She was falling faster. *Now is the moment when you live or die.* The world came down to an inch of iron pin, and how much strength she could put against it. She kicked again and missed. Falling faster. One more time. Her heel connected and she felt it give. The whole frame plummeted and crashed somewhere below her.

Now she hung by both arms outstretched to the keel. The balloon, almost completely limp, was tangled in the keel and hanging around her.

Seven hundred feet below, the earth reached up to drag her down.

ON THE GRANDSTAND WHERE he had hoped to award the medal, President Auguste Pouchet watched the horror unfold above him. Paper flutters from the rockets were all around him; the whole place smelled of gunpowder. Another disaster, another death, another tragedy for France, he thought, and perhaps the final one for him.

But what horrified him most was the look on Yvette's face as she stood beside him. It was a look of triumph.

thirty-two

The Last Moment . . .

---

*H*ARDING HAD BEEN SLEEPING fitfully on a park bench after a bout with a bottle of Romanee-Conti, sleeping until a gendarme tapped him on the shoes with a nightstick to wake him up. The sun was far overhead, and everyone with a place to go was already there. But he had no reason to rush. The contest was over, and, when he thought about it, so was his life.

He wandered the city. He ate tasteless food. He walked past empty houses with broken windows. They looked like paintings of his soul, he thought. He meandered down the Champs-Elysées, watching the pretty girls who strolled along, chattering with one another. "The beautiful shorthand typists," he remembered one of his friends calling them.

Then he went into a *petite zinc* at the corner, rested his elbows on the cool gray stone of the bar, and ordered a pack of Sweet Caporal cigarettes. He looked at the bottles behind the bar, each capped with its own silver siphon, and they seemed to wink back at him in the near dark. He could tell them his life story and they would listen.

Two trips to Paris, two different women, but two failures all the same. Death and pain. His wife dying, holding his hand, not blaming him, although she should have. Alain Chevrier in flames, falling into the Seine. Poor Bishop, waiting until that single terrible moment to blow his head off. And Mary Ann, hurt and anger in her eyes, telling him the truth about himself. "And the pig got up and slowly walked away."

"What did you say?" asked the bartender.

Harding looked up. He hadn't been aware that he was talking out loud.

"Sorry, I couldn't hear you," the bartender went on. "There's too much noise outside."

What noise? thought Harding. Then he heard it too: the hiss and whoosh and bang of rockets fired close by.

He looked out the window. Another rocket shot upward, showering sparks. Then another, and another.

He ran outside and looked up at the Eiffel Tower. There was Mary Ann, 1,000 feet in the air and a quarter mile away.

He ran toward the Tower, bumping into tourists carrying their new Kodak box cameras and high-hatted gentlemen who were flailing with canes, pushing each other out of the way. Bells were ringing in the churches. Auto horns were blaring.

Then he too heard the moan. Harding had heard that noise before, and he would never forget it. It was in New York City, when a jumper had climbed to the top of Madison Square Garden, hung from the statue of Diana and her drawn bow, and then done a "Brody," diving headfirst into the crowd below.

He ran closer, jumping to see over the heads of the crowd. He saw the balloon double up. He heard the engine sputter and die. And he watched Mary Ann drop the framework underneath the balloon. It went crashing into a house only a block away.

Now she was falling from the sky.

Then Harding saw the skin of the balloon billow out around her as a gust of wind took it. The gust actually forced her up a few feet before it died, and she started to fall again.

It reminded him of . . .

That first day. The day when Alain's balloon had exploded. But Alain had survived by spreading the balloon like a kite and riding it down.

Below what was left of the balloon hung the big drag rope. It was so low that it was bumping the rooftops up the street, coming at him like an invitation.

He seized it and started to run, pulling it over his shoulder. No good. Not enough weight.

Then he saw a gang of Apaches, young toughs wearing striped sailors' jerseys and baggy pants with red sashes, hanging out at the corner tobacco store. They were laughing at him, imitating him, and pretending that they were frantically pulling on a rope.

"Come on!" he yelled in French. "Help me pull." He pointed up at the airship falling from the sky.

There was a second of confusion in their faces, then inspiration. They joined him on the rope, and suddenly it went taut. They ran down the street, knocking people sprawling when they got in the way.

A butcher's wagon pulled up alongside. "Jump on back!" the butcher called. "Loop the rope around a hook."

Harding leaped on the wagon and snubbed the rope around a meat hook. Inside the butcher's wagon, ham hocks and open beef sides, their ribs showing, bumped and rattled against the walls as the butcher whipped his horses to full speed. Harding held onto the rope, feeling the rasp of it against his bleeding hands. He was afraid to look above him. A crowd was running alongside the wagon now.

The wagon raced down a side street. Then it careened to a stop. Harding went over backward. Cages of live chickens and rabbits fell on him.

Ahead was a six-foot-high brick wall. The butcher had made a wrong turn.

Harding freed the rope from the hook, wrapped it around his waist, and scrambled up the wall. When he reached the top, he jumped into 100 arms that were waiting on the other side. Hands seized the rope and pulled it. Harding was carried above the throng. Then, finally, he looked back.

He saw Mary Ann, her arms outstretched to catch as much wind as possible, framed against the Paris sunset. The remains of her balloon were transparent through the glow of the setting sun, and trailed out behind her like the gossamer fins of an angelfish.

And the whole city, it seemed, was pulling her to safety.

My last vision of her will be like my first, Harding thought. *In flight.*

thirty-three

*T*HE FINAL DAY BEGAN like the first: the city was wrapped in fog.

Mary Ann had spent the night in an elegant hotel, the kind that had brass rails under each step to keep the carpet in place. There was no shortage of money now, and after all those dark nights in the bilge of a boat, she felt that she deserved it. But the telephone in her drawing room never stopped ringing, and messages were constantly being left at her door: three proposals of marriage, numerous offers to go to the theater or be in the theater, even a telegram from Buffalo Bill's Wild West Show.

Reporters crowded outside and every couple of minutes flowers arrived from somewhere. Since she was a mere woman, "protectors" had emerged from all over France to help her manage her million francs. When President Pouchet announced that he was "her best friend," she knew that it was time to leave.

She decided to catch the late train from Gare du Nord that same evening and travel to the coast, where a liner would carry her back across the Atlantic. But before she left, she had to pay a last visit to a real friend. She settled her bill, slipped out the back entrance of the hotel, and took a cab to the eastern outskirts of the city.

When Mary Ann got out in front of the high gates with their winged hourglasses, she wished that she had asked for directions. Père-Lachaise was a city in itself; 106 acres full of stone houses and statues all crowded together and, like the other city surrounding it, also in turmoil. Monument piled on monument up the steep hillsides, and the hills, in rebellion against carrying all this weight, had bulged out as if they were threatening to release their cargo of the dead.

Some of the mausoleums were cracked, scarred and open. Old men sat outside their family tombs, white heads resting against iron doors that were ajar, as if they could hear the call of dead wives and lovers and were waiting to get in.

She knew the place that she was looking for would be at the highest point, near the grave of Honoré de Balzac, so she threaded her way through the narrow lanes, always choosing the path that led up. As she climbed higher, the only sound was the white gravel crunching under her shoes.

The cemetery became more peaceful and open, with grass and trees surrounding the larger plots. Some of the graves had little wooden crosses topped with cupolas, looking like small churches, often with a picture of the departed tacked onto the cross. She wondered what Alain's grave would look like.

As she came closer, she was disappointed. No marker, no mourners. Did anyone remember that he was alive only four days ago? Then, with shock, she saw that someone was on it. She gasped, and the creature raised its head. It was only a cat.

"You can pet it if you like," said a familiar voice.

She thought for a moment that it was Alain. But the voice was real; it was Harding's. He was standing off to the side, leaning against the gnarled trunk of an oak tree.

"This place is full of cats," he went on. "They like the warm earth of the fresh-turned graves. Of course, if you want to, you can believe what the Egyptians said about cats—that they take the spirits of the dead on to their new life."

"I never had a chance to say thank you for saving my life," she answered. "When I felt that pull on the rope I knew that it was you. And when I came down and everyone got done hugging and kissing me they all told me the story about the crazy American and the butcher's wagon."

"I wasn't alone," he reminded her. "There were hundreds of people pulling on that rope. In the end it felt like the whole city was flying with you. I never saw people so happy."

"I looked for you but you never came," she said, her voice more hurt than angry. "So I thought and thought, and finally I knew that if I was going to find you anywhere that you'd be up here."

"Yeah," he nodded, staring at the mound of earth, "I needed to say goodbye to my better self. He was the better part of all of us.

"Look," he said, pointing to a pile of bouquets, small gifts and messages in front of the grave. One envelope had a monogrammed "M" on it. "We're not the only ones who said goodbye."

"Should I open it?"

"I think that he would have wanted you to."

She read: "'To my son. May the earth be lighter for you than the air itself. H.M.' He must have come here just before the end on the night that he died." She took Harding's hand, holding it tightly over the grave. "I want you to come back with me."

He pulled his hand away and stepped back. "I have another grave up here," he reminded her. "My wife." He was staring through the trees at the horizon, facing the city. The hazy sky made it look like an Impressionist painting. In the distance, lined up with two church spires—like the back and front sights of a rifle—was the Eiffel Tower.

"It's so beautiful," she said. "It's a shame he never made it."

"But you did," Harding reminded her.

"What's going to happen to us now?" she asked, not sure that she wanted to know.

"Nothing has changed. The French are angry and afraid. The Germans are arrogant . . . and greedy. In 10 years we're going to see another war, and it'll be worse than last time. That city down there will be destroyed, or at least changed forever. And there will be a lot of holes up here filled with men like Alain."

"No," she said, shaking her head. "I mean, I believe you. But what's going to happen to the two of us?"

Harding looked at her, unwilling to commit to anything. "I didn't know that there was an us," he said. "You can go anywhere you want. For you, the whole twentieth century is waiting. They gave you the million francs, didn't they?"

"Yes. Yvette Meurthe had to hand it to me personally."

"I wish I'd been there to see that. So, you're a rich woman now. You have more money than Bishop ever had."

"Not as much as you think. First, I gave the captain and his wife a lot of money to fix up the *Bethanie*. It was the least I could do. Then, I redeemed all the tools and musical instruments in the pawn shops so that the workers could have them back."

Harding nodded. "That's what Alain would have done."

Both of them stood there, staring down at his grave. Finally, she broke the silence. "You're not going to leave me, are you? You can't. I love you."

When he looked up his eyes were glistening, and she realized with shock that he was trying not to cry, that all the emotion he had once put into painting, and then hidden in a bottle, was there for her to see.

"I was afraid that you were going to say that. I've got a confession to make. I knew that you'd come here too, and I wanted to see you one last time . . ."

"No . . ." she started to say, but he held his finger to her lips.

"Hear me out. The thought of being your summer hero and marching across Europe having adventures is very appealing. And you know that I love you. I've loved you ever since the day that I watched you fly off that mountaintop. But the best gift I can give you is to go away. I'm going to keep moving, because somewhere beyond the River Jordan, I'm going to have to wrestle with my dark angel, and I don't know who's going to win."

"But I need you . . ."

"I thought about that too," he broke in. "I remembered Leonardo and his birds and what he did with them. And let me tell you something about yourself. You don't need me. You've got a gift, a strange, naïve innocence that protects you, that makes you lighter than air. There's a whole world of people out there who'll tell you that you can't win, but you don't know any better, so you just go ahead and do it. You may lose that innocence someday . . . and you probably will. But it's a gift, and I'm not going to be the one who destroys it."

He reached across the grave and grabbed her by both arms, almost hurting her with his intensity. His face contorted as if he only had a few seconds to speak.

"Listen, I don't believe that there's much good in mankind—or in me. But there was that moment when I was pulling on that rope and thousands of arms were holding you up in the sky. I looked around, and you were coming down through the sunset, and it was as if we were all flying together, the whole city, the whole damn world. It was as if Alain and Meurthe and your father and all the others who had died before had come back and reached up to save you. And I thought, maybe for just that one moment we had found that place Alain was talking about, the Region of Fire. You brought it down to earth for us. And here I was, promising myself that I wasn't going to do this again . . ."

He lifted her chin and kissed her. The kiss was soft this time, a mere brushing of the lips, but its warmth traveled down her upturned neck and floated through her. And in that kiss were all the world's possibilities, waiting to be born.

"Goodbye, Marianne," he said, and walked away.

It took a second for her to realize that he was really going, threading his way among the cupolas and gravestones and little metal water pumps.

"You came back before . . . twice," she reminded him.

"Third time's the charm," he called back without turning.

"But what if I really need you?"

"I'll know."

"How will you know?"

"I'll know."

He was still walking and the light was fading. He was rounding the corner of the path down the hill, heading toward the tomb of the medieval lovers, Abelard and Héloïse. Soon he would be out of sight. She searched for something to say that would stop him.

"Harding!"

He turned around slowly, like an actor who has already made his curtain call and wants to get off stage. He looked at her and waited.

"What did Leonardo do with all the birds?" she called down to him.

"He set them free!" his voice rang out.

Then he faced the road once again and walked down the narrow lane in the waning light, while she watched him, watched him until memory alone held his image: a vanishing man in a vanishing city . . . in a soon-to-be vanishing world.

About the Author

ED LEEFELDT WAS TWICE nominated
for the Pulitzer Prize for his investigative work on vote fraud and Social
Security swindles as a columinst for
The Trentonian. The author of the
book, *In Search of the Paper Children*,
an expose on foster care, he has also
been a frequent contributor to *The Wall Street Journal* and his
work has appeared in the *New York Times*. A senior writer at
Bloomberg Markets magazine, his articles garnered two consecu-
tive New York Press Club awards and were deemed a national
finalist in the Investigative Reporters and Editors Contest. Leefeldt
has received fellowships from the National Endowment for the
Humanities, the National Press Association, the Edna McConnell
Clark Foundation, and the National Institute of Mental Health.